THE CIRCLE OF FORTUNE

England, 1323: On the feast day of Saint Peter in Chains, Roger Mortimer — imprisoned by Edward II and facing execution — breaks out of the Tower of London with the help of the loyal Gerald d'Alspaye and escapes to France . . . Alicia de Lacy and her husband, Eble le Strange, support Mortimer's campaign to rid England of Edward II and his hated favourite, Hugh le Despenser. But as Mortimer's power increases, he becomes as corrupt as his predecessors, and both Alicia and Eble are forced to decide where their loyalties really lie . . .

Books by Elizabeth Ashworth
Published by Ulverscroft:

THE DE LACY INHERITANCE
AN HONOURABLE ESTATE
FAVOURED BEYOND FORTUNE

Elizabeth Ashworth is an author based in Lancashire. Her work has appeared in many publications, including *My Weekly*, *The People's Friend*, *Take a Break Fiction Feast*, *The Lady*, *The Times* and *Top Gear*.

ELIZABETH ASHWORTH

THE CIRCLE
OF FORTUNE

Complete and Unabridged

ULVERSCROFT
Leicester

First published in Great Britain in 2014

First Large Print Edition
published 2017

A catalogue record for this book is available
from the British Library.

ISBN 978–1–4448–3260–0

Published by
F. A. Thorpe (Publishing)
Anstey, Leicestershire

Set by Words & Graphics Ltd.
Anstey, Leicestershire
Printed and bound in Great Britain by
T. J. International Ltd., Padstow, Cornwall

This book is printed on acid-free paper

Part One

1323 to 1324

1

August 1323

Saint Peter in Chains

From his cell, high in the Tower of London, Roger Mortimer heard the chime of a bell. It was the feast day of Saint Peter in Chains, and he knew that the guards and kitchen boys would be gathering below to give thanks for the saint's escape.

On his knees beside his pallet bed, Roger vowed that he would build a chapel to the saint at Ludlow Castle if God delivered him from captivity. Roger had not entrusted his life to prayer alone, however. He had good friends who would ensure that he was soon on his way to France.

Roger crossed himself and got to his feet in the gloom. His squire, Richard de Monmouth, was watching him in the light of the one flickering tallow candle that kept them from total darkness.

'Will he come?' asked Monmouth.

'He will come,' said Roger as he stared at the barred and locked door that stood between him and his freedom. 'I trust him,' he said, hoping that he would not find himself dangling from the end of a traitor's rope come morning.

The laughing voices of the garrison drifted up on the afternoon air as men made their way to a celebratory supper in the castle hall. Roger knew that, outside, the summer sun would still be high, and that it would be an hour or two before his rescuer came.

It fell eerily quiet as the men went inside to eat and drink. With the castle gates shut and all the prisoners locked in their cells, most of the guards were free to enjoy the feast — and Roger hoped that Gerard d'Alspaye, the deputy constable of the castle, had arranged for a generous quantity of wine to be served.

Time passed slowly, and neither man spoke as they listened for any sound from outside the door, apprehensive that quiet footsteps might be those of an assassin with a knife rather than d'Alspaye come to free them.

At last, Roger heard a tapping sound. He met Monmouth's eyes and nodded briefly. His heart raced, but it seemed an age before a stone near the base of the wall began to move, and longer still before it was prised away. Roger watched as the edge of a crowbar levered away another. The work progressed faster as the mortar crumbled and Roger brought the remains of the candle to supplement the lantern which d'Alspaye had carried with him.

'My lord?' whispered d'Alspaye.

'Has all gone according to plan?' asked Roger.

'The constable lies unconscious, and most of the men,' he replied as he struggled to remove another stone.

'I think I can get out now,' Roger said, pressing his body close to the gritty floor and beginning to ease himself through the hole head first.

'One more, I think,' said d'Alspaye. 'It will be better than risking you becoming stuck, my lord.'

'Quickly, then!'

Another stone was wrenched away and fell with a thud that made them all pause and listen for footsteps coming up the stairwell; but, apart from slurred singing in the distance, all remained quiet, and Roger lay down again on his back to wriggle through the gap. He stood and slapped the debris from his clothes as d'Alspaye hauled Monmouth through. Then, with the light of the lantern casting looming shadows, they crept down the twisting stairs.

At the bottom, d'Alspaye opened a door into the courtyard. Roger could see several men lying in a stupor. The soporific in the wine had been both fast and effective. They would all have sore heads by morning, he thought — though that would not be the worst of it when his cell was discovered empty.

They flitted into the kitchens. The cook, supervising the scrubbing of the pots, glanced up as they came in. Work stopped as the kitchen boys paused and a whispering rustled across the chamber.

'Back to work!' roared the cook. 'There is nothing for you to see here!'

The man nodded briefly and moved to guard the doorway into his kitchens as they threaded through the trestles. Roger snatched up some remains of the supper as he passed, pushing remnants of roasted fowl into his mouth. He would have lingered to eat more, but d'Alspaye urged him on towards the fireplace, where the great fire with its iron spit and hooks for cauldrons had been covered. He nodded upwards, and Roger reached up to clasp his hands around the warm stones. His feet scrabbled for footholds, and he was aware that clouds of soot were billowing down on his companions below, but he braced his legs on either side of the chimney and inched his way towards the twilight above. Sharp edges cut into his ungloved hands, and the muscles in his thighs burned with the effort, but he was not fully aware of the pain. He watched as the first stars of evening appeared in the widening patch of sky above him, and at last he began to believe that fortune was on his side.

Panting with the effort, he swung himself over the edge of the chimney stack and onto the roof. He allowed himself a moment to regain his breath as he waited for d'Alspaye and Monmouth. It was full dark now, and the night was moonless, forcing them to feel their way to the edge, where d'Alspaye fixed one of the rope ladders that had been kept hidden by the cook. He climbed down first, and Roger waited until he heard the ladder smack against the stone of the wall — the signal that all was clear below. He felt for the rungs, trusting that they would hold him, and began his descent, expecting an arrow in his back at any moment. On the ground, d'Alspaye was pressed close to the wall. He shook the ladder for Monmouth to come down and they waited, only the sound of their breathing and the gentle splash of the river beyond the outer wall breaking the silence.

When Monmouth's feet reached the ground with a gentle thud, d'Alspaye plucked Roger's sleeve, and they ran like spectres across the open ground to the outer wall.

'Stand clear!' whispered d'Alspaye as he took the second rope ladder that he had strapped across his back and tossed its grappling irons upwards. The man had a sure throw, and Roger heard the irons scrape against the wall. He climbed with increasing confidence, and at the top waited for the others to follow him. Once up, they hauled on the ladder, adjusted the irons, and let it snake down the outer side of the fortifications. Roger went first, feeling for only every other rung as he neared the ground. For the first time in almost two years, he was outside the Tower of London. And it felt good.

He waited, wishing he had at least a knife to protect himself. But the guards slept on, and the watchmen on the towers were also likely to be dozing, d'Alspaye having arranged to have refreshments sent up to them on this special day of celebration. Moments later, the other men were down. d'Alspaye whistled softly.

'This way,' he said, and Roger followed him across the marshy ground towards the flash of a small lantern.

'My lord,' whispered the oarsman as Roger stepped into the boat and seated himself. The second boatman extinguished the lantern and, with knowledge of the river that had no need for light, their rescuers grasped the oars and rowed them out onto the salt-drenched tide and across the Thames to Greenwich.

Monmouth was out first and held the boat hard against the bank as Roger jumped ashore.

'I will see you well rewarded for this,' he told the boatmen. 'I will not remain in France and watch England suffer under this tyranny. I will come back. And when I do, I will not forget what you have done for me this night.'

'May God go with you, my lord,' said the oarsman, 'and hold you in His keeping.'

'And also you,' replied Roger as they were swallowed up once more by the black night.

A horse snickered nearby, and Roger turned in alarm.

'Fear not, my lord,' said d'Alspaye. 'They are your own men.' He pushed a small lantern into Roger's hand. 'Hold this steady,' he said as he struck a flint and lit the wick. Roger shielded the light from the breeze. Then, holding it up as he heard the hooves come nearer, he recognised one of his men-at-arms with his favourite horse, ready saddled.

'Ned!'

'It's good to see you, my lord.' Ned passed him the reins. 'Mount up,' he advised. 'There are only a few hours until sun-up, and by then they will be on our trail.'

Needing no urging, Roger put his foot to the stirrup and pulled himself into the familiar saddle. The last time he had ridden this horse had been into the ward of Shrewsbury Castle, where the Earl of Pembroke had guaranteed that King Edward would grant him a pardon. But the man had lied. Instead of a pardon, he had been taken to the Tower, where he had expected certain death — a fate he would, at one time, have preferred when faced with the clemency of life imprisonment in one windowless and airless cell. But when d'Alspaye had brought the news that he was to be executed after all, life had suddenly seemed too precious to forfeit; and, as Roger and his men headed for Portchester, he was glad that his friends were willing to risk their own necks rather than see him hang.

The lightening of the sky on the eastern horizon came as a mixed blessing. They could press the horses on at speed, but the peasants in the fields would have no qualms about betraying their passing to the king's men for a few silver pennies. Roger hoped that when the men and dogs were sent after them, they would first search the road to Dover, where he might be expected to take ship to France — whereas the route he had planned was taking them in an altogether different direction.

Around dawn they paused, and his men-at-arms produced food and drink. Roger gulped thirstily. The night had been hot, and the day promised intense heat to come as the sun rose, a fiery orange. Despite the beauty of the morning, there was no time to linger, and the men mounted up again and pressed on — four armed and armoured, one in the clothes of a gentleman, and two in rags.

They rode on through the heat of the day, trying to avoid towns and villages where their appearance might cause comment. Instead, they chose tracks through fields and woods and did not rest, not even when the sun completed its circuit of the sky. Roger slumped in his saddle, hit by a wall of fatigue. He had not slept for over a day, and the unaccustomed physical exertion of his escape had left him exhausted.

'Do you need to rest, my lord?' asked Ned, drawing his horse alongside him. Roger shook his head.

'Not until we are safely out of England,' he replied. 'If I fall asleep, tie me to the saddle and ride on.'

It was dark again as they approached Portchester. They did not ride into the town, but skirted around it and came to the coast, where a boat was waiting. They unsaddled the horses, stripped them of their bridles, and left them grazing on the shoreline as they clambered into the small craft. Roger feared that the boat might sink under the weight of so many men, but the swain seemed to know his business, and set the sail to make the most of the breeze. As the land retreated behind them and the waves slapped higher against the hull, splashing Roger's face with welcome coolness, he hoped that the horses would be collected as arranged. They were valuable animals and he was sorry to have left them behind.

'I owe you my life,' he told d'Alspaye, leaning forward in the dark to grasp the man's hand. 'I will not forget it.'

'There are many who regret your treatment at the hands of this king, and they are angry at the way Thomas of Lancaster abandoned you. They look to you as the man who might rescue England.'

'I am flattered by their faith in me,' replied Roger as he felt the boat surge beneath him. He rested his head on his arms, too tired to even contemplate doing more than surviving until he reached France. The saving of England would have to wait until another day.

★   ★   ★

It was daylight when a hand on his shoulder woke him.

'We are here, lord,' said Ned.

Roger scanned the small harbour. Some fishing boats were tied up at the wharf, but the only men he could see in the dawn light were waiting with a string of horses.

'Courtesy of your cousin,' said Gerard d'Alspaye.

As soon as the boat bumped the harbour wall, Roger grasped the ladder and soon had his feet on French ground. Stiff and sore as he was, he was about to kneel and kiss it, when he saw a squire dressed in de Fiennes' colours coming towards him.

'Geoffrey?' he said, recognising his son, yet finding him changed. The last time he had seen him he had been a boy, but now he was a man with a moustache and broad shoulders.

'Father!' he greeted him with a wide smile. Roger opened his tired arms and embraced his son.

'It is good to see you,' the older man said.

'And you, Father.'

As the heir to his maternal grandmother's French lands, it had been decided that Geoffrey should be placed in the household of his cousin, Robert de Fiennes, so that he would know and understand French society.

Although Roger had been saddened at the news of the death of his wife's mother, it had been provident because it meant that Geoffrey's estates could now provide an income whilst he was in exile.

'My lord?' A voice interrupted them, and Roger nodded. He knew that they must make haste; it would be foolish to linger. Geoffrey brought him a horse — a sturdy chestnut that Roger thought might work well in the lists. He was hoping for the chance to participate in some of the French tournaments once he had regained his fitness. It would be a good way to earn some extra cash, and to show the kings of both England and France that he was still a good horseman and soldier.

The sun rose hotter than ever as they took the road towards the de Fiennes estates in Picardy. Roger could feel it burning the back of his neck, but it was a discomfort he welcomed after his time in the dark cell, only able to guess at what the weather outside might be like.

It was a full two days' ride to reach his cousin's home, and Roger could not remember ever having felt so tired in all his life. After he had been welcomed, he was shown to a chamber with a window, a feather bed and, best of all, a tub of hot water in which to bathe. Roger stripped the grimy rags from his filthy body and got into the tub, watching as a flotilla of fleas and lice floated, drowned, to the surface. He picked them off with distaste, splashing water amongst the floor rushes as he did. If he had been at home, his wife Joan would have come to soap the cloth and scrub the ingrained dirt from his skin. They would have laughed. He would have flicked water at her and she would have told him off for wetting her gown, saying that she would have to remove it and put it to dry. And it would have ended with them in bed together.

He was worried about Joan. After his own arrest, she and their youngest son had been taken from the abbey at Wigmore and imprisoned. His two eldest sons, Edmund and Roger, had been taken to Windsor, and three of his daughters were locked up in nunneries. He felt angry. What kind of king took revenge on women and children like that? And now that he had escaped, he was concerned that they would fare even worse.

'What will you do now, Father?' asked Geoffrey when Roger was clean and dressed in fresh clothes.

'I will present myself at the court of King Charles as an ally of France.'

'And then?'

'I am not certain,' he admitted. 'But I will fight for France in any war against King

Edward.' He stared out of the window. It was good to be here and to be reunited with his son. But it wasn't enough. He wanted to free the rest of his family. He wanted his lands back. He wanted vengeance.

2

August 1323

The Prophecy of Merlin

Alicia de Lacy woke in panic. Her dream had left her drenched in sweat and she pushed the bed covers aside, trying to slow the thudding of her heart.

'Alicia?'

'Did I waken you? I'm sorry,' she said, stretching out her hand towards her husband.

'Were you dreaming?' he asked, putting a protective arm around her. He was sleeping naked because of the heat, but his body felt cool against her burning skin. He kissed her lightly. 'Do you want to talk about it?'

'I was at York Castle, locked in a chamber there.' Alicia shivered as a breeze rattled the shutters. Eble pulled the covers over them and Alicia turned towards him. 'I suppose it was thinking about Saint Peter in Chains that brought it back,' she said.

Although she had not been chained in a cell, she had only been allowed to go free from York Castle after she had signed all her lands and twenty thousand pounds over to the king. In her dream the king's chamberlain, Hugh le Despenser, had been shouting at her, threatening her with a witch's death if she did not sign the parchment he waved in her face. And as he had thrust it towards her, it had caught fire; the flames spread to her gown, and she had felt the unbearable heat as the fire consumed her.

'Try to sleep,' said Eble.

'I don't want to sleep again,' she whispered. He would leave her at sunrise to go to Lincoln, where they had business. The king had conceded that, as the Countess of Lincoln, she was entitled to an annual rent of twenty pounds from the profits of the county court; but the sheriff had not paid them. In their reduced circumstances, it was money they needed, and Eble was going to ask the sheriff about his reluctance. He had said that it would be better if Alicia remained behind on the manor at Swaveton. She had objected — she didn't want him to go without her — but Eble had been firm, and she had reluctantly agreed. She knew that he was right. There was much unrest in the country, and it could be dangerous.

She reached to touch Eble's face. He had grown a short beard, and it felt soft beneath her fingers as she stroked his cheek.

'How long will you be gone?' she asked.

'No more than a day or two. Is there anything you would like from the market?'

'No,' she lied. In truth there was a long list of things that she would like: a fine linen tablecloth, new hangings for the bed, fine wines, expensive spices, a book of romances, a well-bred horse. Once such things had all been hers, and it was only when she did not have them that she really appreciated their worth.

Outside, the cockerel crowed. 'I must get up,' said Eble.

'Not for a moment,' Alicia pleaded.

'You are a wicked woman,' he teased her as she caressed his body. She ran a hand down his arm, feeling for the old scar that stood proud from his skin, and rubbed the length of it with her thumb. The desire she felt still surprised her. When she had been the wife of Thomas of Lancaster, her marital duty had been a painful, loveless act, and it was only with Eble that she had discovered there could be pleasure in it.

By the time the light from the window was strong enough to illuminate the colours of the hanging on the wall, Eble had kissed her farewell and gone. Alicia lay in the warm bed, her hands fondling the soft fur of her pet cat, Guarin, who must have slipped into the house past Eble as he went out. She studied the tapestry that showed a young squire who gazed at a lady on a white horse. She remembered how she had helped her mother make it, back at Pontefract Castle, in the days when her father had been one of the most important men in England. The coloured threads that they had woven together had created a story of love that Alicia had believed in, until her faith had almost been destroyed by her first husband. But Eble le Strange had kept the story alive with his love for her, and even now she thought of him as the young squire and herself as the lady.

She had been rich once. From her mother she had inherited her lands and title, the Countess of Salisbury, and from her father the title of the Countess of Lincoln, although all of the de Lacy lands were forfeit to the king when her husband was executed as a traitor. The king had also taken the lands that were rightfully hers, leaving her with only a few manors to hold for her lifetime. He feared that she might be the focus of another rebellion, and in truth she would be glad to see Edward lose his throne and Despenser meet the fate he so deserved. She hated them both with an anger that made her hands itch for a sharp blade or a blunt axe.

* * *

Eble pushed his way through the crowds. It was market day, and the stalls jostled for space around the castle gate, selling wares from pies to belt buckles. His meeting with the sheriff had elicited only a promise that the overdue rents would soon be paid, and Eble had warned the man that he would take legal action if the money wasn't forthcoming by the next quarterday. He was angry that the sheriff had treated him as if he were a mere irritation to be wafted away. He had not even been able to claim the distinction of being announced as Sir Eble le Strange, and being a plain 'messire' did not gain the same respect. Perhaps he ought to call himself the Earl of Lincoln. He had the right, as Alicia's husband; but to him the Earl of Lincoln would always be Henry de Lacy, the man who had brought him up from being seven years old and who had been like a father to him.

He walked down the steep hill, away from the market, to seek a gift for Alicia. He had wanted to buy a book last time he was in Lincoln, but had hesitated, knowing that she would reprimand him for spending so much. He had, however, struck a deal with the scribe. It was one that suited them both.

21

The boy who answered the door to his gentle knock stood aside for him to enter. Osbert glanced up and acknowledged him, and Eble settled to wait on a stool until the man had finished his page. The smell of inks and parchment was one that he enjoyed, and he wondered how different his life might have been if Henry de Lacy had arranged for him to take holy orders as had once been suggested. Would he have enjoyed the life of a monk, rising at midnight and dawn to pray, and maybe spending his days bent closely over a desk as Osbert was now?

The scribe finished with a smile of satisfaction, and Eble stood up as he came across to him. 'Do you still have the book?' he asked eagerly.

'Do you have the poems?' asked Osbert.

Eble reached into his purse and took out the folded parchments. Now that the time had come, he was reluctant, and almost snatched them back from Osbert's grasp. He shifted uneasily as the scribe began to read his work, and hoped that he would not reject it as worthless, but the man began to nod.

'These are good — very good!' He looked up and smiled. 'Maybe I have the best of the bargain,' he said. 'I know a customer who will enjoy these stories.'

'They are not that good,' began Eble.

'Do not do yourself a disservice,' repri-manded the scribe. 'They are good, and I will enjoy making them into a book. Are you sure that you would not rather wait and give your own words to your wife?'

'She already knows them well. I still want the book of romances about King Arthur.'

'I have it safe for you,' said Osbert, and he reached it down from a shelf, unwrapping it from a protective muslin cloth. It was bound in leather, and when Eble turned the pages the vibrant colours shone from the illustra-tions, and the words were neat and well-formed.

'I hope your wife enjoys it,' said Osbert as he carefully re-wrapped it and handed it to Eble. 'And if you have any more poems, I would be willing to buy them from you. Come to see me again next time you are in Lincoln.'

'I will,' promised Eble as he tucked the book inside his tunic and clasped the man's hand again. 'It is good to do business with you.'

As he laboured back up the hill, he noticed several small groups of people gathered in excited conversation. They were talking about someone who had escaped from the castle.

'Not this castle, my lord,' said his squire when he reached their lodging house and asked him what he knew. 'Roger Mortimer has escaped from the Tower.'

'Mortimer? From the Tower?' repeated Eble. It was incredible. They said that if you were imprisoned in the Tower of London you could never escape, but it seemed that Roger Mortimer had proved them wrong — and Eble hoped that it was true. He had met Mortimer several times before the rebellion, and he knew that if Thomas of Lancaster had gone to his aid at Shrewsbury, they would not now be living under the tyrannical and corrupt rule of Edward Plantagenet and his chamberlain, Hugh le Despenser.

★　★　★

Alicia was unsure which pleased her most — the gift of the book or the news about Roger Mortimer. She had asked Eble question after question, but they could only speculate on who might have assisted him and how the escape had been managed. She was glad that the man was free, and when Eble said that the king was afraid that Mortimer would gather an army and invade the country, she replied that she hoped he would.

'Do not speak of it openly,' warned Eble as they talked in their chamber. 'It's better not to bring yourself under suspicion.'

Alicia climbed into the bed and picked up her book from the coffer. It was a story she knew well, but never tired of reading.

'It makes me wonder if it is time for King Arthur to return,' she said. 'The country is in such a state that all the signs are there. And what about the prophecy of Merlin?'

'The prophecy that Arthur would return one day to claim his kingdom?' said Eble. 'There are those who claim that Robert Bruce is the next King Arthur — although that is nonsense, because Arthur must be a Welsh prince.'

'Or someone descended from Llewellyn the Great?' said Alicia. 'Someone like Roger Mortimer?'

'Mortimer is no more Welsh than I am.'

'That's not true,' argued Alicia. 'His great-grandfather married the daughter of Llewellyn.'

'It was a marriage made to stop the Mortimers killing the Welsh. Not that it did much good, because Mortimer's grandfather is buried in a tomb in Wigmore Abbey with an epitaph that boasts how much the Welsh feared him.'

'Have you ever met Roger Mortimer?' she asked.

'Yes. He came to Knockin Castle once

when we were planning the rebellion.'

Alicia nearly said *when you left me,* but she pressed a finger to her lips. She had been so angry with Eble when he had abandoned her at Reigate Castle to go and fight alongside his nephew. But now she understood the importance of family lands, and she knew that he had done what was right, even though they had argued about it at the time.

'What is he like?' she asked, her thoughts returning to Mortimer.

'Powerful,' said Eble. 'If I had to choose one word to describe him, that would be it. And not just physically powerful. He has an aura about him. Men follow him.'

'And you?' she asked. 'Would you follow him?'

'Yes,' said Eble. 'If it was a choice between him and the king, then I think I would.'

3

September 1323

Talk of Rebellion

'My nephew is to be married,' said Eble, reading a letter brought by messenger from the Marches. Alicia looked up from her book.

'Will we go?' she asked.

'Would you like to?'

'Of course! I've never been to Knockin Castle. I would like to see the place where you were born.'

'It's nothing special,' said Eble. 'But I would like to go.'

'And not just because you like weddings?' asked Alicia as she watched an expression of hope flit across his face.

'No,' agreed Eble. 'There will be other marcher lords there — people who support Roger Mortimer. It will be interesting to hear what they have to say about his intentions.'

'Do you think Mortimer really will gather an army in France?' she asked. 'It's what people are saying.'

'It's what people are hoping,' replied Eble.

'But he won't be able to do it alone. He will need money and men and supplies.'

'He will need the blessing of the French king,' said Alicia as she wondered what it would mean for them if Mortimer were to take control of England. Would she have her lands returned to her and be able to live the lifestyle she once knew?

*   *   *

It felt good to be travelling, thought Alicia as they rode west. She had been at Swaveton for too long, and it was pleasant to feel a cooling breeze on her face. Though she was wearing one of her old gowns in which to travel, Eble had been persuaded to escort her to Lincoln market, where she had chosen several lengths of cloth. Working diligently, she had stitched a pink gown that hugged her slim body but flowed into a voluminous skirt and had fashionably close-fitting sleeves, fastened with small silver buttons. Eble also had new clothes. He had said that it was an unnecessary expense, and that his best tunic was perfectly suitable, but Alicia had told him that she would not be seen with him dressed in such an old garment, and he had relented and allowed her to measure him for a new one. It was the first time she had made something for him to wear, and she had taken care to make it perfect, from the inner seams to the outer embroidery on the rich blue wool that exactly matched the shade of his eyes.

He turned and smiled at her as they came to the crest of a hill. 'Knockin,' he said, indicating a small village below, clustered between a narrow river and the precincts of a moated castle. Beyond lay the mountains of Wales, glowing like fire as the sun set behind them.

'It's a beautiful place to call home,' she said.

'Until the Welsh make trouble,' remarked Eble, following her gaze towards the horizon.

'I was born not far from here,' she said as they headed downhill. 'Did I ever tell you that I was born at Denbigh? It was after my eldest brother Edmund drowned in the well there that my father went back to Pontefract. Then John fell from the turret . . . ' She felt the tears well up in her eyes as she recalled how she had seen him fall. Even though it was so many years ago, the scene remained vivid in her mind. 'My mother never recovered,' she said. 'Sadness always surrounded her afterwards.'

'Your mother was always kind to me,' said Eble, 'but I remember that whenever she looked at me she had sadness in her eyes

— and she was always telling me to be careful.'

'I heard nothing but the words *be careful, Mistress Alicia* all through my childhood,' she replied. 'But we survived, didn't we?'

She smiled at him, thinking how lucky she was to have him, but he returned her smile with a frown.

'We still need to be careful, Alicia,' he said. 'Mortimer's escape has stirred people up. And when there is talk of rebellion, suspicion is bound to fall on us.'

'Will there be talk of rebellion? Is that the real reason for coming here?' she asked as she saw the tight clusters of tents in the castle ward.

Eble's silence told her all she needed to know. He said little because he did not want to alarm her, but in truth the prospect of a rebellion excited her and she welcomed it.

Alicia had never met Eble's nephew before, but when he came down the steps from the great hall to greet them she saw that he was just as she remembered Eble when he had been a squire in her father's household — blond, brown-skinned and muscular.

Her husband lifted her down from the mare, and Roger le Strange went down on one knee to greet her. 'You are welcome to Knockin Castle, Countess.'

'Please.' Alicia motioned him to rise and extended her hand. 'I am honoured to be a guest at your wedding,' she told him.

He thanked her, then turned to Eble, who embraced him enthusiastically.

'Is all well?' asked Eble with a raised eyebrow.

'For the present.'

'I see that many have accepted your invitation,' he said with a nod towards the crowded bailey. 'It should be a good tournament.'

They went up the wooden staircase into the hall. It was barely large enough to hold two long trestles besides the top table on the dais, but it was clean and felt warm. The white linen cloths were spotless, and the cups and spoons shone.

People were already gathered, and the beeswax candles on the prickets gave off a sweet scent that mingled with the aroma of roasted meat. Alicia realised that supper had been held back to await their arrival.

Roger showed them to seats at the top table and introduced his betrothed, Maud, who curtseyed low to Alicia. She was a pretty girl with thick braids and a generous dusting of freckles across her nose, betraying her mixed Welsh and Irish bloodline. She seemed overwhelmed to be in such important company, and Alicia was reassured that people still held her in high esteem, despite the king's efforts to make her seem worthless.

Eble relaxed as the servant came forward with a basin and towel for him to wash his hands. Travel always held dangers, especially when there were criminal gangs like the Folvills waging private wars on their neighbours. He returned the towel with a word of thanks and looked around the hall to see who else had come. There was William de Braose. He had become an old man since Boroughbridge, although it was no wonder, thought Eble. His daughter Alina and grandson John were still prisoners in the Tower, despite him having put ten thousand pounds and his lands at Gower into the king's hands — and word was that the body of Alina's husband, John de Mowbray, still hung in chains over the castle wall at York as carrion for the crows.

He thanked God that Alicia had been allowed to go free. He knew that he had John de Warenne to thank for it, although John remained loyal to the king, and if war came again he would probably find himself once more in opposition to his friend.

He watched Alicia as she talked to his nephew's betrothed, setting the girl at her ease. Alicia had the same easy manners as her father and a genuine interest in people. He had been proud of her when she suggested that they take supper immediately rather than making everyone wait whilst she changed her clothes and had a maid re-braid her hair. She was nodding now at something Maud was telling her, her eyes intent and the bread between her fingers momentarily forgotten.

Eble ached with love. He could still not believe that Alicia de Lacy was his wife. He had been in love with her since he was a squire in her father's household, when he had thought that she was so far from his reach that he could only ever admire her from afar. He had been distraught when she married Thomas of Lancaster, who had bullied him and John de Warenne mercilessly. John had always vowed that he would make Lancaster sorry one day, and he had not flinched from taking him prisoner after his failed rebellion at Boroughbridge and escorting him to Pontefract, where he lost his head.

Aware of him watching her, Alicia turned and smiled. She looked happy, and he was glad that he had brought her with him; not just because he hated to be parted from her, but because this was where she belonged — seated at the top table in a castle, even if it was only a small castle, rather than being hidden away on a manor in Lincolnshire.

'Will you ride in the tournament tomorrow?' asked his nephew. Eble turned from his contemplation of Alicia and looked at Roger.

'It will look as if I'm afraid if I don't,' he remarked. 'I just hope they take pity and give me a chance.' He grimaced at the thought of the ordeal to come, reflecting that at least John de Warenne and Roger Mortimer were not present, as both could have tossed him to the ground with a glance. He had never been fond of jousting. He preferred to watch or serve as a squire, holding the horses and picking up the broken lances, which was what he had been trained to do. Many of the lords who had come were wealthier and more important than he was — and it was only because of Alicia that he was seated at the top table at all. Below he recognised Fulk Fitzwarenne, the lord of Whittington, the Talbots, the de Greys of Ruthin, Robert de Waterville, Thomas Wake, and even the Bishop of Hereford. He knew that they were all secret supporters of Roger Mortimer, along with others who should have been present, like Hugh Audley, but who were still in the custody of the king. Eble knew that they had not come just to witness a wedding, but to exchange views on what they might do if Roger Mortimer led an invasion.

Next morning Eble ran a hand over the soft
tunic that Alicia had carefully unfolded from
their baggage and handed to him to wear. It
was blue and the embroidery was exquisite,
combining the emblems of their families —
lions both couchant and rampant.

'Would it not be better to wear the other?'
he asked, pointing to the grubby one in which
he had travelled that was lying across the foot
of the bed. 'You have worked so hard on this,
and it's sure to get torn.'

'Put it on!' Alicia told him. 'I want you to
look your best.'

Obediently, Eble pushed his head through
the opening; and as he reached for the sleeves
he felt Alicia pulling the tunic straight down
his back. She smoothed it with her palms and
he felt a rush of desire at her touch, making
him want to pull the garment off again — and
hers as well. She was wearing a new gown.
The pink colour warmed her cheeks and
intensified the dark brown of her eyes. The
pinched and worried look that had spoiled
her pretty face for months after she had been
held at York Castle had faded; she had
regained weight, and the roundness pleased
him.

'I wish I could afford the cloth for a dozen

35

gowns like that one,' he said as she straightened the neckline of his tunic with a look of satisfaction.

'I can only wear one at once,' she said as she turned to the baggage and produced two short lengths of silk. One was saffron-dyed and the other purple. Alicia knotted them together to make a favour. 'Here,' she said as she handed them to him. 'Will you wear my colours at the joust? They will bring you luck.'

And they will remind everyone that my wife is a de Lacy, thought Eble, remembering the many times that he had followed the purple lion on the banner of the Earl of Lincoln.

★ ★ ★

The wedding was a brief ceremony at the chapel of St Mary, which adjoined the castle. The bishop of Hereford officiated and the Knockin chaplain fussed around him, seeming unsure whether to be honoured or insulted by his presence. Alicia cried, and Eble felt his own tears rise as his nephew made his vows and kissed his young bride. He hoped that their marriage would be a fertile one. There had been too much death in the family these past few years, and as Alicia was growing too old to give him sons and daughters of his own, it was children by his nephew who would probably continue the le Strange name.

After the celebratory dinner had been eaten, or in Eble's case toyed with, the men went to arm themselves for the tournament. He had been drawn against Thomas Wake, who was a cousin to Roger Mortimer and married to Blanche, the daughter of Henry of Lancaster. Eble had known him for many years; had seen him joust, and knew that he was skilled. He was going to feel such a complete and utter fool, he thought, when as the senior member of the le Strange family he went sprawling in the dirt.

As no royal patrons were present, the joust was not a conventional round table, but the traditions of the pageant were kept, and his nephew was crowned King Arthur and the new bride his queen, Guinevere. They were led out from the hall with a huge retinue in attendance and escorted to their cushioned seats on the berfois from where they could watch the sport. Alicia sat beside them and gave him a smile of encouragement.

Weighed down by the chainmail and almost sightless except for the eye slit in his helm, Eble mounted his horse and rode it around in figures of eight to loosen up its muscles. The stallion was a wedding gift from John de Warenne that was bred for the joust, and as he settled into the high-backed saddle, Eble could see its grey ears twitching this way and that in anticipation.

'Steady, boy,' he soothed, leaning to pat the horse's neck before settling the gauntlets onto his hands and leaning to take the lance from one of his nephew's squires.

He heard the muffled blast of the herald's horn and turned Trebnor towards the lists. He was aware of the moment of hush before the herald dropped his flag. Then instinct made him spur the horse forward, his sights fixed firmly on the dead centre of his opponent's shield — embellished with the Wake Knot. It was as if time moved slowly, and Eble aimed his lance, unaware of the wind rushing through his visor and the thud of the horse's hooves beneath him. He watched as the blunted point made contact, vaguely heard the screech of metal on metal, and saw a spark fly. He felt the jarring pain as the impact punched his arm to his shoulder socket, and for a moment he thought that he would be thrown, but he gripped the flanks of the horse tightly with his thighs and grasped at the pommel of the saddle.

Seeing the high stone of the castle wall loom closer, he yanked on the reins, and the horse slowed and turned in response to his command. As time returned to its proper pace, he saw that the end of his lance was broken and that he had scored a direct hit. He threw down the splintered shaft and pulled off his gauntlets and helm, hoping that the crowd believed he was wiping away sweat and not tears of relief. Thomas Wake was conceding defeat and leaving the field, and Eble saw Alicia on her feet, clapping her hands enthusiastically.

★ ★ ★

'Did you allow me to win?' he asked Thomas Wake later, as he poured ale into a cup from one of the flagons set on a trestle near the pavilions.

'No,' he replied. 'I would not do you the dishonour. I was expecting to score the first point at least, but you took me by surprise. I didn't think you were that good.'

'Beginner's luck,' replied Eble, offering Thomas the cup and pouring another for himself. 'What do you know of Roger Mortimer?' he asked after a moment as they stood and watched others joust. 'He is your cousin, is he not?'

'Yes, he is.' Thomas Wake studied Eble for a moment, then took him into his confidence.

'He is in Picardy with the de Fiennes,' he told him, 'though he does not intend to stay there.'

'And you will support him if he comes?'

'What do you think?' he asked with a shrewd glance.

'And your father-in-law, Henry of Lancaster?'

'He has good reason to hate the Despensers as well. I daresay there will be enough who will rally to the cause, especially if the army is led by the king of France.'

'You think the French king will invade?' asked Eble, surprised at the suggestion.

'Whilst Edward continues to take the advice of Hugh le Despenser and refuses to do homage to Charles for his Gascon lands, he will only continue to antagonise him — and who knows where that might lead?' replied the younger man before draining his cup and calling for his horse to take on a second challenger, leaving Eble wondering whether what he had said might hold any truth.

4

September 1323

The King's Enemy

Roger Mortimer was aware that his new clothes were hanging on him. His cousin's wife had measured him and decreed that they needed to be a generous fit, as he would soon replace the muscle that he had lost during his imprisonment. Roger knew that she was right, but he had wanted to look his best for his audience with King Charles, rather than a parody of a growing boy whose mother had clad him purposely in an overlarge tunic.

He fidgeted with the sleeves as he waited to be summoned into the privy chamber. His cousin had assured him that Charles was keen to welcome him, but Roger had been kept waiting for so long that he was growing doubtful. At last he heard voices and footsteps approaching. They grew louder, and he composed his face and turned towards the door as it was thrust open to the accompaniment of a short fanfare from a trumpeter. Roger averted his eyes towards the floor and made a bow to the man he hoped would prove to be an ally.

'Sir Roger!' The king greeted him by grasping his shoulders and kissing him briefly on both cheeks. 'I must apologise for keeping you waiting. I had a slight problem with my footwear.' Charles extended one leg that was clad in an intricately laced and very pointed shoe. Then he raised the hem of his long gown to show that the laces of his other shoe were mismatched. 'We have made some simple repairs, but I am scarcely fit to be seen in public,' he said with an apologetic shrug.

'I am sure it will be said that you are setting a new fashion, and soon everyone will demand that their shoes are laced in such a way,' replied Roger, trying to assess whether Charles was seriously perturbed by his mismatched shoes or if he was being humorous.

'I hope you are right!' he said. 'Please, come and be seated. Bring some wine!' he told a servant.

Roger followed the king across to a window seat and watched as the serving boy handed a gilt cup to Charles. The king's resemblance to his sister, Queen Isabella, was strong. Charles had eyes the same shade of intense blue as his sister's, and a similar cleft in his chin to the one that Roger had always found so appealing in Isabella.

Roger accepted a cup of wine and tasted it. It was excellent and he took a second sip, savouring its warmth and aroma.

'I don't suppose you were served with wine of that quality whilst you were a guest of my brother-in-law in the Tower,' remarked Charles as he watched him.

'I was given inferior ale — and not much else,' replied Roger.

'You were not kept as a nobleman, then?'

'I had a cell. But I was shown no favours — except the sparing of my life, for a while.'

'And why do you think Edward changed his mind about that?' asked Charles, although Roger knew that his French spies would have long since informed him of the reason for every decision taken at the English court. And if not spies, then maybe his sister. Roger swirled the red liquid in his cup and wondered how close Queen Isabella was to her brother, how much information she exchanged with him in private correspondence, and how private those letters actually were.

'Edward no longer makes up his own mind,' replied Roger. 'He has it made up for him by Hugh le Despenser.'

'Who is your enemy?'

'Our families have been sworn enemies since my grandfather killed his grandfather at Evesham. He would like nothing better than to see me dead.'

Charles studied him for a moment. 'What are your plans for the future?' he asked.

'To rest. To regain my health and strength. To build up some muscle again so that I might stand some chance in one of your splendid tournaments.'

'Ah! Your reputation in the lists precedes you,' said Charles. 'I shall look forward to watching you compete.' He paused and gave Roger a direct look. 'You are welcome in France and at my court,' he told him. 'But you must understand that my relationship with the English king is a delicate one — one where I must take care not to tread on toes.' He looked down at his shoes and laughed. Then his face became serious again. 'I must also have a care for the welfare of my sister,' he confided. 'In her letters I sometimes detect a note of unhappiness.'

'The king treats her with every courtesy,' replied Roger, although he did not add that Hugh le Despenser frequently treated the queen with open contempt.

Charles nodded. 'That is good to hear. We will talk some more at supper,' he said. It was a dismissal and, after replying that he would be honoured, Roger rose, handed back the half-drunk cup to the boy with some regret, and bowed his way out of the chamber.

★　★　★

Roger Mortimer remained at the French court. He rented a house from a merchant's widow, and the men who had accompanied him from England either remained in his household or found lodgings nearby. He regained his strength and took a few prizes in tournaments, but as the winter approached he became aware that his life had become too comfortable. Thoughts of Joan, imprisoned in a bleak northern castle, plagued his mind in the dark hours of the night when he found it difficult to sleep. He could not simply abandon his family to their fate. But although word was that Edward expected him to approach the English coast with an invading army at any hour, he simply did not have the money or the support he needed for such a huge undertaking.

'Ready?' asked Richard de Monmouth as he passed him a new fur-lined cloak, a gift from his son Geoffrey, paid for from the coffers of his French estates. They were joining the king on a hunting expedition, and Roger was looking forward to both the sport and the opportunity to talk informally with Charles. Trouble was brewing in Gascony, and Edward was doing himself no favours by continuing to antagonise the French king.

In the small courtyard at the centre of the house, Geoffrey was waiting with the horses. They would be staying a few nights with the king at Vincennes and, as well as the horses, their string included a few baggage mules and a pony. Roger offered the remnants of a piece of bread to the chestnut that had proved to be as good in the joust as he had hoped. He had named it Wigmore as a reminder of the land he hoped to wrest back from King Edward. After brushing the crumbs from his hands, he patted it affectionately and gathered the reins. Once he was in the saddle, it responded to the touch of his spurs with a lunge that almost threw him backwards.

'Steady there, boy!' he laughed as his own spirits lifted.

Vincennes was an easy ride to the east of the city. Once away from the crowded and noisy streets, Roger found the soft track under his horse's hooves soothing. If they were lucky, they would flush out some boar. The roast belly of the animal was a particular favourite of his, and the ravenous appetite with which he had left the Tower had not diminished.

When they arrived at the hunting lodge, Roger and Geoffrey were shown inside to where Charles was waiting. His face looked flushed, and a frown shaded his eyes.

Roger bowed and gave him a quizzical look. 'You seem concerned, my lord. Is all well?'

'Gascony!' spat Charles. Roger pulled off his gloves as he waited to hear more. 'The sergeant I sent to Saint Sardos has been murdered and the building work burned to the ground!'

'That is . . . unfortunate,' replied Roger as he began to calculate whether this turn of events might play out in his favour. Saint Sardos lay within Aquitaine on the Gascon border, but the Benedictine priory there was subject to a mother house that lay outside the duchy. The monks had been campaigning for a long time for exemption from the rule of the English king, and the previous year the French parliament had agreed. Plans had been made to build a fortified town there, but now Charles was explaining how his man had been hanged from the very stake with which he had claimed the land for France — and Roger was in no doubt there would be ramifications.

'I have received word that Ralph Basset met with Raymond Bernard just two days before,' Charles told him. 'And I do not believe that was a coincidence.'

'It would seem unlikely,' Roger agreed. Basset was Seneschal of Gascony, and the thought crossed Roger's mind that he could have been acting on the instruction of Edward. Though what Edward hoped to achieve by his continuing defiance of Charles as his overlord for his French lands, Roger was unsure. What he *was* sure of was that Edward was receiving poor advice from Hugh le Despenser, and the thought gave him a sense of satisfaction. As the king's chamberlain, confidante and rumoured lover, Despenser had a huge amount of influence, but it helped Roger to maintain his hatred of the man when he saw him using his opportunities so poorly. 'If there is anything I can do to help . . . ' he told Charles, ensuring that his expression remained one of concern.

'Well it has not yet come to war,' said Charles with a shrug. 'I still hope a peaceable agreement can be reached with my brother-in-law.' He took two cups of wine from the serving boy and offered one to Roger. 'Welcome to Vincennes!' he said with a wry smile.

'Good hunting!' replied Roger, raising his cup. He secretly hoped that it would come to war. Anything that drove a wedge between England and France would help him.

5

October 1323

Retribution

There were two letters awaiting Alicia when she and Eble arrived back at Swaveton. One bore the royal seal. Beside it lay a smaller, slightly crumpled package that looked as if it had been dampened by the rain.

Alicia's hand hovered over them, unsure which to open first. Knowing that the one from the king would probably not be good news, she decided to read that first.

'God's blood!' she swore, and looked up to find Eble staring at her in alarm.

'What's wrong?' he asked.

'I am named in this order not to assist Roger Mortimer! Look!' She shook the parchment at him. 'Why have I been singled out?' she demanded.

'Well it names others besides you,' reasoned Eble after he had taken the letter and read it himself. 'It includes John de Warenne and Despenser himself because they own lands in the Marches, so it does not mean that all those named here are suspected of rebellion.'

'The king fears that rebels will rally to the name of de Lacy,' Alicia told him. 'But I have done nothing to deserve this! It makes me look guilty, and it is an insult to single me out!' She picked up the other letter and opened it. 'Oh, this is too much!' she exclaimed. 'It is from the constable at Pontefract Castle. The king sent men to search for the family strongbox, and it has been taken away. That means he has all my father's deeds and charters . . . ' She gulped back her tears of anger and frustration. 'He is determined to destroy me.'

Eble drew her into his arms. She clutched at the fabric of his tunic and soaked it with her tears, caring nothing now for the cloth, but only seeking the comfort of his embrace.

'All will be well,' he told her; and although his words soothed her, she was not sure that she believed them. Much as she loved him, she was aware that Eble had not been brought up to understand court politics any more than he had been trained to take an active role in a tourney. Her father had taught him to be an excellent squire, and his way with words made him an adept scribe, but his future had been that of a supportive member

of their large household. He was straightfor-
ward and honest, and Alicia was unsure
whether or not he could survive in a world
where intrigue and deception were the
required skills for men to prosper.

★ ★ ★

As Eble le Strange rode into the bailey at
Conisbrough, he saw John de Warenne
coming towards him with a smile of welcome.

'It's good to see you!' said John. 'Come
inside. The groom will see to your horse.
How is Alicia?' he asked as they walked
towards the keep.

'She is well, but . . . ' Eble hesitated, and
John turned his shrewd grey eyes on him.

'But she is Alicia. And one Lincolnshire
manor will never be enough for her.'

'True,' said Eble as they ran up the steps
and out of the howling wind into the comfort
of the brazier-warmed hall. He and John had
been close since their boyhood in the de Lacy
household, and the intervening troubles,
which had resulted in them fighting on
opposing sides at Boroughbridge, had not
spoiled their friendship. It was John's
intervention that had saved him from the
dungeon at York Castle after the battle, and it
was John who had helped Alicia gain her

51

freedom. They both had reason to be thankful to him.

'I sometimes wonder if Alicia is disappointed in me,' admitted Eble as they settled on cushioned benches by the fire. It was a thought that had troubled him since his marriage. He knew that Alicia had viewed him as her saviour when he had helped her leave Thomas of Lancaster, but his decision to support his nephew by joining Lancaster's army had made her very angry; and although they made up their differences soon afterwards and she had agreed to marry him, he was still unsure of her. He worried constantly that he was not worthy of her.

'Why would she be disappointed in you? Surely you're up to being an attentive husband?' asked John with a grin.

'That's none of your damned business,' Eble told him.

John laughed. 'Well if you need any advice . . .'

'Yes, I think everyone knows how knowledgeable you are on that subject.'

'You should have joined me in the women's chambers whilst you had the chance. I suppose it's too late now that Alicia has her eye on you.'

'I would never be unfaithful to her,' said Eble.

'You never were,' replied John, 'even when she was not your wife. I suppose I should have some admiration for your restraint and single-mindedness, but I couldn't have remained celibate all those years. You might as well have been the priest the Earl of Lincoln wanted you to be.'

'And what about you?' asked Eble. 'Are you still faithful to Maud?'

John shifted on the bench and transferred his cup from hand to hand in a way that was more eloquent than any reply. Eble was surprised. Maud de Nerford had been John's great passion. Although he had bedded many women before her, he had never fallen in love until the day he met Maud, when he rescued her pet dog from under the hooves of a destrier at a tournament. It was for Maud that he had tried to seek the annulment of his marriage to his child bride Jeanne de Bar, the niece of the king. And it was Lancaster's refusal to support his petition for a divorce that had added to their enmity.

'And what of your wife?' asked Eble.

'She is living in the queen's household. I think she is happy enough.'

'And Maud? Is she happy?'

'Why shouldn't she be? I don't flaunt other women under her nose, and what she doesn't know will not harm her — but I have my needs,' he protested.

Eble didn't reply. He knew John well enough to know that nothing he said would make a difference, and he had not ridden all the way to Conisbrough to fall out with his friend, but to discover what he knew about the rumour that the French king had confiscated Gascony.

'Edward is furious,' John told him. 'After the trouble at Saint Sardos, the Earl of Kent and the Bishop of Dublin were sent to try to make peace with Charles; but when Kent heard what the local people had to say, he decided that they had a legitimate grievance. So Kent has decided to resist the French seizure, and Edward has asked me to rally troops to go to assist him. Will you come?' he asked.

Eble frowned, and now it was his turn to twist a cup between his palms as he considered how to answer. The thought of a trip across the Narrow Sea in John's company was appealing. Much as he loved Alicia, he also felt bound by the narrowness of their lives at Swaveton, and he was tempted by the idea of riding as part of an army against the French.

'Alicia — ' he began.

'Is your wife,' John reminded him. 'And you will never make a success of this marriage until you accept that she is subject to your will and not you to hers.'

'That is harsh.'

'But true,' insisted John. 'You will never be happy if you allow her to rule you. And neither will she.'

Eble was about to argue but decided against it. He drank the last of his wine before speaking. 'I will think on it,' he told John, knowing that despite what his friend advised, he would not go unless it was with Alicia's blessing. He had hurt her badly once, and he was not prepared to hurt her again.

* * *

In the end, Eble found that he had been out-manoeuvred by the king, and his decision was made for him. Back at Swaveton a few days later, Alicia greeted him at the door with a letter in her hand.

'I opened it,' she confessed. 'It bore the royal seal, and I could not spend two nights and days fretting about its contents.'

'Is it bad news?' he asked.

'I'm not sure,' she replied as she handed him the parchment. He saw that it was an order that appointed him supervisor of the array for Lincolnshire.

'This is a surprise.' He looked up and met

her eyes. 'I was under the impression that Edward did not like me.'

'This is Despenser's doing,' said Alicia. 'The man is more cunning than a whole pack of foxes.'

'So you think it's a matter of keeping your friends close, but your enemies even closer?'

'Does Despenser have any friends?' sneered Alicia. 'But it must mean that they think the threat of an invasion is credible. What did John say? Does he know where Mortimer is?'

'John is going to Gascony to assist the Earl of Kent at Saint Sardos. He asked me to go with him, but I will have to stay here now.'

'And Mortimer?' asked Alicia again.

'Was entertained by the Count of Boulogne and is now in Toulouse, if the spy network is to be believed.'

'Then he must be trying to raise support as everyone says. I wish he would hurry up! I am tired of living like this.' She waved a hand contemptuously around the hall of the manor house. 'And I will support anyone who will help me get back the lands that are rightfully mine.'

6

April 1324

A Spy at Court

Lady de Vescy watched as the queen frowned over the letter.

'This makes me so angry!' said Isabella. 'And it is all Despenser's doing! I am sure my husband would never have acted so cruelly.'

'What has happened?' asked Lady de Vescy.

'Joan Mortimer has been sent to the castle at Skipton and her children have all been imprisoned elsewhere. It makes me weep to think of it.'

Lady de Vescy was not surprised at the news. The letter she had sent to Gerald d'Alspaye, warning him that the king and Despenser were planning to murder Roger Mortimer, had been timely enough to help him win his freedom; but this backlash of cruelty against his wife and family was not unexpected.

'Skipton is a bleak place,' she commented, 'and far enough north to make any thought of rescue impossible. I suppose that is why

Despenser has had her sent there.'

'He is a heartless bastard. I don't know why Edward likes him so much. Well, I do,' she said as her lip curled in disgust.

Lady de Vescy was sorry for the young queen. Isabella had come to England from France as a girl of only twelve years old, and her marriage had never been an easy one. At first her husband had disregarded her in favour of Piers Gaveston — the man he had called his brother. After Gaveston's death, Edward had turned to Isabella, and they had been happy for a while. She had been a good wife to him and given him four children. It was true that Edward had taken lovers during that time, but the queen had not minded so much because they had at least treated her with respect. But Despenser was different. He had pursued and flattered the king with the intention of making him fall in love so that he could hold power over him. Despenser would do anything for power. Even bed a king.

Lady de Vescy was sad for the king too. She had known Edward since he was a baby and felt a maternal love for him, but these days she didn't know him at all. He had become a stranger to her since Despenser had taken him over. At one time he would have taken advice — from her or from Henry de Lacy. But Henry was long dead, and her own influence had been curtailed, first by Thomas of Lancaster and now by the Despensers. She would have gone back to Italy long ago, except for her fondness for the queen and her promise to Henry to have a care for his daughter, Alicia. She missed Henry and his solid good sense. Edward would have listened to him, she was sure, and Henry would have taken steps to ensure that Hugh le Despenser did not rule the country as king in all but name, with Edward as his willing consort.

'I will write to the constable at Skipton and exhort him to take good care of Lady Mortimer, or risk my wrath!' said Isabella. 'Although whether he will take heed of me, I do not know.'

She sent a girl to fetch her scribe and began to walk about the chamber, picking up books and needlework and then setting them down again as if she had no taste for anything.

'Does the king know where Roger Mortimer is?' asked Lady de Vescy. She knew very well that he had gone to join his cousin in France, but was anxious to discover if Edward had had news of his whereabouts.

'My husband does not confide in me,' snapped the queen. 'Although I doubt he would keep quiet if he did know,' she added.

'Despenser believes he has gone back to Ireland.' She paused and fixed Lady de Vescy with her bright blue eyes. 'Do you know that he had the audacity to ask me if I had helped the man escape?'

'Why would he suspect you?' Lady de Vescy asked, her heart beating a little faster.

'He is convinced there is a spy at court,' replied the queen, and Lady de Vescy was glad that the scribe chose that moment to arrive with his quills and ink. It saved her from having to make a reply, and meant that the queen turned away from her and did not see the flush she felt burning on her cheeks. It was a dangerous game that she was playing, and one she had chosen not to share with Isabella, even though she knew it was only the queen's influence that kept her at court and in control of her lands rather than being reduced to a state of penury like Alicia de Lacy.

As she turned her attention back to her needlework, the door was thrust open again and the king made an unannounced entrance. He was bare-headed; his fair hair was awry, as if he had been running his fingers through it; and a dark flush coloured his cheeks. She rose to acknowledge him, relieved to see that Despenser had not entered the chamber with him, although she could see him lurking

60

outside, and guessed that whatever the king had come to say, it would have had its origins with him.

'My lord?' said Isabella, her face betraying a futile attempt to assess her husband's temper.

'I want you to write a letter to your brother.'

'What do you wish me to say, my lord?' asked Isabella as the king waved away her scribe to make room for his own clerk.

'I want you to convince him that he must end this dispute in Gascony.'

'How can I do that, my lord?' she asked.

Towering over her, Edward folded his arms and glared down. 'Peace between England and France was the reason for our marriage,' he said. 'Tell your brother that if war breaks out between the two countries, then it follows that our marriage has failed!'

Lady de Vescy watched as the queen stared up at her husband, whose face was contorted with suppressed rage.

'Perhaps,' said Isabella, after a moment, 'it would be better if you would allow me to go to France and mediate with Charles in person.'

'Go to France to meet up with your lover, Mortimer, you mean?' shouted Edward, matching the queen pace for pace as she backed away from him. 'Do you think I don't know that it was you who helped him escape from the Tower?'

'My lord!' She held up a hand, the palm towards him, and Lady de Vescy saw her look of panic. 'Who has told you such lies? Who has planted these seeds of hatred for me in your mind? They are not true, and I refute them all. I am your faithful and loving wife,' she protested. 'I would never do anything that would displease you.'

They stared at one another, and Lady de Vescy knew that the name of Hugh le Despenser hung unspoken on the air between them like a miasma. A moment of doubt flickered across Edward's face.

'Someone at court helped Mortimer,' he replied, and when his eyes caught hers, Lady de Vescy felt the hot blood suffuse her cheeks and she looked down, hoping that Edward would not see the guilt that was surely written on her face.

'My lord, it was not me,' the queen insisted.

Edward stared at her. 'Then write the letter as you are bid,' he told her and, although he seemed less angry, Lady de Vescy saw that his suspicion that Isabella had betrayed him was not diminished.

Isabella nodded dumb agreement. As the

scribe dipped his quill into the inkhorn and allowed it to hover over the parchment, awaiting her words, she protested that she did not know what to say. Within a moment Despenser was in the chamber, dictating words and demanding only that the queen take the quill and add her signature and seal before the letter was sanded and taken away for a messenger to deliver to France.

Seeing that Isabella was trembling after the men had gone, Lady de Vescy poured a cup of wine from the flagon on the small coffer.

'I did not help Roger Mortimer,' protested the queen as she took the cup, 'but if I knew who had I would ... I would take this necklace from around my neck and give it to them as a gift.' She fingered the rubies that fell from her throat to the rise of her breasts. 'And I would thank them and ask them to make good use of the jewels to raise men and money to oppose my husband. Do you think that is wicked of me?' she asked.

'No, my lady. I don't.' Lady de Vescy almost confessed to the queen, but instead she turned away and stared at the greyish sky beyond the window. Although she loved Isabella, she was aware that in these turbulent times it was better to trust no one; and only her brother, Henry Beaumont, and her chaplain, who acted as her messenger, were aware that she was the spy in the English court.

★ ★ ★

Roger Mortimer read the letter through twice, then folded it and put it into his pouch, wondering if he could use Edward's distrust of the queen as a weapon against him. He liked Isabella. Not just because he found her physically attractive, but because she had intervened on Joan's behalf, and because he believed that she was a good person. She had not had an easy marriage, and if what he had just read was true, her position in England was becoming untenable.

He wondered whether he ought to give some money to the priest who had tracked him through France, but the man seemed adequately dressed and shod, and Roger thought he might consider it an insult to be treated as a common messenger.

'Is Lady de Vescy in good health?' Roger asked him, taking the wine jug and pouring another cup for his guest.

'She is afraid,' the priest told him. 'If she is discovered, she will be sent to the Tower, and with the queen fallen from favour she would no longer be able to protect her.'

'And what news of her brother?'

'My lord Beaumont is improved since his release from the Tower. Even a short spell there can take its toll on a man's well-being, as you well know, my lord.'

'Edward has forgiven him for his outburst, then?' asked Roger, who had heard several accounts of the meeting at Bishopsthorpe, when the king had ordered Henry Beaumont from the chamber and Henry had replied that he would prefer to be absent than present, for which remark Edward had had him imprisoned for contempt.

'They have made up their differences — at least, the king believes so. In truth, my lord Beaumont is still angry about the truce with the Scots. It means he will lose his claim to his wife's land there and the right to style himself the Earl of Buchan. And he is not the only one to have lost faith in the ability of the king to rule.'

Roger studied the priest and found himself wondering how such men managed without the company of women. He and Joan had been married young, about the time that such desires had begun to trouble him, and whenever they had been parted before, he had had other concerns to keep his mind from the temptations of the flesh. Even in the Tower and during his first days in France, he had not thought much of it. But now that the tournament season was over and he had little to do but wait on the whims of kings, he was filled with a restlessness that was tightening its hold on him day by day. So far he had avoided the prostitutes who stalked the precincts of Charles's court. In the past he had never concerned himself with such women, not wanting to partake of a flesh that had been touched by so many others; but recently he had found himself looking upon them with a more considerate mind and fingering the silver coins in his purse.

He consciously put the thoughts aside and gave his full attention to the priest. 'Edward appears to have neither the ability nor the will to rule,' he remarked. 'When I hear stories of him deserting his court to fraternise with ordinary men as they go about their tasks — digging ditches and building walls — I do not wonder that the lords and barons despair of his kingship.'

'There are some who remain loyal,' replied the priest. 'The king is sending infantry under the command of John de Warenne to try to relieve the siege at La Reole.'

'God's teeth!' swore Roger before apologising to the priest for his blasphemy. 'Does the man never know when he is beaten? He cannot possibly succeed.'

'He will listen only to Hugh le Despenser.'

Roger snorted. 'No good will come of that. It is like a game of chess, when an opponent keeps on moving their pawns and knights in the feeble hope that they might see a way to win.'

★ ★ ★

When he heard the news that the English army had rioted because they had been neither paid nor fed, Eble le Strange was glad that he had not gone to France with John de Warenne. It had been difficult enough to raise even a few men from Lincolnshire. Most were tired of fighting futile battles for a king they had begun to hate, and as Eble had ridden around the villages and manors he had met the same refusal over and over again. Even men who had left the king's army without permission, because they were so embittered, were not persuaded by the threat that they would be arrested and hanged without trial if they did not return forthwith. They told Eble that they preferred to farm their land in peace and, although Eble feared for the consequences if his deception were discovered, he sent messages back to the king saying that the men could not be found.

'The king's days are numbered,' said one as Eble sat astride his horse and watched the man continue to harness up a team of oxen to plough his fields. 'It will not be long before Roger Mortimer brings an army, and then we will be rid of him and Despenser. And the sooner the better, as far as I'm concerned.'

Eble heard similar sentiments wherever he went, sentiments that he sympathised with. The whole country was biding its time until Roger Mortimer came and, like the coming of the Christmas feast, it was an event that everyone was anticipating with pleasure.

Even Alicia was excited by it. She compelled every friar or merchant who passed by Swaveton to come to table in the hall and tell her what they knew of the affairs in France. And little by little they had begun to piece together a picture of what was happening. The king and Despenser were expecting Roger Mortimer to invade East Anglia at any moment. The Earl of Kent's campaign in Gascony had been a disaster. He had been forced to surrender, and the French king was insisting that Queen Isabella go to France to negotiate a peace; but Edward was reluctant to agree, even though his continued refusal to make terms with Charles would result in him losing all his French lands.

'And where is Roger Mortimer? Does anyone know?' Alicia had asked the friar who had recently travelled through France on his way back from Rome.

'He has gone to Hainault, my lady,' the friar replied. 'But Hainault is not that far away from France, and Count William will prove a powerful ally.'

Part Two

1325 to 1326

7

March 1325–April 1325

The Negotiation of a Truce

As Lady de Vescy felt the deck of the ship rise beneath her feet, she said a silent prayer of thanks to be out of England and free of the threat of discovery and imprisonment. The winter had seemed endless, and even now it was still very cold. Beneath a canvas awning, the queen was visibly shivering despite her fur-lined cloak and hood; and although Jeanne de Bar held her hand and whispered words of comfort, tears slid unchecked down the queen's pale face.

Isabella had been so happy and thankful when the king had relented and given her permission to sail to France to intercede with her brother Charles in the dispute about Gascony, but Despenser's sly plotting had soon destroyed her moment of happiness.

Although the French king had asked that his sister bring her eldest son, so that he could pay homage for the duchy in his father's place, Edward had refused to let the prince leave England and had seized all the children from Isabella's household and put them into the care of Lady Despenser.

Lady de Vescy could still hear the screams from Eleanor and Joan as they had been dragged from their mother's arms by Despenser's men. He had not even had the consideration to send women for the little girls.

'Do not complain so,' Edward had told Isabella afterwards. 'I never had any intention of allowing the children to go with you to France. At least if they are here, it will give you reason to complete the task of negotiating with your brother and return to me. Lady Despenser will take good care of them.'

'If so much as one hair on their heads is harmed . . . ' Isabella had begun with a clenched fist.

'They are my children as well!' Edward had shouted back. 'Do you think I want them harmed?'

Then he had stormed from the chamber, and Isabella had collapsed in tears and had not stopped crying since.

There was a crowd of people on the quayside waiting to welcome them as they approached the harbour. Ordinary people, who had come to welcome Isabella home to the land of her birth. They let out a small cheer and waved scraps of fabric as she came down the gangplank to mount her horse.

The sun came out from behind the scudding clouds, and Lady de Vescy felt it warm on her back as she settled into her saddle. Birds were singing in the woodlands, and the warm breeze dried the tears from Isabella's cheeks. As they passed by the small hamlets and villages, people came out to watch the procession go past; and when they were told that the fine lady was Isabella, Queen of England and sister to their king, they smiled and waved. The sergeant-at-arms was instructed to hand out silver pennies from the fund that Edward had given his wife for her expenses.

When they reached Poissy, Charles was waiting to greet them. They were led through the palace to the king's privy chamber, where they were seated on cushioned benches and served with good French wine and thin spiced wafers.

'How are you?' Charles asked his sister. It was no polite enquiry. Lady de Vescy saw that his concern was genuine.

'Better for being out of England,' Isabella told him. 'You have my gratitude for persuading my husband to allow me to come.'

'Then I was not wrong to think that you

were unhappy in England. Is your husband cruel?' he asked, fingering the ornate dagger that hung from his belt.

'He does not beat me,' Isabella assured her brother. 'But cruelty can reveal itself in many ways. He has taken all my children from my care. He knew that if I had been allowed to bring them, I might never have gone back.'

'He holds them as hostages to ensure your return?'

Isabella nodded. 'I have been instructed to be back in England no later than midsummer.'

'Does he take lovers?' asked Charles.

'Only the one,' replied Isabella. 'But surely you knew that?'

'I have heard rumours, but I was not sure whether to believe them . . . '

'Despenser has complete power over Edward,' said Isabella. 'He listens to no one but him. That is why he will not come to pay you homage for his lands in Gascony. It is because Despenser tells him not to.'

'It was my intention to force him to come by confiscating the land,' said Charles. 'I was surprised when he sent his half-brother to declare war. Still, he proved incompetent, and the lands are mine now.'

'And will you keep them from my son as well?' asked Isabella.

'I have no quarrel with you, sister,' said Charles. 'And the prince is my nephew. I am willing to make a truce with your husband, and I will not withhold the lands from the prince if he is made duke and comes to France to pay homage to me.'

'Nothing would please me more than to have my son at my side,' Isabella told him.

'How old is the boy now?'

'He is thirteen.'

Charles nodded. 'Old enough to be betrothed.'

'There was talk of him being betrothed to a daughter of the Count of Hainault.'

Charles sat for a moment, twisting one of the many rings that adorned his fingers. 'Hainault,' he repeated. 'Now that is interesting. You may write to Edward and inform him that I am willing to sign a truce if he meets my demands, but also say that you must remain here. Say that there are complications that must be addressed. And also, tell him that he is welcome at my court. Invite him to come here.'

'What about Despenser?' she asked.

Charles frowned. 'No. He is not welcome. The merchants hate him for the amounts he stole from them during his exile. The man is nothing more than a common pirate, and if he sets foot on French soil he will be arrested and made to stand trial.'

Isabella thanked her brother, and they kissed again before she retired to the chambers that had been prepared for her use.

Once they were settled, the queen asked for her clerk — a new one who had been appointed by Despenser. He was a surly little man who had been violently seasick on the voyage — an affliction which Lady de Vescy told Isabella was probably a punishment from God — because although the man was a priest, there was nothing but his neat handwriting that she could find to commend him.

The other ladies of the household were dismissed. It was probable, thought Lady de Vescy, that they had also been promised full purses to send secret messages back to England, and their sulky looks betrayed their annoyance that the queen would say nothing in their presence. But Lady de Vescy knew that they were not above listening at keyholes; and when she opened the door for the clerk to leave with the carefully worded letter, she checked that there was no one there before speaking.

'If the king agrees to come and Despenser is left alone in England, then Henry of Lancaster will not hesitate to take him prisoner,' she said.

'I would not be sorry,' said Isabella.

'Do you think Edward will come?'

'I don't know.' Isabella walked to the window and stood twisting the tassel that hung from the belt of her green gown. 'If he were parted from Despenser's influence, I might be able to reason with him.'

Lady de Vescy heard the sadness in her voice. She knew that there had been a time when Isabella had loved Edward. She suspected that she might still love him, but Edward had turned away from all those who had once cared for him when he had become obsessed with Despenser.

★   ★   ★

When Roger Mortimer read the letter from Charles, it was the mention of the possible betrothal of Prince Edward to a daughter of William of Hainault that made him pause to consider. That morning he had seen William's second daughter, Philippa, sitting reading on a window seat. At the time his thoughts had been for his wife, Joan, who took similar pleasure in the reading of romances; but now he thought back to what he had seen with a different purpose. He judged that the girl was around ten or eleven years old. She was plump and had dark hair and eyes like her father. Her skin was not fair enough for her to be considered a beauty, but she was of a similar age to Prince Edward; and although they were second cousins, a dispensation was possible. It was a match that might serve him very well, he thought, and he decided that it was time he returned to the French court.

★ ★ ★

Isabella got up from the window seat and smoothed her skirts as the chamberlain showed Roger Mortimer into her apartments. When he had sent a messenger asking if she would see him, she had agreed without hesitation. She was keen to reacquaint herself with this man who had been cunning enough to organise his own escape from the Tower of London, and who had reduced her husband and Despenser to despair as they sought him across England and the continent.

He swept into a low bow before her. 'Your grace.'

'My lord Mortimer,' she replied. He was much changed since the last time she had seen him. On that day he had looked thin and grey and unkempt, but the man who stood before her now had an air of assurance and confidence.

'I trust I find you well, my lady?'

'I am quite well, thank you,' she told him as she beckoned him towards a seat in the window embrasure, as far from her ladies' prying ears as was possible. She watched as he settled himself on the bench opposite her and crossed his legs. 'You look in better health than the last time we met,' she said, raising her gaze from the muscles of his thighs to his face.

'My accommodation has somewhat improved, my lady.'

Isabella felt herself blush, as if his imprisonment had been her fault. 'I am pleased to hear it,' she said. 'I do not think my husband was justified in holding you a prisoner. I was glad when I heard of your escape. It cannot have been easy.'

'I am not a man to be afraid of a challenge,' he replied. 'And I have good friends.'

Isabella glanced towards the hearth, where her ladies were gathered. Each head was bent to a task, but she was aware that their ears were straining to catch every word of her conversation. Roger caught her look and she saw that he understood her dilemma.

'It is a wise man, or woman, who knows who are friends and who are enemies,' he remarked in a loud enough voice to be overheard. 'I hope that you will consider me your friend, my lady,' he added quietly.

'I need friends,' she whispered. He nodded, and she noticed that the sunlight caught the silver highlights in his hair, although she did not think that he looked aged; and she found the creases at the corners of his eyes attractive. She saw his look of amusement at her scrutiny. He seemed aware that he was a handsome man and that women found him pleasing.

'Will you walk with me in the orchard?' he asked. 'The blossom is fragrant on the apple trees, and the weather here is warmer than in England.'

'I think that some fresh air would benefit me,' said Isabella. 'I will ask Lady de Vescy to fetch my cloak and to act as my chaperone.'

She saw his spark of interest at the name. 'I did not know that Lady de Vescy had accompanied you,' he said. 'It seems that you are not friendless after all.'

As they made their way across the inner courtyard, Isabella saw Lady de Vescy exchange a glance with Roger Mortimer and give a slight shake of her head. She wondered what it was about. As far as she knew, they were not on familiar terms, but they seemed to share some secret. She must ask her friend what she knew of Mortimer, because Isabella found she had an insatiable interest in this man who was the sworn enemy of her husband.

When they came to the fence that surrounded the orchard to keep the pigs and wild boar out, Roger unlatched the gate and stood back to allow her to pass through. Pink petals floated along the slender branches of the trees, and underfoot the grass was verdant with new growth.

'We will not be overheard here,' said Roger as he closed the gate. 'And I know that I can speak freely in the presence of Lady de Vescy.'

Isabella gave her companion a sharp look and was met with a smile of contrition.

'You?' she asked her as the truth struck her with clarity. 'Was it you who helped Mortimer escape?' She could scarce comprehend that her friend should have kept such a thing from her. She had thought that they shared everything.

'There were many times that I almost told you,' replied Lady de Vescy. 'But when lives are at stake, it is sometimes best to keep your own counsel.'

'Shall we walk?' suggested Mortimer, diffusing the tension between the two women. He turned to Isabella. 'Your brother has spoken to me about your troubles. If there is any way that I can assist you, please know that I am yours to command.'

Isabella looked up at him. It was hard to

think that anyone could command him. He appeared to be everything that her husband was not — dark where Edward was fair; competent where Edward was inept; and very sure of himself, whereas Edward always needed someone to advise him.

'Do you think your husband will be persuaded to come and perform homage for his French lands?' he asked her.

'I do not know,' she said. 'He would be foolish not to. Aquitaine has belonged to the English crown since the days of Queen Eleanor, and Ponthieu is my husband's inheritance from his own mother.'

'Your brother suggests that your son should be given the titles of Duke of Aquitaine and Count of Ponthieu, and come to pay homage in the king's place.'

'Yes. My brother would be content with such an arrangement.' She met Roger Mortimer's dark eyes again. 'And if it comes to a choice between that and the loss of his lover, then Edward may agree. He will not risk the life of Despenser.'

'You do not like Despenser?' asked Roger, catching her derisive tone.

'He has stolen my husband from me,' she told him. 'I hate him. Every day I pray that some evil will befall him and that he will end in hell! Have I shocked you?' she asked, wondering what he would think of her.

'I can understand the depth of your feelings, my lady,' he replied, as he ducked his head under an overhanging branch. 'You must know that I also have only hatred for Hugh le Despenser. Besides, he will kill me if I do not kill him first.'

'And do you intend to kill him?' she asked.

'Yes,' he said quietly. 'I do.'

'Henry of Lancaster might do it for you if Despenser is left alone in England. Or Henry Beaumont,' she said, glancing at Lady de Vescy.

'But it is not likely that Edward will come to France and leave him behind.'

Isabella shook her head. 'No, not after what happened to Gaveston. Edward would never take that risk. But he cannot afford to continue a war with France,' she told him. 'Or with you.' She hesitated. 'My husband and Despenser are convinced that you are about to invade at any moment. Is there any truth in that rumour, my lord?'

'Would you like it to be true?' he asked.

'I would like to see Despenser removed, but I do not wish any harm to my husband. He is the father of my children, and at one time there was affection between us.' They walked in silence for a few paces. 'I would be content to remain in France, except for my children,' she told him.

'You must miss them very much, my lady.'

'I do. Especially my little girls. I worry about them. I hope that Lady Despenser treats them kindly.'

'I am sure that she does.' Roger laid his hand on her shoulder and Isabella was shocked. It was beyond the bounds of what was acceptable, but the gentle pressure was comforting, and she did not move away or voice any objection. When she looked up at him again, she saw an air of satisfaction on his face as he dropped his hand to his side.

'What would you like to see happen?' he asked her.

Isabella could not answer straight away. She was more used to being told by men what to think. No one had ever asked for her opinion before.

'I would like to see my son become king,' she said at last. 'People say that he is like his grandfather and that he has it in him to rule diligently. But he is not yet fourteen.'

'He could rule, with someone to guide him as regent,' suggested Roger.

'But for that to happen my husband would have to die.'

'Not necessarily,' he replied. 'But first we would need to have your son under our control.' He spoke as if they would act together, and she found that it was a concept that did not displease her.

'If my husband could be persuaded to send my son to me, would you claim him as your king and help me to rule England in my husband's place?' she asked, hoping that she had understood him correctly and was not making a fool of herself.

'If that is what you desire, my lady.'

'Yes,' said Isabella. It was not something that had occurred to her before; but, walking beside this strong and intelligent man, she suddenly realised that what he suggested might be possible — and that with him at her side, she would have the confidence to usurp her husband's throne. 'But I would not want my husband to be killed,' she added.

'Of course not, my lady. My quarrel is with Hugh le Despenser, not the king. But Edward has had too many chances, and failed too many times. I do not think he is fit to govern England.'

'What would happen to him?' asked Isabella.

Roger stared across the orchard. 'We would have to imprison him,' he said at last. 'Not in the conditions in which I was held, of course. He would be treated well. But there is no other option if you want him to stay alive.'

Isabella turned to Lady de Vescy. 'What do

you think?' she asked her.

'I think that what my lord Mortimer suggests has merit. I think that you would be wise to heed his words.'

Isabella nodded. 'We will need money for ships and men,' she said.

'Leave that to me,' said Roger. 'The most important thing now is for you to persuade your husband to send Prince Edward to France. And on no account must you return to England,' he warned her. 'Promise me that you will stand firm, no matter how much pressure is brought to bear on you.'

'I will,' Isabella told him, and his face melted into a smile that caused a feeling of fluttering in her stomach which bewildered and unsettled her. She wanted him to reach out and touch her again, and when he did not she offered him her hand. He took it lightly and lifted it to his lips. His thick moustache brushed her fingers, and a tremor ran through her at his touch.

'I am your servant, my lady,' he said, although Isabella was beginning to suspect that he was the servant of no one.

8

May 1325

A Matter of Trust

When Alicia received the message that Henry of Lancaster was coming to Swaveton, she was thankful that she had a new gown and would not have to receive her late husband's brother looking like a dairymaid. Now, as she stood beside Eble at the manor house door waiting to greet their visitor, she wondered what had brought him, and whether it might be to her advantage.

Henry rode into the courtyard with a small escort, and she was grateful for his consideration. It would be less costly for them to feed and accommodate only a handful of men. He dismounted, handed the reins of his horse to a man-at-arms, and then came towards them, pulling off his riding gloves.

'Alicia,' he said. 'I hope I find you well?'

'Tolerably well,' she told him. 'Please, come inside. I have refreshments prepared for you and your men.'

They followed her into the hall, seeming to fill it with the rattling of spurs and the clanking of swords against chainmail. It was telling, thought Alicia, that they had chosen to ride armed.

Edith was overseeing the distribution of food and drink from a trestle below the window, and Alicia followed Eble as he showed Henry to the dais and offered him the chair. Henry took it with a nod of thanks and drank thirstily.

'It saddens me to see you in such reduced circumstances,' he said to Alicia, putting the cup down. 'What has been done by this king is not justice for either of us.'

'I count myself lucky to be allowed my life and my freedom,' she replied. 'And to be married again.' She glanced at Eble. 'I would be far worse off without my husband to protect me.'

Henry looked at Eble. 'Sit down,' he said. 'There are things we must speak of. Things that will affect all our futures.'

Eble, rather than sitting on the bench, perched on the edge of the table so that he could look down on their visitor. His fingers fiddled with the handle of his dagger, although his face had taken on the bland expression that he had learnt to use to his advantage as a squire.

'What troubles you, my lord?' Alicia asked Henry.

'Apart from having my land and titles withheld from me?' he asked. 'Though you know well enough how that feels.' His gaze strayed to Eble. 'You fought for my brother at Boroughbridge? Against the king?'

'I did,' replied Eble without a change of expression.

'And would you be willing to fight against Edward again?'

The direct question surprised Alicia.

'I'm the son of a marcher lord. What do you think?' replied Eble.

'The king has made you supervisor of the array.'

'That does not mean he trusts me.'

'But you are a friend of John de Warenne?'

Eble folded his arms. 'John de Warenne and I have known each other since we were boys. We might not always see eye to eye on political matters, but we do not allow that to get in the way of our friendship.'

'Is that wise?' asked Henry.

'Yes,' Eble told him. 'John had me released from the dungeon at York after Borough-bridge, which probably saved my life. I owe him a lot.'

'Would you oppose him in battle?'

'I did at Boroughbridge.'

'But if you came face to face with him on the field?' insisted Henry. 'Would you kill him?'

'No,' said Eble. 'We would spare one another's lives.'

'Is this relevant?' asked Alicia. The two men reminded her of stags, circling and assessing the strength of the other before locking horns.

'I need to know whom I can trust,' said Henry. 'And I am not sure of your husband.'

'Why do you need to be sure of him?' she asked. Henry took a breath to speak, and she thought he was about to tell her that it was nothing he would discuss with a woman. The look on his face so reminded her of Thomas that she felt physically sick and wished him gone from her table. But, she reminded herself, despite the resemblance, he was not the husband who had treated her so badly.

'I need to be sure of him, because when Edward goes to France to pay homage he will be unable to take Despenser, which will give me the chance to move against him.'

'You can be assured that we will give you every assistance to be rid of that man!' said Alicia. 'He has everything that is rightly mine. All my mother's lands — '

'Mine as well,' interrupted Henry. 'And with Despenser out of the way, there is a chance that we can get them back from the king.'

'And if Edward does not go to France?' asked Eble. 'What then? Will you still take on Despenser?'

'It would be difficult,' admitted Henry. 'I cannot afford to raise a rebellion without the income from the Lancaster lands — and Despenser knows that, which is why he withholds them.'

'And what of Roger Mortimer?' asked Alicia.

'He faces the same problem. He also needs funds to raise an army; and whilst Charles of France has some sympathy with his cause, he does not seem willing to dip into his purse whilst he can seek a peaceful settlement.'

'And is there no one else who will help Mortimer?'

'He has visited many courts. Most recently he has been in Hainault, seeking help from Count William.'

'And if Mortimer comes?' asked Alicia. 'Will you support him?'

'Will you? And your husband?' asked Henry as Eble shifted restlessly on the table.

'Of course,' said Alicia. 'As I said, we will support anyone who can help us be rid of Despenser.'

Henry rested his gaze on Eble. 'You will

have my support,' he told him.

'Good,' replied Henry with a nod of satisfaction. He reached for his cup and waited for Eble to take up his as well. 'To the downfall of Hugh le Despenser and the restitution of our lands,' he said.

9

September 1325

The Question of Homage

'Your husband sends his regrets,' Charles told Isabella, throwing the letter across the table towards her. 'Apparently he has been taken ill at the last moment, and rather than boarding ship, he has sent the Bishop of Winchester to negotiate on his behalf.'

'I'm sure his illness must be genuine,' said Isabella. She had been sure that Edward would come as he had promised in his letters. She had believed that once he was in France, away from the influence of Despenser, she would be able to persuade him to make peace with her brother. But having to negotiate with the Bishop of Winchester was a different prospect altogether.

'Will you see the bishop?' asked Charles.

'What shall I say to him?' she asked.

'Tell him that if your husband will not come, the only acceptable alternative is for him to give the lands to your son and send the prince to pay homage instead.'

'It is a solution that would please me,' said Isabella as she watched her brother twist a ring on his finger.

'Have you spoken with Roger Mortimer?' he asked.

'Yes.' She wondered if Mortimer had confided in him the plan to invade England and replace the king with his son.

'Mortimer tells me that Count William of Hainault would be willing to marry his daughter, Philippa, to your son if he were made the Duke of Aquitaine. Would you be willing to approve such a marriage?' he asked. 'I think the count could be persuaded to help solve your problems if his daughter were to be the future queen of England.'

'I would have no objections to the marriage,' Isabella told him. 'If it could be arranged.'

'Good. But do not mention any of this to the bishop,' Charles warned her. 'Tell him that he must make it clear to Edward that the Gascon lands will be forfeit if this matter of homage is not resolved by the end of the year.'

★ ★ ★

John de Stratford, the Bishop of Winchester, was a middle-aged man with a benign air.

'Bless you, my child,' he said, making the sign of the cross over Isabella as she bent to kiss his ring. 'I am pleased to see you in such good health.'

'I hope that my husband's illness is not severe,' she said, after the bishop had related Edward's apologies to her.

'He was at Dover, and we were all set to sail when he was taken with a fever,' explained the bishop. 'His physician forbade him to travel. It was very unfortunate.'

'Unfortunate indeed, especially at such a delicate stage in my negotiations with my brother,' she told him. 'Charles is very anxious that my husband should not delay any further and must come to do homage in return for the restitution of his Gascon lands.'

They sat down at the table that had been prepared for them to dine privately in her chamber. She waited whilst the bishop said grace and blessed the food, then nodded to the serving boys to remove the lids from the platters, and urged the bishop to help himself from the steaming dishes.

'There is, of course, an alternative,' she said as she watched him break his bread and dip it into a bowl of savoury mutton. 'The king could grant the lands to our son, Edward of Windsor, and he could come to my brother's court to do homage in my husband's place.'

97

The bishop continued to chew his meat, then reached a finger into his mouth to pick out a remnant from between his teeth. 'It is a possibility,' he agreed at last. 'But perhaps it would be better if you spoke to the king about this yourself.'

'I would have done if he had come,' she said. 'Perhaps when he is recovered I will be able to discuss the matter with him.'

The bishop did not immediately reply, and the silence unnerved Isabella. She fumbled with her spoon, unsure whether to fill her mouth with food or to keep it empty so that she could speak her mind.

'I have brought this,' said the bishop at last, as he reached for something concealed within the folds of his robes. He handed her a letter bearing her husband's seal.

'Do you know its contents?' she asked him as she fingered it suspiciously.

'I do, my lady. The king requires that you return with me to England.'

Isabella stared at the bishop. Edward and Despenser had made an unexpected move.

'But I am in the midst of delicate negotiations with my brother,' she protested. 'If I return to England now, then everything I have done here will be void. Surely the king knows that?'

The bishop gave a slight shrug of his

shoulders, as if the whole affair were a burden he wished to be rid of. 'I am only the messenger, my lady,' he told her. 'I cannot account for what is in the king's mind. But he is adamant that he will provide you with no more money if you do not return.'

'I will not go,' she said. 'He cannot force me.'

'Indeed, it would be difficult for the king of England to send an army to France to compel you to return,' said the bishop without altering his expression. 'What would you have me do?' he asked.

Isabella hesitated, unsure of the man. Was he an ally of her husband, or could she persuade him to help her? 'Will you return to England with the suggestion that the king invests our son with his French lands?' she asked him. 'My brother will provide you with a letter that confirms such an arrangement would be acceptable to him.'

The bishop scratched at his tonsure then reached to help himself to more meat, adding a generous quantity of sauce. Isabella watched him, her own food still untouched.

'Yes,' he agreed at last. 'I am willing to do that, although I can make no promises that the king will agree.'

'I think he will find that he has little choice,' replied Isabella.

Although she had avoided being forced to sail back to England with the bishop, Isabella remained anxious about her children. She did not believe that Edward would harm them, but she feared that he might try to turn them against her and the thought of her husband making them hate her was more than she could bear.

When the news came that Edward would allow their son to come she wept with relief, and when the prince arrived she scarcely waited until he had dismounted before she hurried forward and gathered him into her arms.

Accompanying the prince was Lady de Vescy's brother, Henry Beaumont, and he kissed her hand before greeting his sister with a warm embrace.

'I see that you are back in the favour of the king,' remarked Lady de Vescy to her brother, 'and that my letters on your behalf have not gone unheeded.'

'Indeed, you are to be commended for your excellent letters,' said Henry with a grin. 'The king speaks well of you, and I was honoured to be entrusted with the safety and well-being of the prince.'

'And the king suspects nothing?' asked Lady de Vescy.

'No. And more to the point, neither does Despenser,' said her brother.

'That man is not as clever as he likes to think,' remarked Isabella, smoothing down a strand of her son's fair hair and brushing some dried mud from his sleeve. 'But your sister is cunning,' she told Henry. 'Even I had no idea it was she who was sending letters to Roger Mortimer.'

'And are we sure we can trust Roger Mortimer?' asked Henry Beaumont.

'Yes, I'm sure we can,' replied Lady de Vescy. 'It saddens me to have to act against the king, but he will see no reason where Hugh le Despenser is concerned, and the time has come to be rid of that man.'

'And no one wants rid of him more than Mortimer,' said Isabella.

★   ★   ★

Lady de Vescy placed her hand on the sleeve of her younger brother and allowed him to escort her into the great hall, where Charles of France was waiting to receive his nephew. Catching a glimpse of the Bishop of Exeter in young Edward's retinue, she frowned and tightened her hold on Henry's arm until he inclined his head towards her.

'I know,' he whispered, following her gaze.

'Ever since we sailed, that man has had the look of a cat that has lapped at the milk behind the dairymaid's back. I just hope that he has no plans to disrupt this ceremony with some trouble of Despenser's making.'

Charles rose from the throne at the approach of his sister and stretched out his arms to greet the prince. Isabella put a hand to her son's shoulder and urged him forward, smiling as Charles embraced the boy and received his kiss of homage for the lands in Aquitaine of which he was now duke.

The ceremony complete, they made their way to the feast. At the top table, the king and queen of France were seated beside Isabella and her son, and the Bishop of Exeter had also been given the honour of a place on the dais. Boys came in with jugs and towels for hand washing, and when that was complete the bishop rose to his feet, scraping back his chair and glaring around at the gathering. One by one people fell silent, expecting him to say grace, but he turned his hawk-nosed face towards Isabella, cleared his throat, and began to speak directly to her.

'My lady,' he began in a voice that resonated around the hall. 'Your husband, our gracious lord Edward, has entrusted me with his demand that you return to England forthwith. He will tolerate no more excuses. It is my duty to remind you that, as Edward's wife, you are legally and morally obliged to return to him. The king has sent me with enough money to pay your debts, but that money will not be forthcoming unless you return with me.' He paused and glanced at Charles, who was watching him with an expression of utter disbelief at the insult to his sister. 'This is the king's final word on the matter,' added the bishop. 'My lady, you have no choice but to comply.'

There was a moment of tense silence, and the assembled guests watched as Isabella stared down at her platter. Then, with fierce and angry eyes, she looked up at the bishop and addressed him directly.

'I agree that I am Edward's wife,' she told him. 'But someone has come between my husband and myself and is trying to break that sacred bond. I will not return to my husband until that intruder is removed. In fact,' she said, 'I shall consider myself to be a widow — and I will assume the robes of widowhood and mourning — until that man is gone from my husband's bed!'

The silence that followed was broken within seconds by gasps of amazement and delight at her words. Spontaneous applause broke out as people expressed their approval, and the bishop turned to Charles, expecting him to rebuke his sister for her outburst.

'My lord, surely you will not condone the speaking of such treason?' he appealed to him.

Charles shrugged his shoulders. 'My sister came here of her own free will, and may freely return if she so wishes. But if she prefers to remain, I will not expel her.'

Then Charles raised a hand and beckoned the waiting procession of servers to come forward with the bread and salt, all thoughts of a blessing forgotten. The minstrels began to play, and as people turned to discuss the events with their neighbours, the bishop had no option but to sit down and stare moodily at the table.

10

October 1325

The Widowed Queen

Isabella looked up as the Frenchwoman she had employed to sew her new gowns was ushered into the chamber. She was a plump woman whose fingers looked podgy, but her needlework was beyond reproach.

'Will you assist me?' Isabella said to Jeanne de Bar as she put down the book she had been reading.

It was two days since she had told the Bishop of Exeter that her marriage was over and she intended to dress as a widow. She had been shocked when he stood up and repeated the demands of her husband, and for a moment she had thought she must comply, but the anger that had been burning within her for so long had taken hold like fire in a thatch, and she had said what had been on her mind for a long time. She had tried her best with Edward. She had even loved him, especially when the children were born and he had been affectionate and attentive towards her. His affair with Piers Gaveston had been put aside then, and although she knew that he visited the tomb at Langley, she had been able to live with it. A dead man could not harm her. But a living one could, as had been so amply demonstrated when Hugh le Despenser had been appointed as the king's chamberlain.

Edward had complained about him at first and said that he hated the man, but little by little things had changed. Edward seemed to have less time for her. He stopped coming to her bed. At first she thought it was because of all the troubles with the rebellions and battles that had beset England during those years, but now that she looked back over events she could see clearly what she had not noticed at the time. Hugh le Despenser had inveigled himself into Edward's affections. He had sought out the place that had been left empty after the death of Piers, and he had filled it, taking control of the king's body and his mind.

Despite the bishop's words, Isabella knew that Edward did not desire her for any wifely duties. What he did want was control over her. He had taken a huge risk by allowing the prince to come to France; and now that the homage had been done and the lands were safe, he wanted them both back.

'My lady?' Isabella turned and lifted an arm as Jeanne began to unfasten the blue gown that she was wearing. From now on she would wear only white, and her hair and throat would be completely covered by a wimple and veil. She would show the whole of France that she mourned the death of her marriage to the English king.

She did not, however, intend to look as if she had taken the mantle and the ring. The kirtle that Jeanne lifted over her head was of superb quality, edged with vair fur and embroidered with discreet traces of gold thread. The silk felt cool as it rippled down her body, and Isabella was pleased to see that it fitted well and clung in all the right places. The seamstress nodded her approval, and Isabella held herself still as the woman took her needle and thread to adjust the fashionably buttoned sleeves.

As she waited, Isabella pictured the dark eyes and firm mouth of Roger Mortimer, and wondered how he would respond to the sight of her in her new gown. Perhaps such imaginings were not the most fitting thoughts for a widow, she mused. Or perhaps they were. For widows were free to marry again.

The woman snipped the thread with her silver scissors and stepped back to admire her handiwork.

'Make sure she is paid well,' said Isabella to Lady de Vescy as she picked up the silk veil and allowed it float down around her head. Jeanne helped her to arrange it so that not one strand of her hair was visible before pinning it with a jewelled clasp.

'Do you wish to see yourself?' asked Jeanne, reaching for the burnished steel mirror.

'No,' said Isabella. 'I am in mourning.'

'Yet you make a very fetching sight,' observed Lady de Vescy as she counted coins into the palm of the seamstress.

⋆ ⋆ ⋆

Roger Mortimer could not take his eyes off Isabella when she walked into the hall and took her place on the dais. She had been true to her promise to dress as a widow, and she might have been a vowess, except that the silk of her kirtle was so fine that with every movement he could see the shape of her thighs.

Her son followed her, waiting until his mother was seated before taking his place beside her, and Roger felt the pain of jealousy as he saw the loving smile that Isabella bestowed on the boy.

The blessing was said and the platters

uncovered, but Roger found that it was an appetite of an altogether different sort that was on his mind. He caught Isabella's eye as he reached to help himself to more of the dish of spiced cod, and she gave him a smile that made his blood surge.

⋆ ⋆ ⋆

One by one, Isabella's ladies came to express their regrets and explain that it was vital they return to their homes in England. Isabella presented each one of them with silver coins and thanked them for their attendance. She was glad to be rid of them. They were all spies, and it was no wonder they wanted to go running back to Despenser now that she had openly expressed her disdain for him. And it was not as if she could no longer afford to be generous. Edward might think she was still reliant on him, but he had overlooked the fact that, as her son was now the Duke of Aquitaine and Count of Ponthieu, she could prevent money from those lands going to England and channel it to provide for her own expenses.

'Ow!' she protested as Lady de Vescy dabbed her face with lavender water after plucking her eyebrows.

'It will take away the redness.'

'It doesn't feel as if it will.'

'Trust me. I know you want to look your best,' remarked Lady de Vescy as she gathered the bowl and strips of linen. Do you want me to stay?'

'I'm not sure,' confessed Isabella. 'He is so much of a man.' The thought of Roger Mortimer made her shiver with apprehension as she imagined him, tall and imposing, in her chamber. 'But I need his help if I am to claim the throne of England for my son.'

'You can trust him. He will not do anything to hurt you,' said Lady de Vescy as they heard approaching footsteps and Mortimer was admitted.

'My lady,' he said, making a bow. Isabella offered him her hand, and his fingers were warm and his lips warmer still when he took it and kissed it. 'I hope I find you in good health?'

'I am well, thank you,' she replied. 'Please, be seated. I am eager to hear what you have to say.'

He settled himself on the window seat opposite her and rested the ankle of one leg on the knee of the other. He was wearing a dark green tunic of a finely woven wool, and dark brown hose. His beard had recently been trimmed, and he was appraising her as thoroughly as she was assessing him.

She clasped her hands nervously in her lap as she heard Lady de Vescy close the outer door behind her. She had never been completely alone with a man before, except her husband, and then only on the most intimate of occasions. She wished that she had told Lady de Vescy to stay, and hoped that she remained within earshot, although she knew it was most unlikely that Mortimer would leap across the space between them and attempt to ravish her.

'You're not afraid of me, are you?' he asked gently, watching her expression.

'Should I be?' she challenged him.

He spread one hand in a gesture of innocence. 'I am your loyal servant, and I seek only to serve you.'

'You do not seek to serve yourself then?' she asked, meeting his eyes and seeing the moment of hesitation as she caught him on the wrong foot.

'I will not insult you by saying that my plans will not have benefits for both of us,' he said. 'But, as I have discovered since I left England, I cannot act for myself alone. I can only act in your defence — and in the defence of your son.'

'And how is it to be achieved?' she asked him. She knew that her brother would not fund an army for their rebellion. She had cautiously raised the subject with Charles herself, and he had told her that with the homage of the prince, his truce with Edward would stand; and although he would allow her to stay in France if she chose to, he would not waste money raising an army to invade England. She had been disappointed, but she knew that her brother's mind was not easily changed once it was set, and that as far as he was concerned Roger Mortimer would need to look elsewhere for funds.

'There are those who will help us if they will reap some reward from it,' said Mortimer. 'Do not forget Count William.'

'My son tells me that his father made him vow not to marry without his consent.'

'And will the boy keep the promise?'

'Edward made him swear on some holy relic, and he is afraid to break his word.'

Mortimer sighed. Putting his foot to the floor, he leaned forward with his elbows on his knees. 'Perhaps the promise of a marriage will be enough for Count William,' he suggested. 'I take it the prince made no vow regarding a betrothal.'

'It is a fine line,' said Isabella, watching as the possibilities flitted across his shrewd face.

'But surely he will listen to you,' replied Mortimer. His smile conveyed a total belief in her powers of persuasion, and Isabella felt a flutter of fear rise from the depth of her stomach to the pulse at her throat. She could not decide what she felt about this man. Part of her wanted to snatch up her skirts and run from him, but at the same moment she found herself wishing that he would come closer to her, touch her, even kiss her. She was confused by him. Edward was the only man she had been intimate with, and although the things that had happened between them had not been unpleasant, she had always felt slightly relieved when the act was over. She had never looked at Edward and experienced the feelings that were troubling her now.

'If the prince will agree to a betrothal with Philippa of Hainault, then Count William will back us. We can invade England and put your son on the throne. And you will rule as regent.'

'You do not plan to take the throne for yourself, then?' she challenged, wondering if she could trust him not to throw her and her son into the confines of one of his border castles once he had power within his grasp.

'I am no king,' he replied. 'Only those of royal descent may wear the crown. Except for those who abuse their power, as Edward has. Then they deserve to have it taken from them.'

'But you must not kill him,' she insisted,

still worried that her agreement to his plan might result in Edward's death. She could never allow that. Even if she no longer loved him, she did not want him dead — that wish was reserved for the odious Hugh le Despenser.

'I cannot promise he will not be killed in battle — if he chooses to fight — but if he is captured I will show him the same mercy that he afforded to me. Although I will not spare the life of Despenser,' Mortimer warned her.

'Despenser I would gladly see dead,' she told him. 'But not . . . ' She almost called him her husband, but the word would not form on her lips. 'Not Edward,' she said. 'He is the father of my children.'

She watched as Mortimer placed his hand over his heart. 'As God is my witness, I will not kill him. Do you trust me?' he asked her.

'I have little choice if I want to return to England. I may have one son with me, but John and my little daughters are still in the care of Despenser's wife, and I will not abandon them.'

He nodded. 'I too have children who are imprisoned . . . and my wife,' he added. It was on the tip of Isabella's tongue to ask him if he loved his wife, but she hesitated, not wanting to know the answer. She did not want to hear this man confess his love for another woman. Besides, a wife whom he had not seen for years was hardly a wife at all.

Mortimer moved to sit beside her. His knee nudged hers, and as he took her hand she felt her heart begin to pound with a mixture of fear and excitement. She saw that his eyes were even darker than usual, and she could not look away from him. After he had held her with his steady gaze for a moment, he leaned forward and brushed her cheek with his lips. His breath was hot and smelt of spices.

'Together we will rule England. I promise,' he said.

He took his leave of her, saying that he would come again soon and speak to her son as well. Isabella watched him go with a mixture of relief and regret. Her face tingled from his caress. She looked at her wedding ring, remembering the day that Edward had placed it on her finger — the day he had eyes only for Piers Gaveston. Then she reached for the keys that hung from her belt and went to unlock the small coffer in which she kept her jewels. She lifted the lid, twisted off the ring, and dropped it inside before firmly locking it again.

★ ★ ★

Lady de Vescy raised her eyebrows as Roger closed the door behind him. He nodded.

'As long as we can persuade young Edward to agree, then we can begin to move,' he told her.

'The boy will listen to his mother,' said Lady de Vescy. 'They are close, and he is not likely to turn down the opportunity to be crowned king.'

'But young enough not to be able to rule alone,' said Roger.

'Nothing is certain yet,' Lady de Vescy warned him.

'Have you had word from your brother?' he asked her. Henry had returned to England with those who had declared themselves loyal to the king, but had promised to ride about the country to discover who would back the rebellion.

'It is early days. But he will play his part,' she assured him.

'I hope I will not need to remain here much longer,' he told her. 'The widow whose house I am renting has sent me a letter saying that she desires it back. It is an annoyance I could have done without. If only she had waited a week or two longer, I would have been ready to leave anyway.'

'There are beds here,' suggested Lady de Vescy. 'Most of the queen's household has returned to England, so you and your men could take their places.'

'Will the queen agree?' he asked. It was a tempting offer if Isabella did not object, and would mean that he could keep a closer eye on who came and went from her chambers.

'I will speak to her and convince her of its advantages,' promised Lady de Vescy.

⋆   ⋆   ⋆

'So you are not concerned about what people might say?' Roger asked Isabella the next day, after Lady de Vescy had sent a messenger with a note to say that he might move himself and his men into the palace apartments.

'You know as well as I do that there are some who have already accused me of taking you as my . . . lover.' She hesitated over the word, and the blush that suffused her cheeks made him want to crush her against his body and kiss her pink mouth. He glanced away as the sound of voices broke the moment of tension between them, and saw Jeanne de Bar with the young prince beside her in the doorway. Isabella held out her arms to her son and he came forward, but as he did so, Roger noticed the look of disapproval on Jeanne's face that she had found him alone with the queen.

'Can we trust her? Jeanne, the Countess of Surrey, I mean?' he asked when Isabella had sent her away on some errand.

'Of course. She has been my friend and companion for many years,' said Isabella, brushing a speck of lint from Edward's tunic.

'But she is also the king's niece,' pointed out Roger. 'It may be wiser not to confide in her.'

'Confide what?' asked Edward, looking from his mother to Roger and back again. 'Perhaps you would like to confide in me.'

'That is why my lord Mortimer is here,' said his mother, putting a hand on his arm. 'Come and sit down and we tell you everything.'

'Philippa of Hainault,' said the boy when his mother had explained what they planned. He looked at Roger. 'Have you seen her?' he asked. 'What is she like?'

'She is pretty,' he told the boy. 'And she is willing to become your wife.'

'I would need to see her before I decided,' said Edward doubtfully.

'Of course you would,' said his mother. 'We would not ask you to do anything against your will.'

'And what about my father?' he asked. 'What will happen to him?'

'No harm will befall your father,' Roger

assured the boy, realising that he must choose his words carefully to avoid alienating the prince. 'The truth is that he never wanted to be king. He finds it difficult, and so becomes too reliant on those who give him poor counsel. I have no quarrel with your father,' he told him. 'It is Hugh le Despenser who is my enemy. And it is Hugh le Despenser who has brought such grief to your mother.' He paused as the boy turned to Isabella.

'My lord Mortimer speaks the truth,' she told him. 'Despenser has been an evil influence on your father, and it is he we want to be rid of.'

'Then why not be rid of him and allow my father to remain king? asked the prince.

'Edward,' said Roger, sitting down beside the boy and meeting his eyes in what he hoped would seem an adult exchange. 'I think that your father would be happier if he did not have the burden of kingship bearing down on him. You know that he is happiest when he is away from court and mixing with the common people. You have seen how he likes to turn his hand to tasks such as thatching a house or shoeing a horse. When he is at court he is uncomfortable and unhappy . . . whereas you — you are more like your grandfather. You have kingship in every fibre of your being. I think that your father would be grateful to have the responsibility taken from him, and although your shoulders are only young, your mother and I would be there to help and guide you. It is not a task that should daunt you or make you afraid.'

'But what would happen to my father?' insisted Edward. Roger hesitated. He saw that it might not be so easy to manipulate the prince as he had first thought. He was used to his own sons obeying him without question, and he was perturbed by this self-assured boy who did indeed seem every inch a monarch.

'He would be held securely at first, perhaps in a castle, but kindly treated and would want for nothing. In time, after he had agreed his abdication, perhaps he might be happier in an abbey or somewhere where he could live out his life in peace.'

'My lord Mortimer has vowed that your father will not be harmed,' said Isabella. Roger watched the boy as he turned to his mother with doubt clouding his eyes. 'We can trust him,' she told Edward.

Roger waited, trying not to show his impatience. Without the consent of this child, their plan would come to nothing; and whilst he was tempted to take the boy by the shoulders and shake him until he nodded his assent, he knew that he must tread carefully.

Isabella loved her son, and if he wanted to grow close to her then he must make every effort to appease the boy as well.

'You will be crowned king,' he told him. Surely no boy could resist that, he thought. And he was right. Edward began to nod, imperceptibly at first and then more decisively.

'Very well,' he agreed. 'I will accompany my mother to Ponthieu to raise money and troops, and then we will follow you to Hainault. And if I like Philippa, I will agree to be betrothed to her, but I will not marry without my father's consent.'

Isabella smiled and squeezed her son's hand. Roger resisted the urge to ruffle his blond hair and instead got to his feet and gave the prince a solemn bow. 'You can be certain of my loyalty, your grace,' he told him.

Part Three

1326 to 1329

11

September 1326

Invasion

Roger Mortimer felt a rush of anticipation as the fleet of ships crept through the early morning mist towards the English shoreline. He was looking forward to repaying the debt of vengeance he owed Hugh le Despenser and then claiming back what was his — and more. Beside him, Prince Edward was watching the small fishing harbour loom into view and, as the turning tide lapped against the wooden hull and gulls screamed overhead watching for food, Isabella came out from the canvas cover where she had been sheltering and stood beside them. She looked pensive and was biting her bottom lip with her small, even teeth, and for a moment Roger's thoughts were distracted. But there was work to be done, he reminded himself, as he watched his son, Geoffrey, supervising the tying up of the first ships. There were men and horses to unload and feed, orders to give, troops to organise. Then there would be a long march westwards, where he hoped he would be joined by a good number of those who had pledged their support.

It was pity that Henry Beaumont had landed himself in captivity again, he thought. He was a reliable ally, and what harm would it have done him to swear allegiance to the king and Despenser even if he didn't mean it? There were times when a man with too great a conscience could be a liability.

'Are you cold, my lady?' he asked as he noticed that Isabella was trembling despite the thick woollen cloak that shrouded her. She shook her head.

'Just a little fearful,' she admitted.

'You are safe with me,' he reassured her. 'I will not allow any harm to befall you or your son. The people will welcome you. You'll see.'

She smiled up at him, and he was stirred to see the naked trust in her eyes. Her confidence had been won more easily than he had hoped, her regard for him driven by her hatred of Despenser. He had not even had to bed her to render her in thrall to him, but he would do, by and by, when the chance presented itself. It was perhaps better not to rush these things, but he knew that it was the most effective way of holding her to his will.

Of the prince he was less sure. He had played to the boy's vanity with his promise that he would be king, but Edward was too near to manhood to be duped for long. He would need to step carefully to keep his trust. It was fortunate that he seemed genuinely attracted to Philippa of Hainault, had taken his betrothal vows without fuss, and had even kissed the girl's cheek in a sorrowful farewell before boarding ship, promising that he would send for her as soon as England was his.

The ship nudged the wooden jetty, and snaking lengths of rope were thrown to the sailors already ashore to secure her. The wooden ramps slammed down on the harbour, and Roger offered his arm to Isabella to help her disembark. Fires had been lit, and there was an appetising smell of bacon rising through the morning air as he led her to where a tent had been pitched for her use until they were ready to leave.

'Welcome home, my lady,' he said as she settled onto a stool. Then, leaving Lady de Vescy to organise the servants who were bringing the food and drink, he bowed out and walked back to watch the horses being brought ashore, shaking the drops of seawater from their coats. The horizon was filled with the ships that Count William had provided, and the Hainault mercenaries were efficiently docking and unloading them by turn. It would be the morrow or even the day after before they were ready to move, but Roger wished the time was ripe. He had waited five years for this, and he wanted to see Despenser and the king in chains.

★ ★ ★

Alicia poured a cup of the best wine and carefully handed it to Henry of Lancaster. They were down to their last barrel because of all the visits they had received of late, despite the ever more desperate letters from the king forbidding her to have any contact with those suspected of supporting Roger Mortimer.

Henry sat down with her and Eble in the small solar that also served as their bedchamber. They had dismissed the servants.

'Good wine.' Henry nodded in approval, then glanced towards the curtain that separated them from the main hall.

'You can speak freely,' Alicia assured him, reaching to fondle Guarin, who was brushing himself against her legs in the hope of a titbit.

'Roger Mortimer needs to know that he can rely on you,' he told them, keeping his voice low.

'My family are marcher lords. We have

always supported Mortimer,' replied Eble, 'although I am not in any position to promise men and arms.'

'I understand that,' said Henry. 'But as Alicia's husband, it is important that I am certain where you stand.'

'So it is imminent?' asked Eble.

'The king thinks so, judging by the tone of panic in his letters,' scoffed Alicia as she rubbed the cat's ears.

Henry smiled. 'Mortimer has landed in Suffolk with over a hundred ships provided by Count William of Hainault.'

'Enough to transport over a thousand men and horses,' replied Eble, calculating the logistics with ease.

'Mortimer plans to march in search of the king, and Despenser, and needs every man he can to join him.' Henry paused. 'You do know what I am risking by telling you this?' he asked.

'You know that you can trust me,' protested Alicia.

'Yes, my lady, but . . . '

'And you can trust my husband,' she assured him. 'You have my word that he is loyal to this cause.'

Eble leaned forward to replenish their guest's cup. 'I am with you,' he said. 'I have told you before that you need have no doubts about me. The way my wife has been treated is an abomination, and I am determined to help get back the lands which are rightfully hers.'

Henry of Lancaster took another drink, wiped his mouth and looked satisfied. 'Whether or not we are successful depends on men like you,' he said.

'I will not let you down,' repeated Eble. 'We will be rid of Hugh le Despenser and we will regain our lands.'

Two days later, the messenger wearing royal colours brought more letters from the king. By now Alicia knew that his name was Hob, and that he had a wife and five children. She gave him a silver coin and told him to take some refreshment in the kitchen and rest his horse before he began his return journey. It was not his fault that he was the bearer of missives she would rather not receive.

He had brought a letter addressed to Eble, as supervisor of the array, and one for her. When opened, their contents were similar. As well as the usual dire warnings of further reprisals against her if she supported the king's enemies, the letter revealed that Edward was aware that the queen and Roger Mortimer had entered the realm by stealth with foreign mercenaries. It also warned them that Henry Beaumont had been imprisoned at Warwick Castle for refusing to swear to the king and Despenser that he would live or die for their part. The implication was unspoken but clear, and Alicia trembled as she remembered her time at York.

The letter to Eble said that he must raise men to go in force against the king's enemies and arrest and destroy them. Only the queen, the prince and the Earl of Kent were to be saved. And anyone who rendered to the king the body or the head of Roger Mortimer would be rewarded with a grant of a thousand pounds.

'Just think what we could do with that much money,' remarked Eble as he put his letter down on the trestle for her to read. Alicia knew that he was jesting, but she did not laugh or even smile.

'Eble.' She reached out and put her hand on his arm. 'Have a care for yourself,' she said, finding that her throat was tightening with emotion. 'I could not bear it if something happened to you.'

He drew her into his arms, holding her close against him. 'I will come home,' he promised, although they both knew that the choice was not his, but was in the hands of God, and that all they could do was pray.

'I wonder if Henry will ask for intercession at the tomb in Pontefract?' she said. 'I hear that the miracles performed by my late husband continue.'

She felt Eble's arms tighten around her. 'I doubt he will waste the time,' he reassured her. 'Does it still trouble you, this cult of sainthood for Thomas?'

'You and I both know he was no saint,' she said as a shiver ran through her at the thought of him and his cruelty. 'I consider it a blasphemy.'

'And you worry that God might act against those who pray at the tomb?'

'I just worry,' she said. 'So many tragedies have befallen me in life that I cannot trust the happiness I have with you. I feel as if it will be snatched from me at any moment.'

Eble bent his head and kissed her, allowing his lips to linger as she clung to him. He did not repeat that he would come home, and she did not tell him again to be careful.

★ ★ ★

As dawn approached, Eble watched the men arrive in the courtyard at Swaveton. Some were on horseback and wore armour, others came on foot protected only by padded gambesons and armed with sharpened sticks. They told Eble that they had come to join him and Henry of Lancaster in support of the queen, and he thanked them and sent them into the hall, where Alicia was overseeing a breakfast for those who were to ride out.

By the time the sun had crested the horizon, the hall was filled with men, laughing and talking in excited voices. After the years of waiting, since Mortimer's escape from the Tower the time of change was imminent, and there was not one amongst them who would be sorry to see Hugh le Despenser brought low.

When all the bread was eaten and the ale finished, Eble led them outside. Alicia stood beside him as the stable-lad brought out his horse, ready saddled and brushed until it shone the colour of an iced pond in the morning light.

Eble bent to kiss her cheek. She looked pale and weary, and he knew that she had cried herself to sleep the previous night despite his trying to distract her with lovemaking. She put a hand on his arm, and her face told him everything she wanted to say but could not. He nodded and put a foot to the stirrup. He would stay alive, he vowed to himself, because he could not bear to think of the sadness it would cause her if he were killed.

They joined Lancaster's army on the road south and met up with Mortimer and the queen at Dunstable, where they received word from a spy that the king and Despenser had fled from London, where they had feared the people would turn on them. The army turned west and followed them towards Wales, where Despenser held lands. The queen had put a price of two thousand pounds on Despenser's head — twice the reward being offered for Mortimer — and more and more men were either refusing to fight for the king, or were joining the queen's forces, saying that Despenser had grossly insulted her and must be brought to justice.

As they approached Oxford, Lancaster sent for Eble. 'The queen is anxious,' he said. 'I promised that I would send someone trustworthy ahead to ensure that there will be a welcome and the city gates will not be closed in our faces. Are you willing?'

'Of course, my lord,' replied Eble, wondering if this was a test of his loyalty, or if Lancaster merely considered that he was expendable should the citizens prove true to the king.

'And when you have smoothed the way, will you also ride to the friary and arrange lodgings for the queen and her household?'

'And Mortimer?' asked Eble.

'No.' Lancaster shook his head. 'He will lodge with the army at Osney Abbey, outside the walls. It is important that the townsfolk do not fear their houses will be looted.'

As Eble approached the gates of Oxford, he saw a group of men riding out towards him. He reined in his horse and waited, wishing that he had a larger escort. The approaching men far outnumbered his party, and it would be a sorry thing if he should die here rather than in battle. He watched the men come nearer, and when they were within hailing distance the Oxford men also drew rein.

'Greetings!' called one, eyeing Eble cautiously. 'We have come to welcome the queen and to present a gift of a silver cup.'

Eble let out a breath of relief and waved one of the men forward. It seemed that wherever they went, the people were looking to Queen Isabella to bring about change, and it was only a matter of time before the regime of the king and Hugh le Despenser was finished.

★ ★ ★

Roger Mortimer watched as the Bishop of Hereford placed the blessed host on the tongue of the queen in the city cathedral. Isabella, still dressed as a widow, made the sign of the cross and bowed her head. After a moment she moved to the chair that had been set aside for her and, as the bishop walked slowly up the steps to the pulpit, an expectant hush fell over the congregation.

The bishop looked around, and his gaze met Roger's for a moment. 'My text for today,' he began, 'is from the book of Genesis. I will put enmity between thee and the woman!'

As his sermon, already read and approved by Mortimer, unfolded, the congregation was left in no doubt that Isabella was the woman, and that the snake who had come between her and her husband was Hugh le Despenser. The bishop told them that the snake would be crushed underfoot, and all around him Roger could hear the murmurs of assent. There was a growing belief that God and right were on their side, and that they could bring Despenser to justice. It was enough for now, he thought. Let them believe that once Despenser was removed, the queen would be reunited with her husband and that good would prevail. He had no intention of allowing that to happen, of course, but he would keep his true objective to himself for the time being.

★   ★   ★

As they rode towards the castle at Wallingford, Isabella heard the trumpeting of the horns. She could make out the men on the battlements and her stomach fluttered; but when the gates were pulled open to admit them, she realised that the garrison had been gathered to greet her. The constable came forward, bowed low and held out the keys to the castle.

'I am your servant, my lady,' he told her.

Beside her, she saw Roger Mortimer suppress a smile of satisfaction as he swung down from his horse and grasped the keys on her behalf.

'We will be here for a few days,' he told the man. 'The queen needs to rest. Do you have news of the whereabouts of the king?'

'At Tintern, my lord,' said the man, 'hoping for the arrival of Welsh knights.'

'He may have a long wait,' remarked Roger as he turned to assist Isabella.

After freeing her feet from the stirrups, she slid down into Roger's grasp. As soon as she was safely on the ground, he moved away from her with a slight bow, but she continued to feel his touch. Ever since they had left Hainault, he had masterfully led her army with skill and intelligence, and her husband and Despenser had run before them in fear. But Roger had kept a respectful distance from her, only meeting her in the presence of others and confining their conversations to matters of tactics and planning, and it had left her dissatisfied. Now he offered her his arm, and she placed a gloved hand on his mail sleeve as he escorted her to the great hall, where he glanced around to ensure that all her needs had been met. She watched as he turned to her, dark eyes glowing with pleasure. She wanted to reach out and touch him. She wanted to feel the softness of his beard against her cheek. She wanted to feel his firm hands pressed around her waist again.

'I think that our next move should be to issue a proclamation of our own,' he said, throwing down his gloves onto the table. 'One that makes it clear you have come to rescue the country from the evil influence of Hugh le Despenser.'

'Yes,' agreed Isabella. 'When Edward hears it, he may come to his senses and rid himself of Despenser.'

'And what then?' Roger asked her. 'Will you cast off your widow's weeds and return to your husband?'

Isabella felt the blood fire her cheeks as he continued to look at her, waiting for an answer. 'I do not know,' she said at last, feeling flustered. Her moment of discomposure was calmed by Lady de Vescy.

'My brother is here!' she told them. 'He

was released from his cell — and he has brought you a gift, my lady.'

Isabella looked towards the doorway, where Henry Beaumont was waiting to greet her. In his hand he held a sack, the bottom of which was wet and blackened with liquid, and she could not imagine what it contained.

Henry came forward and bowed before holding out the sack. 'I have been asked to give you this, my lady,' he said.

Uncertain about taking it, Isabella hesitated, and Mortimer reached past her and put the sack on the trestle that was being laid for supper. He prised open the knots in the rope that held it closed and spread the sacking.

The first thing Isabella saw was the top of the head with its trademark tonsure, around which the greying hair was plastered to the skull with congealed blood. Her hand flew to her mouth as the bile rose in her throat, though she found it impossible not to look at the dead and glazed eyes of the Bishop of Exeter staring back at her.

'Well,' remarked Roger. 'This is quite a gift.'

As he spoke, his voice seemed to fade, and hall drifted out of focus as Isabella hoped that the layer of floor rushes was deep enough to soften her fall.

When she regained consciousness, she was unable to recall where she was, the day, or the time. She became aware that someone was laying her gently onto a soft mattress, and was puzzled to see the concerned eyes of Roger Mortimer looking down at her.

'If I had known what the sack contained, I would not have opened it in front of you. I apologise.'

With his words, she recalled the gruesome sight, and struggled to sit up as she felt the contents of her stomach surge. She waved a hand wildly, needing a basin or bucket, but before she could make him understand, the torrent spewed from her and she vomited across her skirts, the bed cover, and over Roger's hose and tunic. Swallowing down the remains of the vile, burning liquid, Isabella stared at Roger in horror as he stood up and looked down at himself.

'Oh God, forgive me!' she burst out. 'I am so sorry, my lord. Will you call for one of my ladies?'

'No need,' he said grimly as he pulled the tunic cautiously over his head and threw it into a corner before peeling off his soiled hose. Isabella watched as he poured water into a basin from the jug on the coffer. Where were her ladies? Where was Lady de Vescy?

He washed his hands and dried them on a linen towel before bringing water and a cloth and placing them beside her. She sat on the edge of the bed and wrung out the cloth before trying to wipe the spreading stain from her white gown. As she did, she felt him pull the bedcover from beneath her and throw it onto the pile of items to be dealt with by the laundress. She really ought to call for Lady de Vescy, she thought. It was madness to be alone in a bedchamber with a man who wasn't her husband — especially when he was clad only in his undershirt and braies.

'Let me help,' he said as he watched her attempts to clean herself. He took the cloth from her hand and wiped the front of her gown, pressing against her breasts as he did so. 'I really think you should take this off before it begins to stink any worse,' he advised.

She reached to unlace her gown as she felt the wetness seep through to her chemise. 'Will you call for Lady de Vescy?' she asked him again.

'No need,' he said, gently pushing her trembling hands aside as she struggled with the cords. His firm fingers quickly undid them and he eased the bodice from her shoulders. 'Stand up,' he said, and as she obeyed him she felt the garment pool to the floor around her ankles. As she stepped out of the soiled skirts, she knew that what she was doing was wrong. She glanced towards the door, but Roger shook his head and moved to place the wooden bar that would hold it shut. Isabella was unsure if the sudden spasm in the pit of her stomach was fear, or excitement, or an indication that she was about to be sick again. She folded her arms, holding the finely woven fabric of her damp chemise close to her. Why should she be afraid? she asked herself. It was not as if she was a virgin, as she had been on her wedding night. She had known her husband's body many times; had borne him four children. She knew well enough what was about to happen.

She washed her hands and face thoroughly in the water, then took the cup of wine that Roger offered her. She drank, relishing the taste and the way it soothed the burning in her throat.

'The Bishop of Exeter . . . ' she began.

'Not now,' he said as he took the cup from her and set it down. He reached for the pin that held her wimple in place and allowed the fabric to fall loose. His eyes were fixed on her hair, and he began to unpin that as well until her braids hung down. He lifted one and, after pulling off the tippet that held it, he began to loosen the strands until he was able to ran his fingers through them. Then his eyes met hers, and she answered his look of query with a slight nod. She could not refuse him.

She felt his warm hand close around the back of her neck as he pulled her towards him. A moment later his lips were on hers, and she allowed her body to lean into his so that she could feel the hardness of him against her belly. She could taste the wine on his tongue. Part of her wanted to push him away and tell him that it was wrong, but she wanted more and did not protest when he laid her on the bed. He began to stroke her gently — her breasts, her stomach, her thighs, until she grasped his hand in hers and guided it between her legs, holding his fingers there clasped within her own.

'Please,' she said, desperate for fulfilment. Then he smiled his slow smile as if he was satisfied that he had made her beg, and she eagerly parted her legs for him as he pushed down his braies and pinned her, helpless, beneath him.

★　★　★

'The bishop of Exeter,' she said again as they lay side by side on the bed, recovering their breath and their senses. 'Do you know who killed him?'

'Londoners have gone mad since the king fled the city,' he told her. 'They killed John le Marshal, then went after Stapleton. He tried to reach the sanctuary of St Paul's, but they pulled him from his horse by the north door, dragged him to Cheapside and cut off his head.' He propped himself on his elbow and looked down at her, as if wondering if he needed to pass her the basin again. But she did not dwell on the remains of the bishop.

'John!' she said. 'My son — he is in London!'

'He is safe,' Roger reassured her, pressing his palm to her cheek. 'Apparently the Londoners have appointed him guardian of the city.'

'But he is a nine-year-old boy!' she protested, pushing his hand away and getting up from the bed to reach for her chemise. 'I must go to him. He has no one else to protect him now that his father has fled.'

'No,' said Roger.

'But what if he is harmed?' She pulled the garment over her head, noticing that it was ripped. Her travelling coffers had not yet been brought in, and she was about to go to the door and call for her women herself, when she felt Roger's hand close around her wrist.

'No,' he repeated. 'We will send a bodyguard to watch over John, but we will not turn away from our pursuit of the king.'

She tried to pull away but he held her firmly, and when she looked up into his face she saw that something had changed. By giving herself to him, she had acknowledged not only her need for him, but her subservience to him. She realised that now there was nothing she could do without his consent.

'I have sons in London too,' he told her. 'I understand your concern, but we must not let it distract us. First we will rid ourselves of Despenser. Then we will go to London.'

'You're hurting me,' she said, and he released her without another word. She sat rubbing her wrist as he fastened his braies. She was powerless without him. He had charge of the army that accompanied them. Men had pledged themselves to her, but in reality they obeyed him, and she doubted that any would ride with her to London without his permission. She hated Despenser for what he had done, but now she wondered if she had exchanged one tyrant for another.

'You have changed,' she told him.

'No,' he said as he looked down at her. 'It is you who now sees clearly. Braid your hair, and I will send Lady de Vescy to help you dress.'

With that, he opened the door and walked out in his undergarments. 'My lady has spewed over the both of us,' she heard him say. 'Bring me some fresh clothes.'

12

October 1326

Revenge

Eble watched as the mercenaries from Hainault surged towards the walls of the castle at Bristol. The foot soldiers went first, holding their shields above their heads to protect themselves from the torrent of arrows raining down on them from the battlements. Behind them came the ram, and as the foot soldiers tossed grappling irons to the top of the stone walls, the sound of the sturdy tree trunk being pounded against the locked gates resounded across the sultry air. The castle belonged to Despenser, though not for much longer, thought Eble.

Suddenly there was a roar as the gates buckled and a portion of the wall began to crumble. The men who had scaled the walls were engaged in hand-to-hand combat along the battlements and, as the gates finally gave way, Eble was one of the first to gallop into the ward, striking out with his sword as the grey wheeled to his command. Above the noise he heard a thud behind him, and glanced to see that he had been lucky not to be knocked from his horse by the falling body. It was not one of their men, he noted with satisfaction as he raised his sword to fend off an attack from an oncoming assailant dressed in Despenser's colours.

He turned again, squinting through the slit in his helm, and was disappointed to see that it was all over. Apart from the ringing in his ears, silence had fallen, and he heard Roger Mortimer order that any prisoners should be chained. Eble watched as an elderly man in expensive armour was hauled to his feet, only to be pushed to his knees in front of Mortimer, who dismounted his horse and struck the man a blow that sent him prostrate in the churned mud. It surprised Eble. It was out of character with the unspoken rules of warfare, and the Earl of Lincoln had always taught that prisoners, especially those of the nobility, should be treated with respect. He had expected better of Roger Mortimer.

'Who is that?' he asked Henry Beaumont, who had ridden up beside him.

'The elder Despenser,' he replied. 'Mortimer hates him as much as he does the son.'

Eble watched as the old man stirred. Blood was running from his nose and dripping from his chin. He clasped his hands, begging for mercy, but Mortimer sneered and ordered him chained and dragged to the dungeon with the other prisoners.

'It seems harsh,' said Eble, uneasy at the pointless attack.

'Don't forget he was responsible for the murder of Thomas of Lancaster,' Henry reminded him. Eble did not reply. Both he and Alicia were well rid of Thomas of Lancaster, but it was the return of Alicia's lands that had driven him to join this rebellion, not the torture of old men.

'It cannot go on much longer,' said Henry Beaumont as the iron gate of the dungeon clanged shut. 'The king is defeated.'

'What do you think he will he do?' asked Eble as they dismounted to join the throng who had liberated a quantity of cold meat and ale from the castle kitchens.

'Run. Isn't that what Edward always does when there is trouble?'

★ ★ ★

A few days later, Eble heard that the king and Despenser had indeed run. They had sailed from Chepstow, probably intending to make for Ireland, but a westerly wind was holding them back and, if the rumours were to be believed, they were paying a friar to pray that it might change direction.

'However much they paid, Mortimer must have paid more to keep it blowing against them,' remarked Henry as the wind whipped the hood from his head. He and Eble were standing at the top of a turret at Bristol Castle, watching the churning sea in the distance.

'What was the meeting about?' Eble asked him. He was angry and frustrated that because of his lack of status, he had been excluded from Mortimer's group of confidantes, and had been forced to climb the hundreds of steps to the battlements to seek out someone who would tell him what had been said.

'Mortimer plans to appoint the prince to govern the country in his father's absence. Though I doubt he'll be absent for long unless this wind abates. Let's go down,' suggested Henry. 'There's nothing to see up here.'

Eble followed him into the calm of the twisting stone staircase, wondering exactly what Mortimer was plotting. As each day passed, it became clearer who held the authority. Rumour was that the queen had begged for the life of the elder Despenser to be spared. He was an old man and had been kind to her in the past. But Mortimer had refused, and the man's trial was set for the morrow. There was no doubt what the verdict would be, and the turn of events was troubling Eble. He wished he could talk things over with Alicia; she had inherited her father's ability to shrewdly sum up a situation. Instead, he did the next best thing and found himself a quiet corner to write her a letter. He told her everything that had transpired, then added that he loved her, and wrote a rhyming couplet that was intended for her eyes only. With a smile, he closed the parchment and sealed it with the small stamp that he kept attached to his belt. It would not be cheap to pay someone to ride all the way to Lincolnshire with it, but he had promised that he would keep her informed.

The next day, Eble watched as the elder Despenser was dragged into the hall before Mortimer, Henry of Lancaster, Thomas Wake, and others. They all bore the old man a grudge, and he looked half-dead already, with his badly swollen face. He was not allowed to speak, but Eble doubted he could have said anything coherent, and he looked unaware of his fate as they took him down the hill to be hanged on the common gallows in the town. Afterwards they would cut off his head. And then they would continue their pursuit of his son, who had been forced back to dry land along with the king.

The leaves were blown from the trees in the autumn gales, and night frosts took hold, as Eble followed Henry of Lancaster's army across open country. The king had sent an embassy headed by the abbot of Neath to bargain with the queen, but in a response that mirrored his own pleadings five years before, Mortimer had sent the man back with the message that only complete surrender was acceptable. The king had refused and was still evading them.

Eble squinted into the low sun as someone called out and pointed towards a group of horsemen picked out in black against the horizon. Lancaster's trumpeters sounded a haloo that echoed across the valley as they urged their horses to pursuit. Their quarry turned at the sound and began to kick the flanks of their own horses in panic; but as he galloped at an exhilarating pace, with the wind stinging his eyes, Eble saw that they were gaining on the king and Despenser. Lancaster sent men left and right, and as the king's party approached the river they became trapped between the two flanks and the deep water. The king's escort of men-at-arms closed around him, but they were too few to fight; and as Eble reined in his horse, panting and amazed at the turn of events, Lancaster called out for the king to give himself up.

'You have nowhere to run to, Edward!' he told him, as his guards were forced aside at sword point and Despenser was dragged from his horse.

'Desist!' shouted the king as he saw the men strike his friend. 'Desist, I tell you!'

'It's over, Edward!' shouted Lancaster. 'Throw down your sword and come quietly! I swear that I will treat you honourably!'

The angry and outraged king glared at the two guards who held Despenser fast, and then at his cousin, Henry of Lancaster. After a moment in which he looked as if he might try to continue his defiance, he sank in his saddle and, in a gesture of defeat, flung his sword to the ground.

'You will be sorry for this day!' he growled at Lancaster as they moved forward to secure him.

'Take his reins,' Lancaster told Eble. 'And if he utters a word of complaint or tries to escape, see that he is bound hard to his saddle.'

'Where are you taking him?' wailed the king as he saw Despenser being dragged away.

'To the queen at Hereford,' Lancaster told him. 'Let her decide his fate.'

*　★　*

Isabella watched the smile spread over Roger's face as the jeering of the crowd drowned out the trumpets and the drums. Much as she hated Hugh le Despenser, she was frightened by the pleasure Roger was taking in this. And she knew it was not entirely for the insult to her. Mortimer had vowed to be revenged on the Despensers long ago, not just because of his own imprisonment, but to settle the longstanding feud between their families.

The shouting and drumming reached a crescendo as Despenser came into view, blood pouring from every inch of his bare flesh and a crown of nettles crammed onto his head. The crowd had already dragged him from his horse, and it looked as if they might tear him apart before the charges were even read out. But Roger wanted him to live a little longer, and sent men to hold back the mob.

Isabella had thought that she would relish this moment, but she barely recognised the man before her. He was cowed, and so badly beaten that he was struggling to remain on his feet, even though his guard prodded him with a sharp sword every time he swayed or staggered. Every bone of his body was visible because he had tried to starve himself to

154

death in captivity rather than face his accusers. His face was a swollen mass of bruises, and one arm hung by his side as if it had been broken. Now that he came nearer, Isabella could see that his skin was scrawled with biblical verses denouncing his arrogance.

He collapsed to the ground and had to be pulled up as the charges against him were read. Roger and Henry of Lancaster had sat up late into the night writing down every evil act they could remember that Despenser had ever committed.

'By investigation of the prelates, earls and barons and all the community of the realm, it was found to be well known that your father and you were traitors and enemies of the realm.' The crowd fell silent to hear the accusations. The charges spoke of Despenser's unlawful return from exile before Boroughbridge, his forcing of the king to ride against the earls and barons, his murder of Thomas of Lancaster, his killings of many others and his wicked treatment of their widows. 'And God, by his mercy, sent our good and gracious lady, Isabella, and her son and the good men who have come in their company to this land, by which the realm is delivered.' At these words the crowd let a huge cheer, and Isabella briefly met the eyes of a man she recognised as Eble le Strange.

He was the husband of Alicia de Lacy, one of the widows whom Despenser had treated badly, and she saw him nodding in agreement at the charges.

'By common assent you are declared a thief and a criminal, and for this you will be hanged. And, because you are a traitor, you will be drawn and quartered, and the pieces of your body sent throughout the realm. And because you were exiled by our lord the king and by common assent, and returned to the court without authorisation, you will be beheaded. And because you were always disloyal and procured discord between our lord the king and our very honourable lady the queen, you will be disembowelled, and your entrails will be burnt. Withdraw, you traitor, tyrant, renegade; go to take your own justice — criminal, traitor, evil man!'

As William Trussel stepped back with a final flourish of his parchment, the crowd let out a roar that vibrated through Isabella. Roger Mortimer raised a hand, and the men who guarded Despenser roped him to four horses. As their riders spurred them forward, he was yanked from his feet and dragged along the rough ground as the crowd ran alongside, cheering and throwing anything that came to hand.

Henry of Lancaster escorted Isabella to

where the high gallows had been erected so that the crowd could witness the spectacle. A man was adding kindling to a smoking fire, and the sound of knives being sharpened on a whetstone echoed from the stone walls. Roger Mortimer followed at a discreet distance, and it was Henry who took the place beside Isabella at the table that had been set for a feast. She arranged her skirts and hoped that she would not need the bucket. On her other side, her son, Edward, was quiet, and she laid her hand over his in a moment of reassurance.

Despenser was dragged up the ladder. A noose had already been placed around his neck, and after the rope was secure he was pushed to dangle, choking in front of them. Some of the crowd stared in silence, other shouted insults and obscenities. Then the traitor was hauled back to the ladder and his arms and legs were tied, although he was barely moving and Isabella was unsure if he was still conscious. An executioner climbed the second ladder with a sharpened knife in his hand and, leaning towards Despenser's naked body, he grasped his penis and testicles in one hand, sliced them off in a gush of blood, and threw them down into the fire. The crowd bellowed their approval, and Isabella swallowed and forced herself to think of all the wicked things that Despenser had done.

There was less blood than she expected when the traitor's belly was sliced open and his entrails dangled on the end of the knife for all to see. The crowd began to stamp their feet and chant, 'Burn them! Burn them!' Isabella waved away the page who was offering her food. For all her prayers that she might be rid of Despenser, she found it hard to watch such a brutal display.

13

November 1326–January 1327

Abdication

'Thank you for the books, my lord,' said Joan after she had greeted Roger with a kiss. His wife looked old, he thought, as he compared her dried and creased skin with the fresh bloom that still adorned the cheeks of Isabella. 'It was a kindly gesture,' she added.

'I know how much you enjoy reading,' he said. 'I was sorry when I learned that your books had been taken from you along with your other possessions.'

'Sorry?' she said, with a glint of anger that reminded him of the girl he had once loved. 'You were sorry? Was that the extent of it, my lord?'

'What do you want me to say?' he asked. He had come to the manor at Wigmore to try to make amends, but it seemed that his wife was not going to make it easy for him. 'I regret what happened to you. But you are free now and the traitor is dead. What more can I do?'

She turned away and went to sit on a bench near the hearth. It was a cold day with a hint of sleet hanging in the air, and Joan rubbed her hands together over the flames. She was stick thin, and he wondered how much she had been given to eat at Skipton Castle; barely enough to keep her alive, he surmised.

'I've brought cloth for new gowns,' he said in another attempt at appeasement. 'For you and the girls.'

'Is it true?' she asked after a moment.

'Is what true?'

'That you are the queen's lover.'

He knew that he should deny it, that he ought to take her in his arms and reassure her. He would have done once, but five years had passed since their last meeting, and she was almost a stranger to him now.

'Then it is true,' she said, with a sadness that touched his soul.

'Joan.' He went to sit beside her and took her hand. It felt brittle, like aged parchment, and he could feel every bone under his thumb as he rubbed it back and forth. 'Joan,' he said, 'much has changed.'

'Indeed it has. What will you do with me now?' she asked.

'Joan.' He touched her cheek and wiped away her tears. He thought about kissing her but could not bring himself to do it. 'Joan, you are still my wife.'

'In name only,' she replied as she pulled her hand from his. 'You do not love me anymore.'

'I do love you,' he lied, desperate for this meeting to be at an end.

'No,' she whispered. 'I am not blind, my lord. Look at you. Look at your fine clothes. You are still a handsome man, and I am grown old. Five years at the French court has been kinder to you than the five years I have spent in Yorkshire.'

'I am sorry,' he repeated.

'So you said.'

'I will see that you have everything you need. You can live here, or at Ludlow. It is your choice.'

'I should like to live at Ludlow, with your permission.'

'Of course.' Relief flooded through him that she was going to be reasonable.

'And will you come to see me sometimes?' she asked.

'I will be busy . . . ' he began, thinking of all the other challenges that were ahead of him now that the Despensers had been dealt with.

'I'm sure you will be.' He heard her sob and reached out to put a hand on her shoulder. He was about to say once more that he was sorry, but even he acknowledged that it was inadequate. Yet he could think of nothing that would serve better and, after a while, he left her to cry whilst he went to inspect the manor and arrange for the work that needed to be done.

* * *

Eble followed Henry of Lancaster to an upper chamber of the palace at Westminster, where the king was being held.

'Tell the king that the Earl of Lancaster is here,' he said to the man who was guarding the door. Henry's use of his brother's title surprised Eble. He had not been officially given the status of earl, although it was his right, and it seemed that using it now was sending a clear message to the king that things had changed, and that the bestowing of such titles was no longer in his power.

The guard opened the door and announced Henry, who motioned to Eble to accompany him. The chamber was hung with Flemish tapestries, and rushes lay in a thick layer on the floor, but it was gloomy because the window was shuttered and barred. Edward was sitting on a stool, dressed from head to toe in black. He looked up at them with weary eyes, and

Eble saw that he had been weeping. He did not acknowledge them, but returned his gaze to the floor and absently wiped his nose on the sleeve of his gown.

'I have come to take you to Kenilworth Castle,' Henry told him, standing with one hand on the hilt of his sword as if anticipating a refusal, but the king merely gave a shrug of his shoulders.

Henry nodded to Eble, who approached the king. He felt awkward, not quite knowing how to act. This man was his sovereign lord, and yet here he was assisting Henry of Lancaster to take him into captivity. Eble made a slight bow.

'Do you need any assistance, my lord?' he asked.

'Assistance?' asked the king. 'What sort of assistance do you offer?' He stared at Eble. 'I know you. You are the squire who married the lady Alicia de Lacy.'

'I am Eble le Strange, my lord, and Alicia de Lacy is my wife.'

'Small wonder then that you are embroiled with these traitors and murderers,' he told him. 'It grieves me that your wife has become my enemy, when her father was always by my side.'

'It is time to leave,' interrupted Henry of Lancaster.

'It seems I am in your hands for the present, cousin,' replied the king as he got to his feet. 'Do you plot to cut off my head?'

'You will be treated as my honoured guest.'

'I will remember this day and everything that has passed,' warned Edward as a page helped him on with his cloak and hood.

'And I have not forgotten what was done to my brother!' replied Henry, as his fist tightened around his sword hilt and he glared at the king in open anger.

'Do you mean to steal my throne as well as my freedom?' asked Edward, drawing on leather gauntlets.

'I mean to take what is rightfully mine,' Henry told him.

★ ★ ★

The journey north was cold. Sleet stung their faces, and the peasants remained huddled around the hearths of their small thatched dwellings. No one paid much heed as the king passed by.

When they reached Kenilworth, the king was taken to a small apartment of rooms with a few of the loyal servants who had accompanied him, and Eble was dismissed to travel home to Swaveton in time to spend Christmas with Alicia.

164

She came out into the yard to meet him, wrapped in layers of wool against the sharp frost. But her smile was warm, and she hugged him tightly and raised her lips to his as he held her against him, regretting every hour that they had been apart. She kept her hand in his as they watched the horse being led away to the stable and Eble's pack of belongings carried inside the hall to be sorted. She only let him go to pour him ale, to which she added herbs, and then plunged the hot poker from the fire into the cup to heat it. It tasted good and warmed his veins, and he glanced around with satisfaction at the clean and neat hall as Alicia drew back the cloth from the platters of bread and meat that were laid out on the trestle awaiting his arrival.

When he had changed his shoes and hose for dry ones, they sat near to the fire, and he gave her what news she had not already gleaned from the travellers who had eaten at her table.

'I cannot say that I am sorry to hear of Despenser's death,' she told him. 'The man showed me little mercy. What do you think will happen now? Will Edward rule with the guidance of a council again?'

'I doubt it,' said Eble. 'I think the queen intends to depose him and have her son crowned in his place.'

He watched Alicia frown as she considered the consequences of that.

'From what you tell me, it is the queen who will rule her son, and it is Roger Mortimer who will rule the queen,' she said.

'I thought that you supported Mortimer?' he asked, puzzled by her tone of disapproval.

'I supported him because I wished to see the removal of Hugh le Despenser. I never supported him as an alternative king, despite his descent from the legendary Arthur,' she said. 'If the king is deposed, I should rightly support his son, but the boy is too young to rule alone. He would need guidance, but that need not come from Mortimer.'

'Then who?' asked Eble.

'Henry of Lancaster has a claim as well,' she said. 'Do not forget that if Thomas had become king, Henry would be his heir.'

'And you would be queen of England,' said Eble, as he pictured the image of the wheel of fortune that was painted on the wall of the nearby church. Alicia had almost reached the pinnacle before she had been cast down again.

She reached out and tightened her fingers around his hand. 'I would never have been happy, as I am happy with you,' she told him. Her dark eyes gleamed and he almost threw down his food, picked her up and carried her to the bed in the chamber at the far end of the hall. But it must wait, he decided. He needed to wash thoroughly and put on clean under linen first. He was aware that he smelt after so long in the saddle, and Alicia was always so clean and fragrant.

'Who is the most likely to return my lands, do you think?' she asked, her own thoughts still on politics. 'I will support whoever promises to treat me fairly.'

★   ★   ★

Roger Mortimer watched as the acrobats twisted themselves into impossible shapes and leapt like fleas across the floor of the hall at Wallingford Castle. Isabella sat beside him, and on his other side the prince was laughing at the antics being performed for them. To an onlooker's eyes, it seemed that his invasion had been successful. The king was in prison and the prince believed that power would soon be his when his father abdicated and he was crowned. But as Roger relished the fun of the Christmas feast, he knew that his position was still fragile. He did not trust Henry of Lancaster, who had begun to call himself earl; and with daily reports of fresh miracles being performed at the tomb of his brother,

Thomas, Roger was becoming concerned about the growing number of people who were expressing support for him. Whilst the king was in his custody, Henry was in a strong position to persuade men to take up arms in his cause, and another civil war was the last thing Roger wanted. He had the queen, he had prince and he had the army from Hainault, but he was unsure whether that was enough.

'You are quiet,' Isabella said, the edge of her hand touching his on the table. 'Is everything to your satisfaction?'

'It is all well done,' he said. 'My thoughts were taken up by worries about the king.'

'Lancaster has him safe,' she said. 'Is that not enough for now?'

'Yes,' said Roger with a smile, covering her hand with his. 'I am guilty of letting my concerns run away with me rather than enjoying the pleasure of your company.'

★ ★ ★

Two days before the feast of the Epiphany, Roger Mortimer attended the queen and the prince on their journey to London. The city had calmed since the appointment of Richard de Bethune as mayor, although there was no sign of a welcoming crowd as they rode in through the gates with their heads bent low against a flurry of snow. Isabella was looking forward to seeing her son, John, and her face had a look of anticipation. Roger was less optimistic. There had been no word from Kenilworth, and he was worried that the king would not arrive for the parliament in three days' time.

When Bishop Orleton arrived, he came alone. He told Roger that Edward had refused to accompany him and that Henry of Lancaster had refused to force him.

'Do we need him to be present?' asked Roger. 'With all the representatives of the commons as well as the lords present, it may be possible for him to be deposed in his absence.'

'I think it could work to our advantage, my lord,' said Orleton. 'A king who refuses to come to parliament is not worthy to rule. What the king has done is against God and nature. It will be better for all if the prince is crowned in his place.'

* * *

'Make sure you enquire about my lands.' Alicia's last words were still on Eble's mind as he saw the walls of London on the horizon. He reined Trebnor to a walk as he passed through the city gates, noting the presence of many men wearing the colours of the Count of Hainault. It seemed that Roger Mortimer was keeping his foreign mercenaries close by in case of trouble. Eble made his way through the narrow streets towards an inn near the river. On the way, he passed by the house on Shoe Street that had belonged to the Earl of Lincoln. By rights, he should have been able to ride in through the familiar archway and lodge there, but the house was still in the hands of the king.

The inn where he was to stay was near the wharf, and the stench of fish vied for supremacy with the smell drifting up from the communal privy. It was busy, and Eble was shown to a chamber he would have to share with several others. There was a reek of sweat that he could have sliced with his knife, and his hand strayed to its handle as he took stock of the other occupants. He would stink as badly as any of them after a few days sleeping in his clothes, he thought. Alicia had stitched a secret purse into his undershirt where he had his money, and he had no intention of removing it for anyone.

He nodded to the other guests and put his pack down on the pallet. The coarse linen sheet that covered the mattress seemed clean enough, and he had no intention of inspecting the bed more closely, though he would not be surprised to wake and find himself bitten half to death by morning.

'Here for the parliament?' asked one man as he studied Eble. 'Have you come far?'

'Lincolnshire.'

The man nodded. 'What do you make of it?' he asked. 'We're well rid of the Despensers.'

'The Despensers were no friends of mine,' said Eble.

'Do you support the king then?'

'I will support him if he rules fairly,' said Eble, not wanting to commit to any faction whilst he had to sleep beside the man. Communal living was hard enough when you were a squire or on campaign, but at least you had some inkling as to who were your friends and who your enemies.

'They should get rid of him,' said the man. 'Put the boy on the throne instead. Fresh start.'

Eble nodded. It seemed a good idea in principle, but he had come to agree with Alicia that putting the prince on the throne would be tantamount to crowning Roger Mortimer, and that outcome troubled him.

★   ★   ★

Parliament was delayed whilst they waited for the king. Eble heard that Mortimer had called a meeting of the lords, and he was irritated and angry that he had not been issued with an invitation. Mortimer knew his circumstances, and Eble believed that as Alicia's husband, he had a right to be present.

He called for his horse and rode to the palace at Westminster, where Mortimer was residing in the company of the queen, and asked to see him. He was told to wait, and spent almost an hour kicking his heels on the bench outside the presence chamber as he grew increasingly angry and frustrated.

At length the door was opened, and Roger Mortimer came out with a smile and an extended hand of welcome. 'Eble. What can I do for you?'

'My wife has tasked me to enquire about the status of her lands,' he began without preamble. 'The lands that were stolen from her by Hugh le Despenser. Now that he is dead, my wife is anxious to know when she will receive them back.'

'I can understand her anxiety,' said Roger. 'And I commend you for bringing this matter to my attention. I will look into it,' he promised. 'But, as you know, there are more pertinent matters vying for my attention at the moment.' He paused. 'You fought against the king and the Despensers at Borough-bridge, didn't you?'

'I did, my lord.'

'Then can I rely on your support? I am asking men to attend the Guildhall to swear an oath to protect the queen and her son — and to depose the king. Will you swear?'

Eble met Mortimer's dark eyes and saw the bargain that he was offering. Support against Edward in return for Alicia's lands.

'I will swear,' he said, after a moment's consideration. Alicia would never forgive him if he did not secure her inheritance, and besides, Mortimer could not hold power forever. Prince Edward might only be thirteen, but it did not take many years to make a man out of a boy.

'Thank you.' Roger grasped his shoulder briefly. 'And you will attend the parliament tomorrow?'

Eble nodded. He was about to say that he would also like to attend the meeting of the lords that night, but Mortimer had already turned away, and he did not dare to call after him.

★　★　★

Westminster Hall was heaving with bodies the next morning. The lords were seated on benches near the front and the commoners were packed in behind them. Eble eased himself into a vacant place and was thankful that he was tall enough to see over the heads of the crowd.

Promptly at nine of the clock, there was a fanfare of trumpets and the queen entered, her hand on the sleeve of Mortimer's tunic as he escorted her to the throne. Then Mortimer turned to the assembly and waited until a hush fell.

'I have here,' he told them, 'a letter signed by Richard de Bethune, mayor of this city, and the citizens of London. They ask that every one of you will swear to support the queen and her son, our royal prince, Edward. Last night, all the lords of the land met together and they discussed the matter at length,' went on Mortimer. 'Their unanimous wish is that the king should be deposed. This is not my wish alone,' he told them. 'This is not for my wellbeing, but for the wellbeing of the realm.'

'The king is not fit to rule!' burst out Thomas Wake, jumping to his feet. Murmurs of assent spread across the hall until most men were nodding their agreement, and any who remained unsure were given dark looks that pressured them into conformity.

Bishop Orleton rose to his feet. 'An unwise king destroyeth his people,' the bishop quoted. 'If God has seen fit to warn us of such a thing in his holy bible, then we ignore that warning at our peril.'

His words roused the crowd to a frenzy. 'Away with the king!' shouted someone, and the chant was taken up and filled the hall. 'Away with the king! Away with the king!' It was all exquisitely arranged, thought Eble as someone jabbed their fingers into his ribs and glared at him until he reluctantly joined the chorus.

'Is this the will of the people?' demanded Thomas Wake, now standing on the bench and appealing to the crowd with his arms spread wide. 'Is it the will of the people that Edward should be deposed and his son made king in his place?'

With the assurance of the bishops that this was indeed God's will, the crowd roared their approval. Then a door to the side of the dais was opened, and through it came the prince.

'Behold your king!' cried the archbishop. The trumpeters sounded a note; and the crowd, as if they had been well rehearsed, did not hesitate as they began to sing: 'All glory, laud and honour, to thee redeemer king . . . Thou didst accept their praises; accept the prayers we bring. Who in all good delightest, thou good and gracious king.'

★ ★ ★

A week later, Eble stood in the hall at Kenilworth Castle. When Edward was led in, he stared around, then swayed on his feet and had to be supported by Henry of Lancaster as the bishops read out the charges against him. He had been found incompetent to govern. He had allowed others to govern for him to the detriment of his people and the church. He had refused to listen to good advice, instead pursuing occupations unbecoming to a monarch. He had lost Scotland and lands in Gascony and Ireland. He had allowed representatives of the holy church to be imprisoned, and other nobles to be killed, imprisoned, exiled and disinherited. He had failed to ensure that there had been justice for all, but had governed for his own profit — and allowed others to do the same — against his coronation oaths. He had fled the country in the company of a notorious enemy of the realm, leaving the realm without government, thereby losing the faith and the trust of his people; and the people agreed that there was no alternative but to depose him.

Eble could not help but feel pity. It was belittling to see the man brought so low, and Eble could not help but remember how golden Edward had seemed at Alicia's wedding to Thomas of Lancaster. He had been in awe of Edward then, and he hated the way that he was being treated now.

The bishop rolled up the parchment and waited until Edward looked up. 'You are given a choice,' he told him. 'You can abdicate in favour of your son, or, if you resist, the throne will go to one who is not of royal blood but who is experienced in government.'

The threat was unspoken, but everyone in the hall understood the implications; though whether Roger Mortimer became king in name or by deed, it made little difference, thought Eble.

'I greatly lament that I have utterly failed my people,' whispered Edward, 'but I could not be other than I am. I have always done my best. I am sorry that people have so hated my rule.' He paused and took a deep breath to steady himself. 'If the people will accept my son then I will abdicate in his favour,' he told them.

Then Sir William Trussel stepped forward and renounced homage on behalf of all the lords of the realm, and Thomas le Blount broke his staff of office.

'The royal household is no more,' he announced, and Henry of Lancaster grasped his cousin's arm and led him from the hall as he wept openly.

14

February 1327

I did not take — I received

Alicia was bitterly disappointed. The chamber that had been allocated to her and Lady de Vescy was cramped and had only the narrowest of slits for a window; and, judging by the smell that was rising from outside the poorly plastered wall, it overlooked the cesspit.

She supposed it was better than a disorderly inn, and that she ought to be thankful she was here at all, but it was very different from when she had come to London in the past and stayed at her father's house in Holborn or the royal apartments with Thomas. Neither did she have the comfort of Eble to soften the mattress stuffed with lumps of flock. He was sleeping with Henry Beaumont's men, somewhere on the far side of the courtyard.

'Why so sad?' asked Lady de Vescy. 'At least it is clean and safe — and I will ensure that the queen grants you an audience before you return to Lincolnshire.'

'But will it do any good?' Alicia asked the older woman.

'I do not know. But it is worth trying. The queen is a compassionate woman. God knows she has endured much herself these past years, and I think that she will listen kindly to your pleas.'

Alicia nodded. She had hoped that with Despenser gone and the king removed from power, her lands and possessions would have been returned to her by now. Henry of Lancaster had been granted his earldom and a portion of Thomas's lands, but all the land that she had been forced to grant to Despenser was now in the control of the new king, which meant that it was in the control of Roger Mortimer, and he might be as unwilling as Despenser to return it to her.

When she was admitted to the queen's apartments, she saw that Isabella had discarded her widow's garb and was dressed in a gown of the deepest blue. It was many years since Alicia had last met the queen, though she noted that the passage of time had treated her kindly. Her face looked older, but not aged, and she wore a bloom that was rarely seen on noblewomen. Alicia recognised it as the look of a woman who was in love, and she had no doubt that it was Roger

Mortimer who was the recipient of the queen's affections. Alicia could hardly blame her. No woman would dispute that he was a very attractive man.

Alicia sat down and smiled at the younger of the two little girls who were playing at their mother's feet. 'I am sure you are glad to have your children back at your side,' she said, trying to imagine how painful it must have been for Isabella to have been parted from them.

'I missed them,' she said. 'It has been hard, but now my life has taken an upward turn on the wheel of fortune, and I am blessed that my son has become the rightful king.'

'Indeed. I think we are all glad of that,' said Alicia. 'And I hope that there will be better times to come.'

'You were also treated badly by Despenser,' said the queen, and Alicia grasped the opportunity to press her case for the restitution of her lands.

'Despenser kept me confined at York for many months, until I was eventually forced to grant him all my first husband's lands, and the Salisbury lands that are mine by right,' she said. 'They were my mother's inheritance, and I am hoping that they will be returned to me now that restitutions are being made.'

'I would have to ask my lord Mortimer

about that,' said Isabella, 'but he is busy with the arrangements for the coronation at present.'

'I believe that you have been granted the castle at Clitheroe,' said Alicia, disappointed that the queen appeared to be dismissive of her petition.

'I am not sure. I think my lord Mortimer may have mentioned it.'

'And what of Ightenhill Manor?' she persisted, visualising the rolling green hills and meadows that she had loved as a child. 'My father used to breed our horses there.'

A look of irritation flickered over the queen's face. 'I will make enquiry — after the coronation,' she said, and picked up the embroidery that she had placed on the bench beside her. It was a clear signal of dismissal, and Alicia made a perfunctory curtsey before returning to her small chamber, where she picked up a steel mirror from the top of her coffer and flung it across the room with all her might.

*　*　*

Roger Mortimer watched as the young Edward knelt on the cushion. He was dressed in an ornate embroidered gown and held himself rigid as John of Hainault raised his sword and touched it to both shoulders, bestowing a knighthood on him ahead of the coronation ceremony.

Roger's gaze did not remain on the king for long, but strayed to where his own three sons were waiting for their turn to receive knighthoods: Edmund, his heir; his name-sake, Roger; and Geoffrey, who had been such a support to him whilst he was in exile. Other young men, especially chosen, stood with them, and the king would knight them after he had been crowned and anointed as was the tradition. But none looked as fine as his own sons, thought Roger. With their dark good looks and exquisite gowns, he thought that they eclipsed the pale boy who was now being led towards the high altar by the bishops of Winchester and London to swear that he would uphold the oaths of kingship.

Roger escorted the queen as the king was brought into the shrine of Edward the Confessor and seated on the coronation throne, beneath which dwelt the rough-hewn rock that his grandfather had taken from the Scots. The problem of Scotland crossed Roger's mind as he watched. There was an uneasy truce with Robert Bruce, and he hoped that it could be upheld. The ruling of England was his concern for the present, and he had no wish to squander vast resources from the treasury on another long and pointless war.

He forced his mind back to the present as Walter Reynolds, the Archbishop of Canterbury, intoned the Latin words of the consecration and anointed the boy on his head and breast with the oil of Thomas a Becket, brought from Canterbury. The bishops placed the crown of Edward the Confessor around the king's head, but held its weight. It was heavy with gold and huge jewels, and they were afraid that the boy would not be able to bear it alone. But it was enough for him to be proclaimed the crowned king, and judging by the rapturous welcome Edward received when he walked out of the doors of Westminster Abbey, it seemed that the people were all of one voice, and that voice was pleasure.

★ ★ ★

Alicia looked closely at the medal that Eble had placed on her outstretched palm. It was one of the specially commissioned silver coins that had been thrown amongst the crowds after the king's coronation. 'How did you come by this?' she asked.

'I caught it,' he said. 'One of the compensations of being a commoner is the ability to mingle with the masses.'

She glanced up at his tone. Although he spoke lightly, she knew that he was hurt that he had been passed over for a knighthood.

She looked again at the engraving on the bright circle in her hand. It showed the young king laying a sceptre on a pile of hearts, and bore the motto: *Given to the people according to their will*. Alicia turned it over, and on the reverse there was an image of the king holding out his hands to catch a falling crown. The motto read: *I did not take; I received*. It was cleverly done.

'He did not need to take the crown,' remarked Eble. 'Roger Mortimer took it for him.'

'I thought you liked him,' said Alicia as she continued to finger the coin.

'I thought that he would be fair,' replied Eble, 'but we are no nearer to recovering your lands, and it seems that most of them are now in the queen's possession.' She watched him as he stood up and brushed the clinging stalks of straw from his tunic. Frustrated by the sleeping arrangements at court, they had slipped away as the last course of the supper was being served and found themselves a secluded comer of the stables. 'And Henry of Lancaster is furious about Pontefract Castle being kept from him, because Mortimer says that the queen has need of it.'

Alicia clenched her hands around the coin until she felt its edges digging into her flesh. Thoughts of Pontefract always stirred up mixed feelings in her. Of all the castles that had once belonged to her father, it was the one that she thought of as home, although she knew it was unlikely she would ever pass through its gates again.

'Will Mortimer continue to allow Henry custody of the king — of Edward of Caernarfon?' she corrected herself.

'He captured him, which gives him the right to hold him prisoner,' said Eble. 'But with the return of his lands and the custody of Edward, he is a threat, and I do not think that Mortimer will allow it for much longer.'

'So what do you think will happen to Edward?'

She watched as Eble's face hardened. 'It would be better for Mortimer if Edward were dead,' he said.

⋆   ⋆   ⋆

When they returned to Lady de Vescy's chambers, Alicia was surprised to see Jeanne de Bar sitting by the dying embers of the hearth, in close conversation with her estranged husband, John de Warenne. As far as Alicia knew, she still hated the man.

'John,' said her husband, greeting his friend. Eble glanced at her, and she gave a slight shrug of her shoulders to tell him that she was also puzzled. Why Jeanne might want to be reconciled with her husband, she could only guess. Perhaps she felt vulnerable now that she had lost the protection of her uncle, and Alicia doubted that Roger Mortimer would continue to pay for her keep within the royal household.

'Eble,' replied John. 'What are you two doing?'

'I was seeing my wife safely to her bed,' said Eble.

'Come and share a drink with us first.' Eble hesitated, but Alicia whispered her assent, curious to know more.

'My lady,' said John, and he handed her a cup of wine. As she sipped from it, she saw Eble exchange a look with his friend, and she noted the slight shake of John's head as he warned him not to ask about what was going on.

'Where is Lady de Vescy?' asked Alicia.

'She is busy with her prayers,' said John and, as a momentary silence fell, Alicia heard the soft murmur of voices from the other side of the curtain. One of them was deep and clearly male, and Alicia presumed it was Lady de Vescy's chaplain — though it was a strange hour of the day for confession.

★   ★   ★

'It was not what I intended,' protested Lady de Vescy.

Brother Thomas Dunheved, the confessor to Edward of Caernarfon, frowned. The moonlight illuminated his tonsure like a halo, but his face conveyed only suppressed anger. 'What did you think would happen, my lady?' he asked her.

She looked away, but found herself gazing at the crucifix that hung in a small alcove, lit by a fluttering votive candle. The face of Christ was tortured in agony, and her soul flooded with guilt at what she had done. 'I wished only to be rid of the Despensers,' she said. 'It was never my intention that Edward should come to any harm.'

'So what did you think would happen?' repeated the priest. His hands were folded into the sleeves of his white habit and he stood quite still, but his displeasure filled the room like a miasma.

'How is Edward?' she asked, thinking of him not as a grown man, but the frightened and lonely child she had once known.

'I was not allowed to see him,' Brother

Thomas told her. 'So I can bring no news of his wellbeing.'

'It pains me to think of Edward captive there,' she said, remembering the towering walls of Kenilworth Castle.

'Did you think that he would be allowed to go free?'

'Yes, of course,' protested Lady de Vescy. 'I thought that once Despenser was removed, the problem would be gone. I thought that the queen would get her husband back and that Edward would rule, perhaps with the guidance of the nobles.'

'Then you underestimated Roger Mortimer,' replied the priest, 'if you thought he would be content with that.'

'But Mortimer was always loyal to Edward,' she protested again.

'Two years in the Tower can change a man's perceptions,' the priest told her.

Lady de Vescy could not reply. The priest was right, but hindsight was a precious thing, and it was easy for him to judge her now. If she had known what would happen, then she might have acted differently, but Isabella had been so sad for the loss of her husband. She had loved Edward, and Lady de Vescy had been convinced that they could love one another again if only the evil influence of Hugh le Despenser could be removed. Yes, she knew that Edward was weak and that he had flaws, but at heart he was not an unkind or cruel man. It was just that he was too easily led astray. She had thought that with good guidance, everything could be made right. She had not realised how difficult it might be to put the spilt wine back in the barrel. And she had certainly not foreseen that Isabella would fall in love with Roger Mortimer.

'What can I do?' she asked at last. 'How can I make amends?'

The priest visibly relaxed at her acknowledgement that she was in the wrong. 'Please,' he said, in a gentler tone, 'be seated.'

Lady de Vescy lowered herself thankfully to the bench. Her legs, as well as her heart, were aching, and she was desperately tired.

'I need you to speak with your brother, Henry Beaumont,' said the priest.

'For what purpose?'

'For the purpose of freeing the rightful king,' said the priest. 'There are others who are willing to assist us, but Kenilworth is a fortress, and unless we can find someone whom we can trust to infiltrate the castle, it will not be easy.'

'And where will you take Edward if you can get him out?' she asked. 'A group of monks cannot simply bring him back to London and reinstate him on the throne.' It was ridiculous, she thought. They would all end up swinging by their necks.

'The house at Scarborough will shield him for the present,' said Brother Thomas. 'You know the place?'

Lady de Vescy nodded. She had endowed the friary there, near to the castle, and the monks were obliged to her for much of their income. And even if nothing more was achieved than a life amongst the cloisters, in the company of other men, it would suit Edward better than the prospect of a lifetime of confinement in the custody of his hated cousin, Henry of Lancaster.

'I will talk to my brother,' she promised, 'and do what I can to make amends. I have sinned,' she confessed. 'Will you give me absolution?'

'May God forgive you,' said the priest, as he made the sign of the cross on her forehead. 'And may God forgive us all for allowing His anointed king to be dispossessed and imprisoned. We are all sinners.'

★ ★ ★

'What's going on between you and Jeanne de Bar?' Eble asked John when he caught up with him in the courtyard.

John hesitated, then took Eble by the arm

and drew him towards the well, where they could see if anyone approached them. 'What do you make of Mortimer?' he asked. 'I know he is a marcher lord, like you. But do you trust the man?'

'Not entirely,' Eble said. 'Though I'm not sure what that has to do with your renewed friendship with your wife,' he remarked, determined not to let John eschew an explanation so easily.

'It has everything to do with it,' replied John. 'Jeanne hates Mortimer as much as I do, and she is determined not to allow her uncle to spend the rest of his life in captivity.'

Eble peered down to where the quavering water was reflecting the light of the full moon. 'What are you planning?' he asked.

'We are planning to free the rightful king and put him back on the throne.'

'We?' asked Eble. 'You and Jeanne de Bar? Who else?' He paused. 'The Lady de Vescy?' he ventured.

'I am hoping so, after tonight.'

'And what about Alicia?'

'I think that by now she will know as much as you do,' said John, glancing up at the window of Lady de Vescy's chamber, where the faint candlelight still flickered behind the thick panes of glass. 'And I am hoping that she, and you, will join our cause.'

15

June 1327–July 1327

Scotland

Roger Mortimer put aside the documents that had been brought for his approval, and listened in growing anger. 'Enough!' he said, holding up a hand to silence the man. 'I have heard enough. Where is Lancaster now?'

'He is in the council chamber, my lord, conducting a meeting about the merits of another campaign against the Scots.'

'Tell him I want to see him,' said Roger, scraping back his chair. 'Get him out of the chamber if needs be!'

Whether Lancaster knew about the rumoured rescue or not, action needed to be taken, thought Roger. He had known that there were some discontents, but he had not realised that there were enough to make an attempt to free Edward of Caernarfon, and to almost succeed. He only hoped that Lancaster had not been party to it.

He turned from his angry contemplation to see Henry of Lancaster glaring at him.

'What is so urgent,' he demanded, 'that you send a message asking me to break up a meeting that you yourself asked me to convene?'

Roger waited a moment before replying. 'Your castle at Kenilworth is not as secure as you think, and your household not as loyal. I have just been informed that your prisoner, Edward of Caernarfon, was almost freed two days ago by his former confessor, Thomas Dunheved.'

He watched with some pleasure as Lancaster's irritation was replaced by disbelief and then indignation that he had not been the first to hear of it. 'Why was I not told?'

'I'm telling you now,' replied Roger.

'Is it true? Who brought the news? Was it one of my men?'

'The truth or otherwise is not the issue here, my lord,' said Roger. 'Whilst Edward remains at Kenilworth, there may be more attempts to free him. I think it would be better if he were taken elsewhere — somewhere not openly disclosed.'

'Where?' muttered Lancaster. 'He could be held securely at Pontefract if you would write to the constable there and instruct him to render me the keys.'

Roger ignored the challenge. He had no intention of returning Pontefract, or any other of the disputed de Lacy lands. He had been generous enough already. 'No,' he said, 'I was thinking of another location.'

'Ludlow? Do you really think he will be safer on the fringes of Wales?' scoffed Lancaster.

'I have not yet made a decision. I must give it careful thought!' retaliated Roger. 'But I will take Edward from Kenilworth and place him where I can be sure that he is secure.'

'And if I don't agree?'

'Then I will take him by force.' The two men glared at one another, and Roger was satisfied when Lancaster was the first to look away. 'What has been said about Scotland?' he asked after a moment, partly to appease Lancaster.

Henry took the cup of wine that Mortimer offered. 'Our spies talk of a build-up of forces along the border,' he said. 'And the other earls believe we should plan a fresh campaign.'

Roger turned aside and tried to disguise the sigh of annoyance that had escaped him with a cough. A negotiator from Bruce had met with him and Isabella in Paris before the invasion, and terms had been agreed that in return for recognition of Scottish sovereignty, there would be no more attacks. But it seemed that Bruce was growing impatient for that agreement to be made official.

'I am sure a diplomatic solution can be found. It would certainly be less costly,' he replied.

Lancaster's jaw tightened. 'You cannot believe that a truce is acceptable. Henry Beaumont does not wish to give up his claim to his wife's lands in Scotland.'

'It is a small price to pay. We must all make sacrifices,' snapped Roger. Although he owed a lot to Lady de Vescy, he was becoming irritated by the constant whingeing of her brother and his aspirations to become the Earl of Buchan. 'I will send word when I intend to come for Edward of Caernarfon,' said Roger. 'I trust that you will have him prepared and that there will be no trouble.'

It would be a relief to have Edward under his own control, thought Roger, although perhaps he would sweeten Lancaster with the promise of his leading an army north. When he considered it, he thought that the young king might enjoy such an expedition as long he wasn't allowed to become embroiled in any actual warfare. The promise of independent sovereignty had been made on the understanding that the Scottish raids would cease, and perhaps Bruce needed to be taught a lesson.

Roger nodded to the clerk to take the

papers to the queen for her signature and then pulled a fresh sheet of parchment towards him and smoothed it under his hand. He would write to his son-in-law, Thomas Lord Berkeley, and to John Maltravers, who had been in exile with him. They would be better custodians of Edward of Caernarfon than the tetchy Earl of Lancaster, and Berkeley Castle was a more secure prison. Then he would write to Count William in Hainault and ask him to send mercenaries for an assault on the Scots.

★   ★   ★

The lake around Kenilworth was calm, and a haze floated above the surface as it was heated by the noonday sun. Roger approached the castle in the company of Berkeley and Maltravers without any display of banners; and although they were accompanied by a guard numerous enough to withstand any rescue attempt by the Dunheved brothers and their adherents, each man had concealed his armour under his cloak. To an unobservant eye, they looked like nothing more than a group of travellers, perhaps on pilgrimage.

There was no sign of the Lady of the Lake as they approached the drawbridge, which had been lowered in response to their horns.

Not that this was really the lake where the lady dwelt, thought Roger, as the hooves pounded on the thick wooden planks and echoed into the abyss below. It was on Welsh land that Excalibur was placed in Arthur's hand.

When they reached the inner bailey, he dismounted and handed Wigmore's reins to a groom before climbing the stairs to the hall. Lancaster was waiting to greet him. A woman whom he took to be one of his daughters was efficiently organising washing water and refreshments, though Henry's welcome was no more cordial than he had expected.

'Is Edward ready?' asked Roger.

'When do you intend to take him?'

'Now,' said Roger.

'Surely not today? I thought you would want to rest your horses and men for one night at least.'

'We will stay to dine,' conceded Roger. 'And then we will leave, with Edward.'

He had no intention of spending a night at Lancaster's hospitality. Besides, it would wrong-foot any would-be rescuers if they left that day rather than waiting for morning, and Roger was not afraid of the dark. Henry gave a shrug of resignation and asked a servant to go and ensure that Edward was fed and made ready to leave by the time their dinner was finished.

The conversation at the table was guarded and mannered. There were exchanges about the weather, the crops, jousting tournaments and the contents of the sauces. No word was spoken about the former king until he was brought into the hall, cloaked and booted, and with a furious face.

'Mortimer.' He greeted Roger with the look of a man who had just stepped in something bad. 'Where do you intend to take me?'

'On a short tour of your former realm, my lord, and then to a cosy chamber far away from the pressures of the courtly life. I am sure you will find it to your liking.' The former king looked too well clothed, he thought. His hair and beard were clean and impeccably trimmed, and he was wearing expensive robes. 'We cannot take him like that,' he said, turning to Lancaster, who was standing by as if expecting a commendation for having cared for Edward so diligently. 'Take that cloak and give him something more appropriate,' he told Berkeley.

'This is not enough to keep me warm,' protested Edward as they stripped his beaver-lined cloak from his shoulders and replaced it with one of rough wool.

'Make sure your tunic is kept covered at all times, or that will need to be changed as well,'

Roger instructed him. 'And put this on,' he said, handing him a well-worn brown hood.

Edward took the item between his fingers and stared at it in distaste. 'I cannot wear this. It looks filled with lice,' he complained, holding it at arm's length as if it might bite him.

'Put it on,' Roger told him, enjoying the feeling of power it gave him to overrule the man who had once been his liege lord.

'Surely it is not necessary to humiliate him like this,' protested Lancaster.

'Of course it is necessary,' replied Roger. 'We might as well take him with the crown still on his head as take him in such sumptuous clothing. He must look like a clerk or a servant.'

In the bailey, Roger led Edward towards the palfrey he had brought. It was a comical-looking skewbald gelding with one side of its face white and the other brown, but sturdy despite its appearance. He had considered bringing a donkey, but Edward was a tall man, and it had been from pity for the animal rather than the former king that he had decided against it.

'You cannot expect me to ride that.'

'Ride it or walk,' he said. Edward stared at him in disbelief, and Roger wondered if the man would ever accept that he was no longer the king. As he walked away to mount his own horse, he saw Edward haul himself into the palfrey's saddle and arrange the thin cloak about him. His hair and beard were covered by the hood, and Roger was pleased to see that he was barely recognisable.

They rode out of the castle in close formation and headed south. Their final destination was the sandstone fortress of Berkeley Castle that guarded the estuary of the Severn near the Welsh borders, but Roger had planned a circuitous route that he hoped would confuse any spies who caught sight of them along the way. At Berkeley he would leave his prisoner in the care of the two men he trusted implicitly — and then he would turn his attention to the Scots.

★　★　★

Alicia followed Lady de Vescy into the monks' dormitory at the Dominican friary in York. All the pallet beds had been removed, and trestles had been brought in and set up the length of the chamber. Where the monks were to sleep that night she was unsure, but it was certain that they would not be lying here. Servants scurried up and down the night stairs bringing embroidered linen cloths and napkins for the tables. Chairs for the queen and her guest of honour had been carried up for the top table, and benches from the monks' refectory had been brought up for the other ladies.

Lady de Vescy had charge of the silverware, and they had come to supervise its placing. The cups and the salt pot shone with the hard polishing they had received and, after she had moved them imperceptibly from left to right and back again, Lady de Vescy nodded her satisfaction.

'I'm sure Sir John will be impressed,' remarked Alicia. She and Eble had remained with the court as it had journeyed north to York to await the reinforcements from Hainault. The previous day, the striped sails of Sir John and his mercenary troops had been sighted sailing up the Ouse towards the harbour. Tonight, Queen Isabella and her ladies were to entertain Sir John whilst the king and Roger Mortimer feasted with the other men in the hall below.

'He should be,' sighed Lady de Vescy. 'I think more money is being spent on the entertainment than on the preparations for war.'

'You sound as if you disapprove.'

Lady de Vescy gave her a warning look. 'Let us get a breath of fresh air,' she said. 'We are only getting in the way here.'

Alicia followed her down the staircase and out into the gardens, where the bare soil revealed the amount of herbs and vegetables that had been dug up and taken to the kitchens.

'Have you seen the Earl of Lancaster?' asked Lady de Vescy.

'Not since he arrived in York. Why?'

Lady de Vescy glanced around again, and then lowered her head and her voice as she spoke. 'Mortimer has taken Edward away from him.'

'To where?'

'No one knows. But Lancaster is in contact with Thomas Dunheved, and there are men throughout the realm who are seeking him.'

'And when they find him?' she asked. 'What then?'

'If he can be freed, he will retake his rightful place.'

'And young Edward?' asked Alicia.

'His time to be king will come,' said Lady de Vescy. 'The boy is scarce fourteen and cannot rule alone. And whilst Mortimer guides him, we are no better off than when Despenser guided his father.'

⋆   ⋆   ⋆

The voices sounded louder each time the outer door opened for the servers to carry in another procession of food. It was becoming impossible to ignore them; and when Eble craned his neck to see what was happening, he caught sight of one of the English archers with an arrow notched in his bow. What on earth was happening? he wondered. Were they being attacked by the Scots even as they sat down to dinner? He glanced to where Roger Mortimer was sitting beside the young king. Neither seemed aware of the uproar outside.

A scream of pain reverberated as the outer door swung open once more. It was too loud to ignore, and Eble climbed over the bench with several other men who were drawing their swords and going to investigate the commotion. Outside, it was apparent that a quarrel between the servants of the Hainaulters and the English archers had spun out of control. The archers had grasped the weapons that were never far from their reach, and one Hainaulter now lay dying in the priory cloisters with an English arrow protruding from between his ribs.

There were men on the stairs that led up to the monks' dormitory, and Eble was unsure how friendly they were. He glanced up and saw a few of the women looking down in horror and fear at the fighting below them. They were trapped, and all Eble wanted to do was force his way through the melee to find

Alicia and ensure that she was safe.

The men from the hall called for the fighting to cease, but both sides were too angry to listen, and arrows flew across the cloister lawn that was being churned to mud beneath the feet of the opponents.

A door banged; and as Eble turned, wondering what to do, the mob moved as one mass and began to spill out of the precincts of the abbey into the streets beyond. He saw that the stairs to the dormitory were clear and he ran up them, two at a time, and into the chamber. The dishes lay untasted on the trestles, and the queen and her ladies cowered against the walls.

'Where is Sir John?' Eble asked.

'Gone below to try to restrain his countrymen,' replied Alicia as she came to him and took his hand. She was trembling.

'Are you harmed?' he asked her.

'No. The fighting did not come further than the steps. But the queen is badly shaken.'

Eble glanced at Isabella. 'My lady, you are quite safe,' he reassured her. 'The miscreants have moved away now, and I'm sure the trouble will soon be contained.' Although, judging by the rising noise from beyond the walls, Eble was not as confident as he hoped he sounded. Alerted to the riot, the feasting below had also been interrupted, and he heard Mortimer calling for his horse to be brought. His hand tightened around Alicia's. The queen was being escorted to her private chambers in the guest house, but he had no intention of allowing his wife out of his sight. Neither would he return to their lodgings, in the house of a gold merchant near the river, until he was sure it was safe to walk the streets. It was not an auspicious beginning to what should have been a joint attack on the Scots, he thought, when the English and the Hainaulters fought amongst themselves.

He led Alicia down the steps in time to see the body of the dead man being carried away by a group of monks. Inside, the hall was deserted.

'When we are in Lincolnshire I crave to be at court.' She shivered. 'Then, when I am here, I wish to be back in Swaveton.'

'Our home has much to recommend it,' agreed Eble, wishing that he could take her back there rather than having to leave her alone in York when he rode for Scotland with the rest of the army.

★ ★ ★

The riot was eventually quelled by Roger Mortimer and Sir John, who rode through the streets and appealed for calm. By the time the bells of the minster had chimed the darkest hour of the night, both sides had slunk off to their beds. Dawn broke on fences and gardens trampled underfoot, and on men whose sobered and throbbing heads made them regret their actions — although many of the mercenaries said that the English were keener to kill them than the Scots, and swore to sleep in their armour from then on.

For a few days an uneasy peace hung over the city, but an attack by the Scots on the lands of some northern barons put pressure on Roger Mortimer to take action. Then, as the army gathered to march out on the first morning of July, a messenger galloped in under the archway of the friary gatehouse. Roger recognised the man as one of the household of his son-in-law, Thomas Berkeley, and he sensed trouble even before the man slid from the saddle of his exhausted horse and fell to one knee before him.

'Bad news,' said the man in reply to his unspoken query as he handed over the creased parchment.

Roger broke open the seal and scanned the contents before uttering an oath that made several men turn towards him.

'Is all well, my lord?' asked John de Warenne warily.

'Yes. It is . . . It is news that my wife is unwell — nothing serious,' he lied, quickly folding the parchment. 'Can you take over here? I must send a reply.'

Having dismissed the messenger to find some food, with a warning to speak of the matter to no one, Roger ran up the steps of the abbot's house where he was lodging and closed the door of the bedchamber behind him. Alone, he took the parchment out and re-read it more carefully. The message was stark. The castle had been stormed and ransacked, and Edward of Caernarfon had been freed.

Roger sat on the edge of the bed and allowed his head to fall into his hands. How in the name of St Peter had such a thing occurred? Berkeley was a fortress, not a barn where a thief might force the door in the dead of night. His son-in-law's excuse that the men had disguised themselves as labourers working on the strengthening of the castle was ironic and hollow. It seemed they had secreted themselves inside the walls and then opened the postern gate for their fellow conspirators, who had spirited Edward away on horseback.

Roger shivered despite the humid heat outside. If he had thought the coming thunderstorm was making his head ache, then this made it throb a hundred times more.

What on earth was he going to do? He was about to set out to fight a fraudulent war on behalf of a fraudulent king, whilst the real king was at liberty in his own realm and, it seemed, was not without support. He stared at the light beyond the narrow slit of the window. This monk's chamber reminded him too much of his own incarceration in the Tower, and he folded the letter into his pouch before going back to the courtyard where he had been inspecting the horses with John de Warenne. What did he know of it? he wondered. He found the man enigmatic; and even though he had sworn his loyalty to Isabella and young Edward, he had only done so after the execution of Arundel. And what did Lancaster know? He had accepted the invitation to lead the army into Scotland with good grace, but was that because he had some ulterior plan?

Roger lingered the collar of his tunic as he came out of the abbot's house. If Edward of Caernarfon garnered enough of a following to claim back his throne, then it would mean certain death for himself and the sons who had so openly supported him. And even if the former king was not set up as a rival to young Edward, without possession of him Roger knew that his power over Isabella's son would be curtailed. At present there was the unspoken threat that his father could be brought back if he did not agree to the plans put to him by his mother; but without that hold, how could he hope to keep the growing adolescent in his power?

★ ★ ★

When the army rode out of York, with trumpets blaring and pennants fluttering, Roger Mortimer stayed behind. Eble shifted his weight forward in the saddle and spurred Trebnor on from the slow pace of the heavy baggage wains to draw level with John de Warenne. 'Why has Mortimer not ridden with us?' he asked.

'Perhaps he cannot bear to be parted from the queen,' said his friend, taking the reins in one hand and making a rude gesture with the other. Eble grinned.

'What do you know about the messenger that came?' he asked. 'Quite a few people commented on the state of the horse and that the man wore no colours.'

'I believe it was a secret letter from Lord Thomas Berkeley.'

'Berkeley? Is that where the Lord Edward is being held?'

'Was being held. The Dunheved brothers have got him out.'

'Truly?' Eble let out a low whistle of admiration. 'That's almost as incredible as Mortimer's own escape from the Tower. What will he do?'

'Mortimer? He'll hope and pray that he can recapture him. He's terrified that there is enough support to put Edward back on the throne and his own head on the block. That's why he has remained behind — hoping for better news.'

'But if Edward is free, why are you riding north to engage with the Scots?' asked Eble.

'Because it is too soon to openly declare my hand. And if I refuse to fight, then Mortimer will cry treason and I will be a fugitive as well.'

'And Edward?'

'He will be taken abroad until we know we can defeat Mortimer.'

'Does Lancaster know?'

'I don't think so, but he has his spies. And he would like nothing better than to take custody of Edward again and use him as a stick to beat Mortimer with. Do not breathe a word,' John warned him.

★　★　★

They rode on at a leisurely pace through Mytton-on-Swale to Topcliffe, where they paused to wait for news from the border. By the time they left to head for Durham, Roger Mortimer had slipped back into their ranks, although he had the look of a man whose mind was elsewhere.

On the fourth morning, Eble pushed back the flap of his tent to reveal a pall of rising smoke. The Scots were burning settlements to the south; but no sooner had the English and Hainaulters strapped themselves into their armour and drawn up their battalions to fight, than the Scots were burning other villages.

'They move too quickly for us,' complained Henry of Lancaster. John de Warenne had taken Eble with him to the meeting at a nearby monastery to discuss tactics, and the gloomy commanders, along with the young king and Roger Mortimer, were seeking a solution to their humiliation.

'They do not travel as we do,' observed Sir John of Hainault. 'Each man carries his own supply of oatmeal beneath his saddle which they bake into flat cakes. They butcher local cattle for their meat and stew it in cauldrons made of hide. It allows them to move quickly. We are held back by our long supply chains of packhorses and wagons.'

'Perhaps we should emulate them,' suggested the Earl of Kent. 'What if our mounted forces were to ride with a loaf of bread strapped to their saddles so that they could eat without having to wait for provisions?'

'It would allow men to move faster, and speed is of the essence here,' said Lancaster. 'The Scots are in retreat, but if we can move to cut off their route across the Tyne they will be trapped and forced to fight.'

'And our numbers far outweigh theirs,' said Kent. 'If the mounted force can hold them until the rest of the army arrives, they will have no chance.'

The men looked towards the king for his approval and the boy nodded in agreement. Eble could see that he thirsted for a real battle, and he remembered what it was like to be fourteen and filled with the belief that war was exciting.

★ ★ ★

The next morning, Eble saddled up Trebnor and tied his ration to the saddle. There was a thirty-five-mile ride ahead of them towards the Tyne. As the rain began, Trebnor fell into step beside John de Warenne's horse, and they pushed on against the prevailing wind and the sudden showers of sharp hailstones that bounced off their armour and flew up into their faces. Eble wished for his cloak and hood as water began to seep inside his mail and soak through the padding of his gambeson, weighing him down in the saddle. But the orders had been to carry nothing other than weapons and the one loaf, which was already beginning to swell in the downpour.

John had ordered his men to ride in formation, but many fell behind as the track turned to a quagmire, and they were forced to dismount and lead the horses through the mud to prevent them being trapped fetlock-deep.

The river was already rising when they reached it and urged the weary horses into the fast-flowing spate. In the dusk beyond, a group of soaked men watched them disconsolately. They held the reins of their horses, whose heads were lowered against the weather, and they looked at a loss to know what to do. The ground was bare, and even if they had been equipped with hatchets and hooks, it was doubtful that any kindling they gathered could have been encouraged into a blaze. Everything was drenched, and even the king looked pale and near to tears as the earls gave him what comfort they could.

'The lad is learning that war is not so alluring now,' remarked Eble to John as he unfastened his loaf of bread from the saddle and the soggy mess fell apart in his hands. His stomach wrenched with hunger and he pushed a handful into his mouth, but found it tainted with the salty tang of Trebnor's sweat. He offered some to the horse, but even he sniffed at it and let out a disgruntled snort before turning his head away. Reluctantly, Eble let it fall and eased himself down onto the soaked ground. He was as wet as it was possible to get, and as night fell he began to shiver with cold and hunger, only thankful that it was summer and that the hours until dawn were mercifully few.

As daylight lightened the eastern sky from a sun that was invisible somewhere behind the thick grey cloud, he saw that the swollen river was now impassable. Their baggage remained somewhere on the far side, and of the Scots there was no sign.

'What now?' he asked John as he watched Henry of Lancaster pacing the edge of the water.

'One scouting party has been sent to look for the Scots, and others to look for the provisions,' said John, who had stood in a huddle with the other earls. 'Meanwhile, we wait.'

'People thought the old king was incompetent, but we were never reduced to this,' grumbled Eble, wondering if he should take off his armour and try to wring some of the water from his gambeson, or whether it was better just to stay wet. He had tried to stave off some of the hunger pangs with a drink of the river water, but it tasted brackish in his mouth, and his stomach rumbled audibly. 'I think that once the water falls, we should cross back and look for our supply wagons,' he said. 'If the Scots come upon us like this, we will be slaughtered.'

He looked behind him as shouting broke out. One scouting party had returned, leading a couple of mules and men were fighting over the contents of the saddlebags. Eble heard Roger Mortimer call to his men to break up the fight at the point of their swords, but those who had bread in their hands were already stuffing it into their mouths as fast as they could, despite the threats. Eble could hardly blame them. His mouth watered at the thought of the food, and he longed to wade into the melee and grab what he could for himself.

Later that afternoon, they mounted up and rode down the riverbank. At Haltwhistle the ford looked passable, and Mortimer sent scouts ahead to test the crossing. Eble watched as the men and horses fought against the torrent. One horse was pulled from its feet by the force of the water and swept away, its rider only missing drowning by clinging to the tail of another man's mount until he was dragged out onto the far bank. But, despite the loss of the horse, Mortimer ordered them across.

Trebnor tossed his head and refused to go in at first, and Eble had to spur him mercilessly to drive him into the water. Snorting and whinnying with fear, the horse lost his footing, and Eble felt him begin to swim. He slid from the saddle, clung onto the horse's mane, and urged him forward. The water lapped around his head, filling his ears and cutting off the sounds of shouting. He had taken off his mail and strapped it to the saddle, but it was still weighing them down, and he was wondering if he could manage to unfasten it and let it sink when Trebnor caught a foothold and scrambled onto the muddy grass, where both Eble and the horse stood trembling with cold and fatigue.

The Earls of Lancaster and Kent had got the king safely across; and although another couple of horses were lost, no men drowned that afternoon. They mounted up and squelched their way towards the burnt-out remains of Blanchland Abbey. As they approached, Eble saw that the baggage wagons were waiting for them and some tents had been pitched, but he knew that the worst was probably not over.

★   ★   ★

The next morning, after the priests had said mass in the remains of the roofless abbey church, they made their confessions and set out to do battle. The Scots were waiting for them, lined up on a steep hill on the far side of the Wear. It meant another river crossing and an assault uphill, under fire, to engage them.

Roger Mortimer watched as the first battalion of archers waded into the water. Lancaster had sent heralds on behalf of the king to ask if the Scots would cross the river to fight on level ground, but they had replied that if the king of England did not want them in his country, he should come to them and force them to retreat. Roger bit his lip as he scanned the area for any sign of an ambush. Lancaster was a fool and would not listen to his advice, and young Edward was so intent on taking his first victory that he listened to anyone who told him it could be done. How had he allowed this to happen? he wondered. His mind had been so distracted that he had failed to take proper care of this matter with the Scots. It had never been his intention to fight. He had thought that a strong army marching north would have been enough to see them off, but it seemed that Bruce was angrier and more determined than he had realised.

As he watched, one of the foremost archers pitched into the water with a Scottish arrow protruding from his chest. His sharp cry reached Roger's ears a moment later, and was followed by more as men were picked off before they could even notch their arrows to defend themselves — and those who did manage to return shots were so unbalanced by the swirling water that their aim was pitiful.

It had to be stopped, thought Roger as he watched the bodies of the dead float slowly downstream. He touched his heels to Wigmore's sides and galloped towards the vantage point where the Earls of Lancaster and Kent flanked the king.

'Call a retreat!' he ordered.

'And allow the Scots to take the day?' demanded the king.

'Retreat and fight another day, when the odds are not against us,' Roger told him.

Edward turned furious blue eyes on him. 'You are not a commander of my army,' he said.

'I may have no official title,' replied Roger,

'but if you value your life you will listen to me. I do not want to return you to your mother as a corpse!'

'Take no notice, your grace,' said Lancaster. 'We can win this day.'

'Nonsense! We must retreat!' shouted Roger, wondering if the man's eyesight was worse than he thought and he really could not see the extent of the Scottish force ranged against them.

The king raised his chin. 'I will listen to the Earl of Lancaster,' he said.

'God's teeth,' swore Roger under his breath as he wheeled his horse. How was he to keep control of this boy? He urged Wigmore back down the slope and galloped towards the Earl of Norfolk, who was leading the vanguard. 'Stand down!' he shouted. 'Stand down, or we will all be killed!'

Norfolk hesitated and glanced towards the king. Then he ordered his men about in obedience to Roger.

⋆　⋆　⋆

'You are a traitor, sir!' shouted the king when they had returned to their camp. 'You wanted the Scots to get away. It is treason!'

Roger watched the anguished face of the boy and was reminded of his own sons, when they were barely old enough to walk, bawling over some disappointment or other. Lancaster and Kent looked as mutinous as the boy over the usurping of their authority, and Roger could see similar suspicion in their eyes.

At least Norfolk and the other commanders had obeyed him. But he knew that although the army had been saved, he had enhanced the enmity between himself and Lancaster. He and Kent were the king's kin, and the boy seemed to prefer their advice now that his mother was not here to control him. That insolence, added to the worries about the whereabouts of Edward of Caernarfon, worried Roger. There was the prospect of him losing the power he had gained if he did not find a way to keep control of the king.

*　*　*

Eble pushed his fingers into his ears in a futile attempt to shut out the noise. For the third night in a row, the Scots were blowing their trumpets and howling like wolves in an effort to deprive the English army of any sleep. Even through the fabric of his tent, he could see the glow of their fires; and when the wind was in the right direction, he could smell the meat cooking in their cauldrons. He groaned and turned over. Mortimer had instructed them to sleep in their armour in case of a surprise attack; and the mail, combined with the thin pallet on the hard ground, was rubbing sores the length of his body despite being wrapped in his cloak. It was torture, and the men were growing increasingly fraught as the days passed. Squabbles and petty disagreements were spilling over into fighting, and Eble thought that if the situation wasn't resolved soon, the English and the Hainault mercenaries would kill one another, leaving the Scots with an easy victory.

He must have drifted back to sleep. When he woke again, it was to a merciful silence; but as he gave thanks for the peace, he heard a sharp crackle and smelt smoke that seemed too pungent to be drifting from across the river. He gingerly parted the flap of the tent to look out.

'God's mother!' he swore, leaping to his feet. Flames had taken hold of several tents, and he could see men moving stealthily through the camp, the light from their torches casting their shadows as they hacked at guy ropes and thrust their spears into the sleeping occupants before setting the canvas alight.

Eble shook the other men in his tent to wake them, and as they raised the alarm he grasped his sword and ran, tripping twice, through the darkness towards where the king was sleeping.

As he approached the tent, he saw it lean to one side and then fall as the ropes were cut. The torch that the Scot carried illuminated him and, without hesitation, Eble thrust his sword into the man. He stamped on the flames that were licking at the edges of the canvas, then pulled at the heavy material. He grabbed at the flailing arm and dragged the king clear of the fire. The camp was filled with shouting and the sounding of horns, which mingled with the screams of the dying. Outnumbered, the Scottish raiders were now withdrawing, and some of the English were pursuing them in the direction of the river; but Eble heard Roger Mortimer shouting at them to let the Scots go and bring water to douse the flames.

He turned back to the figure he had pulled free. The young king, visibly trembling, had got to his feet and was staring around.

'Are you hurt, sire?' asked Eble.

'N-no. I don't believe s-so.'

The boy's teeth chattered, and Eble looked about for a blanket. There was nothing to hand, so he unclasped his own cloak and put it around Edward's shoulders.

'Thank you,' said the boy. 'Have they gone?'

'I think so,' said Eble. He stared towards where men were beating at the remains of the burning tents. The moaning of those who had been stabbed and impaled filled the air as they were lifted and taken to where their injuries could be treated, or the priests could give them the comfort of absolution before they passed to their maker.

'Where is the king?' called a frantic voice.

'He is here. He is safe,' replied Eble as the Earl of Lancaster loomed out of the darkness.

'Are you hurt, sire?'

'No.' Eble watched the boy compose himself. 'They set my tent alight, but this man dragged me free.' He paused and turned to Eble. 'I do not know your name.'

'I am Eble le Strange, sire.'

'Then I am indebted to you — and I will not forget it,' promised the king as he was led away by Lancaster, still wearing Eble's cloak.

16

August 1327–September 1327

The Death of a King

Roger Mortimer touched the lighted taper to the candle before the altar of Lincoln Cathedral, then knelt in thankful prayer. The campaign against the Scots had been a disaster, but he had managed to deflect the blame onto the Earls of Kent and Lancaster and escape with his own reputation intact. And the message brought to him in his private chamber that morning by William Ockley had brought relief from weeks of agony. Edward of Caernarfon was back at Berkeley Castle.

One of the men who had freed Edward, William Aylmer, had been caught at Oxford and had admitted that the Dunheved brothers had masterminded the plot. Other members of the gang had also been arrested and quietly dealt with, but the Dunheveds had so far evaded capture, and Roger knew that they would never be content until the former king was permanently freed.

He rose from his knees and crossed himself before turning to walk down the busy nave. He nodded his head or exchanged a brief greeting with one or two people that he knew, but he was not in the mood for conversation. He came out of the west door into bright sunlight that made him blink for a moment before he headed across the precincts towards the bishop's palace, where the king was residing.

He reached the palace and climbed the stairs to the chamber he had been given, near to Isabella's. There was no sign of her, and one of the servants reminded him that she and the king had gone out hunting with their hawks. With a nod, Roger dismissed the man and sat down at the small table. He drew a sheet of parchment towards him, and after a moment's thought he picked up a quill and dipped it tentatively into the inkhorn. There was some unrest in south Wales that needed his attention, but on the way he would ask his son-in-law, Thomas Berkeley, to meet with him at Ludlow.

★   ★   ★

'Are you sorry to leave it all behind?' asked Eble as he and Alicia rode down the hill from the palace at Lincoln and skirted the

Brayford Pool before heading home.

No.' Alicia turned in her saddle to glance back, then met her husband's eyes. He still looked tired, she thought. He hadn't said much about what had happened at Weardale, although she had heard from others how he had pulled the king from his tent as an assassin was about to strike. 'The court is not the same as it was,' she said.

'Nothing ever remains the same,' remarked Eble. 'We all have to learn to live with change.'

'Did you know that Roger Mortimer also left court today?' she asked him. 'He came to the queen's chamber to bid her farewell. He said that he has been commissioned to investigate an uprising in south Wales.'

'I think he is still angry with the king for accusing him of helping the Scots to get away.'

'Then Mortimer does not find him easy to advise?' she asked.

Eble shook his head. 'The king is like his grandfather in so many ways — and his determination to win Scotland is only part of it. Edward knows his own mind, and he will soon be a man. Mortimer is not finding it easy to make him bend to his will.'

'Perhaps that is a good thing,' mused Alicia as the ground under the horses' hooves flattened out and she urged her mount to quicken its pace. 'A strong king is what this country needs.'

★ ★ ★

Roger Mortimer took the cup of wine from his wife and drank. He was thirsty after the long ride and glad to reach Ludlow, as the fine weather had shaded to rain. Joan had greeted him so warmly that he was beset by guilt at his abandonment of her. She had efficiently arranged for hot water, soap and towels so that he could wash, and from one of the coffers in the bedchamber had produced dry hose and shoes. It reminded him of all the other occasions when he had returned home after a long absence. Roger studied her. She had regained some weight, but the sadness that clouded her face was plain for him to see. He knew that it was because of him, and he wished for a moment that it could have been otherwise. She was a good mother to his children, and they had been happy once when they were both young.

'I have brought the plans for the improvements to the castle,' he told her, getting up to fetch the drawings from his pouch. 'I have decided to build a new solar as well as the chapel of St Peter.'

Her eyes brightened as she looked at the parchment he spread out on the bench between them, and he was wondering whether or not to explain that the new solar was intended for a future visit from the queen, when they were interrupted by a knock on their chamber door. When the chamberlain entered in response to his call, Roger expected him to say that Thomas Berkeley had arrived, but instead he told him that a messenger had arrived from William de Shalford, his lieutenant in north Wales.

'I will come down to the hall,' he said, hoping that de Shalford wasn't going to bother him with trivialities.

The sight of the travel-stained messenger irritated him as the man knelt and handed him the letter. Roger told him to go to the kitchens and find himself some refreshment. Then he broke the seal and scanned the contents.

'God's teeth!' he swore.

'What troubles you, my lord?' asked Joan, who had followed him down.

'William de Shalford has discovered yet another plot to free Edward of Caernarfon. Rhys ap Gruffydd and Donald of Mar are plotting to take him from Berkeley by force.'

'Do you think they could succeed?' asked Joan.

'If a small group of men led by a priest could succeed, then a force gathered by Gruffydd and Mar must be a credible threat,' said Roger. 'At the very least, they could lay siege to the castle and force a battle.'

'What will you do?'

'Find a way to resolve the situation.' Roger frowned as he looked at the letter again, in which de Shalford warned him that he and his friends would die terrible deaths if the Lord Edward was ever freed, and advised him to find a remedy that meant no one in England or Wales would ever again consider delivering the former king from captivity.

He was considering what that remedy might be when the chamberlain returned to say that Lord Berkeley had come.

'How, in the name of all that is holy, did it happen?' demanded Roger once the formal greetings were over and they were alone.

Thomas spread his hands in a gesture of bewilderment. 'They must have come in with the builders and concealed themselves, then opened a door for their accomplices. But the Lord Edward is back in my custody now,' Berkeley reassured him. 'He is held securely, and it will not happen again.'

'I never expected it to happen the first time!' barked Roger. 'I thought that I could trust you!'

'It was an oversight, my lord.'

'An oversight?'

'I was momentarily distracted, my lord. The building work has caused more problems than it has resolved. And I cannot watch the Lord Edward all the time.'

'Then find someone who can!'

'It has already been done, my lord. I have appointed Sir Thomas Gurney as his keeper. He will reside at Berkeley as long as the Lord Edward lives, and he will ensure that no harm befalls him.'

'Yes, I know the man,' said Roger. 'Is he discreet?'

'Yes, my lord. He is utterly trustworthy.'

'Good.' Roger indicated that Thomas should be seated. 'There is a serious matter that you should know about,' he said, speaking more congenially now that he had expressed his displeasure. He opened the letter he had received from de Shalford and showed it to Thomas.

'He does not indicate how large a force they may be,' he said, handing it back after reading it. 'If they force a siege, I am not sure how long we could resist. The cellars are stocked, but without supplies we could not hold out forever.'

'Then we must find the remedy that de Shalford suggests,' said Roger. 'If Edward were to die, then there would be no more of these rescue attempts.'

Roger could see the brown flecks in Thomas's hazel eyes as he stared at him, trying to assess whether or not he was seriously suggesting that they murder the former king. Then he began to shake his head.

'No,' he said. 'No. I will have no part in killing him.'

'Would you rather have him plucked from under your nose again and die the atrocious death that de Shalford hints at?' asked Roger as he put the letter away in a small coffer and turned the key. 'Remember what we did to Despenser. Do you think Edward would have you, or me, treated with any more compassion?'

He saw Thomas swallow nervously. 'How could it be done?' he asked.

'Discreetly,' replied Roger. 'People must believe that Edward has died a natural death. Although I do not really want him dead,' he added as he sat down again and poured more wine. 'If Edward were dead, then it would remove the hold I have over the king,' he admitted. 'Whilst his father is alive and in my custody, he is compelled to bend to my will or run the risk of losing his crown. Whilst I have both father and son, the best pieces are mine to move at will — and I do not mean to give up that advantage.'

Thomas continued to look at him in bewilderment. 'So do you plan to murder Edward, or not?' he asked.

'I do not plan to kill the king,' said Roger. 'I only plan to make people believe that Edward is dead.'

*   *   *

It was an audacious plan, thought Thomas Berkeley, and one that was worthy of Roger Mortimer's cunning. Whether or not such a subterfuge could be pulled off was another matter, but a man who could plan his own escape from the Tower of London and then return to rule a country from behind the throne of a boy king was surely someone who could succeed in this.

The ride back to Berkeley Castle was long, and it was dark by the time Thomas and his small group of men-at-arms had forded the Severn and ridden in over the lowered drawbridge. Torches were burning in their sconces around the inner courtyard as he slid wearily from his saddle and handed the reins to a groom. He gave the order for the watch to be doubled and security raised to its highest level. It would be a disaster if the

Welsh struck before their plans could be put into operation.

Thomas Gurney was sprawled in the chair on the dais when Berkeley went in, and got up reluctantly to make way for him as servants hurried to fetch more food from the kitchens.

'How is our guest?' asked Berkeley as he washed his hands.

'Grumbling,' replied Gurney. 'He does not like being forced to take his meals in his chamber and would prefer to preside in the hall.'

'I'm sure he would,' said Berkeley, helping himself to bread whilst the server carved slices of meat. 'But do not be persuaded by him. Mortimer has been sent word of another plot to free him.' He told Gurney about the letter from de Shalford as he ate. 'So,' he ended, 'Mortimer has decided to remedy the situation. As soon as we receive word from him, we are to do as he has bid.'

Gurney scratched his head and poured himself more wine. 'But where are we supposed to find a body?' he asked.

'People die every day.'

'But not people who are six feet tall and blond-haired,' argued Gurney.

'People will see what they want to see,' said Berkeley. 'And we will ensure that no one looks too closely. An embalmed body with cerecloth covering the face, viewed superficially, will raise no suspicions. Why should it? Why would anyone say that it was not Edward?'

'But the physician who embalms the body will know. How can we buy his silence?'

'We will not send for the physician. There is a wise woman in the village who is perfectly capable of completing the task.'

'And her silence?'

'Roger Mortimer will take care of that,' he told him.

★   ★   ★

The sun had already set, and thick beeswax candles were burning all around the hall for the late supper that Isabella was taking with her son, when the messenger arrived. She knew Sir Thomas Gurney by sight; and as he came forward, drenched with rain and splattered with mud from the road, the lateness of the hour informed her that he carried bad news. Her first thought was that something had happened to Roger, and her heart pounded with fear and apprehension as the man knelt before the king and handed him a letter.

'There is a letter for you also, my lady,' he

said. 'It is my duty to forewarn you that I carry distressing news.'

'My lord Mortimer?' she asked.

'No.' Gurney shook his head. 'This does not concern Mortimer,' he reassured her. 'It is about the Lord Edward.'

'My father is dead.'

Isabella stared at her son. He had opened his own letter and was staring at the script as if he could not believe what was written there. 'How can this be?' he demanded of Gurney.

'Edward?' asked Isabella, gesturing to the man to rise. 'Edward is dead?'

'I am sorry to be the bearer of bad tidings, my lady,' said Gurney.

'How?' asked the king. 'How did it happen?'

'An accident,' said Gurney.

'I wish that I could have seen him one last time,' said Isabella as she turned her own still-sealed letter around in her hands. 'I asked to visit him, but my lord Mortimer counselled against it.' She imagined her husband losing his footing in a steep stairwell, stumbling and striking his head on the stone. She hoped that he had felt no pain.

'May I be excused?' she asked, and her son nodded his acquiescence. 'Come to me,' she told him softly. Through her tears, she saw that his face was filled with shock and sadness. Despite his eager agreement to be crowned king after Edward's abdication, she knew that the boy was fond of his father and that he would mourn for him.

Lady de Vescy and Jeanne de Bar helped her up and steadied her as she walked back to her chamber. She was determined not to weep in public lest people call her a hypocrite; but as soon as the door had closed behind them, she sat down on the bench, and the hot tears fell onto her clasped hands and spotted the silk of her pale blue gown.

★ ★ ★

Thomas Berkeley and William Ockley each grasped an arm of the former king and bundled him out of the postern gate and towards a waiting horse.

'Where are you taking me?' demanded Edward. It was a question he had repeated incessantly since they had unlocked his chamber and taken him down the narrow back stairs. 'Do you mean to kill me?' he asked, pulling back at the sight of the knife that Thomas grasped in his hand.

'Fortunately for you, my lord Mortimer prefers that you stay alive,' muttered Thomas, peering into the moonless night and hoping that none of ap Gruffydd's Welshmen were in the vicinity. Mortimer would surely kill him if he lost possession of Edward now. 'Get on the horse and do not tempt me to bind your feet to the stirrups,' he warned.

'Where are you taking me?' asked Edward again.

'Corfe Castle,' Berkeley told him. It did not matter that the man knew his destination now. It would not benefit him.

'What is that?' asked Edward as Ockley raised his lantern to reveal the shadows of two men carrying something in a sack. Berkeley watched until they and Ockley had gone inside and he had heard the sound of the heavy bolts being drawn across the door.

'It is you,' said Berkeley as he pushed Edward towards the horse. 'Or, at least everyone will believe it is.' He waited until his captive was in the saddle. 'In truth, he is some outlaw from the forest who was poaching rabbits.' He stood close by the horse, feeling the warmth from its body as he continued to speak. 'The man will have a more lavish funeral than he could ever have dreamt of. And even if you escape from me, my lord, no one will believe you when you say that you are Edward of Caernarfon — because Edward of Caernarfon is dead.'

Isabella was drying her eyes on a square of linen when her son came into the chamber. She patted the cushioned bench beside her and he came and sat down.

'I cannot believe that my father is dead,' he said.

'We are always in the midst of death,' she told him. 'And although we mourn your father, it will at least quiet those who criticise what was done. No man now will dare to say that you do not wear your crown by right.'

'It is a high price to pay,' said Edward. 'I never wished my father any harm. I would be angered to discover that he was not well cared for at Berkeley Castle.'

'Every provision was made for his care!' protested Isabella. Roger had assured her that Edward was kept as an honoured guest, with food and drink in abundance, and that he was happy to have been relieved of the pressures of kingship. She had no reason to believe that it was not true, but the tone of her son's voice troubled her. It hinted that Edward might not be so ready to take Roger Mortimer at his word, and she knew that was dangerous. If Edward turned against Mortimer, everything that they had fought so hard for would be destroyed — and she could not allow that to happen.

'You must listen to my lord Mortimer,' she told him as he continued to stare at the floor. She stroked his soft blond hair as she had done when he was still a babe. 'You should have listened to him on the Scottish campaign. He knows what he is about, and he is concerned for your welfare.'

'And what of my uncle, the Earl of Lancaster?' demanded Edward, shaking off her embrace and standing up. 'He is my kin. Surely it is better for me to listen to him and to the Earl of Kent rather than to your lover!'

Isabella stared up at her son. His blue eyes blazed down at her in anger. 'It is true, isn't it?' he asked her. 'It is true what they say, that Mortimer creeps to your bed and into my father's place?'

'You should not listen to gossip!' she replied. 'You are not old enough to understand the complexity . . . '

'Not old enough? Am I not betrothed myself and due to be wed in only a few months' time? Of course I am old enough! And if I ever discover that Mortimer had a hand in my father's death, then he will not live to warm your bed again!'

'Edward!' she called after him. But he had stormed from the chamber, and the door hung half-open as his footsteps echoed down the stairs.

'Let him go,' advised Lady de Vescy. 'He is upset, as we all are. There will be time for reconciliation tomorrow.'

Isabella paused in the doorway and stared into the void of the stairwell. 'You are right,' she said at last, and turned away. Lady de Vescy looked ashen. 'It has been your loss too,' she acknowledged. 'We have all lost a man we once loved.'

★ ★ ★

The court was in residence at Nottingham Castle when Roger Mortimer ushered the wise woman into Isabella's chamber. Isabella stared at her. She was dressed in a poor-quality gown of a greenish-brown colour that was stained around the hem. A coarse linen wimple was wrapped tightly around her head, and in her hands she clasped a silver vase — a far more valuable object than a peasant woman like her could ever have afforded; and Isabella wondered how she had come by it. She looked at Roger, who had cleared the chamber of servants.

'This is Mistress Watkyns,' said Roger. 'She embalmed the body of the man who will be buried as Edward of Caernarfon.'

Isabella stared at him and then looked sharply at the woman whose eyes remained downcast. 'The body of the man . . . ?' she repeated, not sure if her own senses were still dulled by her grief or if he was being deliberately obtuse.

'She has brought you the heart.' He nodded at the woman, and she curtseyed again and proffered the vase to Isabella.

'Is this my husband's heart?' she asked her.

The woman seemed flustered, and looked to Mortimer for guidance. 'Tell the truth,' he instructed her. 'You may speak freely to the queen.'

'No,' whispered the woman. 'I was taken into a chamber at Berkeley Castle and shown a body. I was instructed to remove the heart and to prepare it for burial.'

Isabella stared at the woman and then at the silver vessel in her hands. 'What does this mean?' she asked Roger.

'Can you not guess?' he asked, unfolding his arms to spread them in a gesture. 'Do I need to explain? Edward is not dead.'

17

December 1327–January 1328

Secrets and Lies

'Of course it was murder!' said John de Warenne with a face that betrayed his desire to do the same to the perpetrators. He had recently returned from court, and Eble and Alicia were taking dinner with him at Conisbrough Castle. 'Though the queen and Mortimer seem to be more concerned with making a treaty with the Scots than committing Edward's body to the ground,' grumbled John. 'And do they really think that people will ride across the country to Gloucester in this winter weather?'

'Gloucester?' said Eble. 'The burial will not be at Westminster then?'

'The monks there would have had it so. They asked for the body to be taken to them so that Edward might be buried alongside his father and grandfather, but Mortimer refused. He fears there may be uprisings against him if the funeral procession crosses the country to London. He prefers the burial to be closer to Berkeley.'

'Will you go?' Alicia asked him.

'If the weather stays fair. It is only right. The man was our king,' replied John. 'And you?' he asked, glancing between her and Eble.

'Yes,' she said after a moment. 'I think it is something my father would have wanted me to do. So I shall go as his representative, and to remind the queen and Mortimer that I am still the Countess of Lincoln and by right the Countess of Salisbury.'

★   ★   ★

Dressed in the plainest gown that she owned, and covered by her fur-lined mantle, Alicia followed Eble through the hushed precincts of the abbey of St Peter at Gloucester, where the scent of incense hung thickly in the still air. It was approaching the shortest day of the year, and already it was dark; but around the hearse, where Edward's body lay before the altar, countless candles cast huge shadows across the painted walls.

Despite the shallow covering of snow that lay over the ground outside, many had come to pay their respects to the former king, and there was a crowd around the oak barrier. As they awaited their turn to approach the body,

Alicia saw that the queen and Roger Mortimer had not been frugal. Figures of the four evangelists watched from the four corners of the hearse, and eight gilded angels held the censers from which the incense rose. As the people in front moved aside, Alicia was surprised to see a carved wooden image of the king lying beneath the canopy. She had expected to see an embalmed body. As she took a taper to light a candle, she reflected that it must be some ostentation of the queen's, perhaps a way of recalling the magnificence that had once been Edward's.

She slipped her hand inside Eble's as they turned from the splendour and walked back to the west door and the icy chill. No chambers had been provided for them; and even though Lady de Vescy had said that she might share her bed, Alicia had chosen to remain with her husband in his tent. It would be a cold night ahead, but at least Eble would allow her to warm her feet on his legs without too much protest.

* * *

Isabella glanced up from under her veil and thought that Roger Mortimer looked particularly handsome in his new black tunic. He had played his part well, and the funeral had been a spectacle that could not have failed to impress even the most sworn of their enemies. The church had been crowded, and some had even wept as the coffin was lowered into its resting place and the heavy stone slabs fell with resounding thuds above it. The mass had been magnificent. The choir had sung like angels, and the prayers had been wafted heavenwards on the most expensive incense that gold could buy. Not one person had demanded that the ceremony be stopped and the coffin opened so that they could gaze upon the face of Edward of Caernarfon for one last time. And now that it was over, and the candles had all been snuffed except for one, which would burn constantly for the soul of the deceased, there would be no more plots to free the former king from captivity. Isabella and Roger had nothing more to fear, and could guide the hand of the young king with impunity.

⋆ ⋆ ⋆

'A truce with the Scots?' The king was attempting to sound incredulous, thought Roger as he eyed the boy, who was dwarfed by the bishop's huge carved oak chair. But his voice, which had not yet settled to the deeper tones of manhood, came out as more of a petulant squeak.

'Yes, your grace,' he replied, wondering how long he could keep control over his rising impatience.

'What is your view?' the king asked Henry of Lancaster, who was standing beside him.

'There are men who have lands in Scotland whose loyalties may be divided on the matter,' he replied.

'It is no different from men holding lands in England and France,' interrupted Roger. 'France, being its own kingdom, does not make any difference, and the same will be true of Scotland.' He tried hard to keep his tone respectful and not allow the contempt he felt to show. But having to listen to the views of the earls was becoming more and more abhorrent, and he was beginning to regret appointing Lancaster to head the king's council.

'But what if there is war?' asked Lancaster.

'War is what we are striving to avoid. That is why we are discussing a truce,' replied Roger, thinking that it would be easier to make a child understand.

'I do not wish to give away part of my kingdom,' said Edward. 'Scotland is mine. I prefer to fight and defeat Bruce rather than simply give up.' He glared at Roger. 'Just because we failed last time does not mean we will fail again.'

'We do not have the money or the resources to plough into another campaign,' Roger told him. 'It is better that we make peace.'

'You are not even a member of my council,' the king accused him.

Roger clasped his hands in an attempt to restrain himself from physically knocking sense into the boy. There was no way that he was willing to risk going back on his promise to Bruce. If the man did not get his sovereignty, then what had happened at Weardale was only a taste of what would come. The Scots would ravage the north; and with the wedding of the king planned for next month at York, it was a risk he could not take. If something happened to Edward, the crown would not pass to Isabella, but to the morose Earl of Lancaster, who was still shaking his head.

'My lord Beaumont and Thomas Wake will not agree with you any more than I do,' he said. 'For them and others, there is too much at stake.'

'I agree with the Earl of Lancaster,' said the king. 'And he is the head of my council.'

'Indeed he is, your grace,' said Roger. 'But I am appointed by your lady mother to proffer her views, and she wishes for peace with Scotland.'

'Let us think on it some more,' said Bishop Orleton as the king held Roger's furious gaze in a deadlock of wills. 'Shall we convene again tomorrow when ... when we are not so tired?'

As Edward rose they bowed, some more deeply than others. Once the boy and Lancaster had departed, Orleton grasped Roger's sleeve. 'The boy knows his own mind,' he warned.

'Do you think I don't realise that?' spat Roger. 'There are times when I wonder whether it would have been easier to rule the father than the son.'

'Except that the father is dead,' remarked Orleton.

'Quite so. But the boy will listen to his mother. I will make sure of it.'

Leaving the bishop staring after him, Roger climbed the stairs to Isabella's apartments, but Edward had anticipated him and was already standing with his back to his mother's hearth, looking sulky.

'Leave us!' Roger told the women who had been sitting with Isabella. The Lady de Vescy hesitated and looked at him. 'You as well,' he told her. He had much to thank her for, but her brother Henry Beaumont was one of the flies in the ointment — and besides, she had served her purpose and was dispensable now.

'My lord?' asked Isabella when the women had gone.

'It is nothing to be distressed about,' he told her, putting a hand on her shoulder. 'It is just that we have matters to discuss that are for our ears alone.' He sat down, even though he was in the king's presence. 'I think there is something you should know,' he told Edward.

'Do you think I will be interested to hear it?' he asked, glowering down at him.

'Yes . . . yes I do,' said Roger. 'I think it is time that you knew your father is not dead.'

Edward stared at him as if he thought he had lost his senses. 'I saw him laid beneath the pavement of the abbey church at Gloucester not three days ago,' he said, looking to his mother.

'It was not your father,' said Isabella.

'Not my father?' he demanded. 'If we did not bury my father, then who did we bury?'

'The man's name is not important,' said Roger with a shrug.

'And if my father is not dead, then where is he?'

'He is safe and cared for.'

'Where?'

'I cannot say.'

'Cannot? Or will not?' Edward's eyes

burned into him. 'You lie!' he accused him suddenly, and Roger saw him clench his fists as if he would strike a blow. 'He lies,' he appealed to his mother.

'Edward.' Roger watched as Isabella reached out and tried to take her son's hand, but the boy pulled away from her as if she were white-hot.

'This cannot be true,' he protested. 'I saw my father's body.'

'What did you see?' asked Roger with a growing feeling of satisfaction.

'I saw . . . I saw . . . '

'You saw a wooden effigy, and you saw a sealed lead coffin placed inside an outer wooden one. Others saw an embalmed body shrouded with cerecloth. No one saw your father.'

'But what about those who were with him when he died, and those who stood vigil over his body at Berkeley Castle?'

'William Beaukaire and Hugh de Glanville will say that the body was that of your father,' said Roger. 'But if it will set your mind to rest, there is one person who will swear to you that it was not.'

'Who?'

Roger uncrossed his legs and leaned forward to speak to Isabella. 'Where is the woman, Mistress Watkyns?'

'She is still within my household as you instructed, my lord. I have told her that she will be paid soon.'

'Send for her to come to us,' said Roger. 'I would have the king hear what she has to say.'

★ ★ ★

Edward stared at the peasant woman. She was wearing a gown that he recognised as having once belonged to his mother, and her eyes were downcast.

'Rise,' he told her, and he saw that she stumbled as she pushed herself upright from the floor. Her eyes met his and she looked hurriedly down again. 'Well?' said Edward, though the question was directed more towards his mother and Mortimer than towards the woman who stood with her hands clasped meekly together.

'The king wishes to know the truth about his father,' said Mortimer.

'You are not in any trouble,' his mother reassured her. 'But we want you to tell the king what you told me when you were last summoned before us.'

'About the body?' asked the woman. Her voice was a cracked whisper.

'Yes. You must tell the king whose was the body that you embalmed.'

'I think his name was Janekyn,' she said. 'At least, that is what people called him.'

'Then you did not embalm the body of my father?' asked Edward, unsure whether to believe what he was being told or whether this was some trickery on the part of his mother and Mortimer; a ruse to dupe him into believing that his father still lived.

'No, sire. It was not your father,' said the woman, meeting his eyes. She looked honest, and Edward decided that he believed her.

'What treachery is this?' he asked. He was fighting to stay calm, but his mistrust of Mortimer was increasing by the minute. He looked at his mother, who was sitting on the bench and watching him with imploring eyes. 'Did you know about this?' he asked her.

'What my lord Mortimer has done is in your best interests,' she said. 'He wishes to be a good and loyal advisor. Edward, you must trust us,' she pleaded.

He looked back at the woman. 'Tell me exactly what happened.'

'I am the wisewoman at Berkeley, sire,' she said. 'My lord Berkeley came to me and said there had been a death at the castle and that he needed my services.'

'What services?' asked Edward.

'As well as bringing lives into this world, I am accomplished at easing their passage into the next, and when they have passed over I prepare the bodies for their graves. Lord Berkeley knew that I was skilled in the process of embalming, and he also knew that I could be discreet. I have spoken of this to no one, sire. Only to you and the queen.'

'And Mortimer and Berkeley,' added Edward. 'And who else?'

'I do not know the names.'

'Who else was involved?' asked Edward, though the question was addressed to his mother.

'Thomas Gurney knew, and William Beaukaire. But that is all.' She glanced at Mortimer for confirmation and he nodded.

'And this body is the same one that was buried at Gloucester?' Now Edward glanced between his mother and Mortimer.

'Indeed, the body that was buried was that of a poacher from the village of Berkeley,' confirmed Mortimer. 'And it is his heart that is held in the silver vase.'

'So where is my father?' the king asked once more.

'That I cannot tell you,' insisted Mortimer.

'Do you know where my father is?' Edward demanded of his mother. She shook her head.

'I think enough has been said in front of Mistress Watkyn,' interrupted Mortimer. He nodded at the woman. 'You may go.'

'My lord,' she began hesitantly, 'there is the

matter of the payment I was promised . . . '
Edward watched as Mortimer's eyes hardened.

'You will receive your due,' he said as he indicated the door. The woman curtseyed, then sought Edward's eyes.

'I am sorry if I have offended you, sire,' she said. Edward nodded. He felt momentarily sorry for the woman, and suspected that he would never see her again.

'Go in peace,' he told her, and watched her gather the skirts of his mother's cast-off gown and hurry from the chamber.

An oppressive silence hung on the air, and Edward avoided his mother's gaze and looked directly at Mortimer. 'I will only believe that my father is alive when I see him with my own eyes,' he said. 'Tell me where you are keeping him.'

'I cannot,' repeated Mortimer.

'Then I must believe that what you say is untrue — that the woman was paid to tell the tale she did, and that it is truly the body of my father that lies beneath the pavement of the abbey.'

'Is that wise?' asked Mortimer, and Edward was alarmed at the hint of menace in his voice. 'Remember that you are only king in name by my efforts and those of your mother. We have made you king, and we can take away your crown. Your father is alive, and do not forget that he has the right to sit upon the throne!'

'My father abdicated. Even if he lives, I am still the rightful king!'

'By rule of your mother, who is regent, and by your appointed council. Do not make the mistake that your father made, of thinking that you rule by the gift of God alone,' warned Mortimer. 'The people will not tolerate it — and you have seen how easy it is for a king to be deposed.'

'Do you threaten me?' asked Edward, wishing that he had the height and strength to strike the man.

'Of course not,' replied Mortimer. 'I am here to advise you.'

'Edward, it is true,' pleaded his mother. 'Your father is not dead. I would know if he were.' She looked at him imploringly.

Edward looked away, towards the high window where weak sunlight was lighting the motes of dust in the air. Part of him wanted to believe them. Part of him wanted his father to be alive.

★ ★ ★

The cathedral at York was filled with the sound of joyful singing as the Count of

Hainault put the hand of his daughter Philippa into that of the king at the west door and the young couple walked together towards the high altar to hear mass.

She wasn't a particularly pretty girl, thought Alicia as she watched them pass. She was too dark to be considered a beauty, but Edward looked content with her. She felt for Eble's hand and locked her fingers with his. He smiled down at her and her heart soared with love for him. She still could not believe that God had granted her this man, and she pressed her cheek to the soft fabric of his upper arm and closed her eyes in silent, thankful prayer. The late king and Despenser had been able to take her lands and her money and her goods, but they had not succeeded in parting her from Eble, and he was more precious to her than any of those things.

'Robert de Holland has been given his lands back!' grumbled Henry of Lancaster as they pushed their way through the assembled crowd outside St Peter's towards the bishop's palace where the wedding feast was to be held.

'Really?' Alicia was surprised. The man had turned traitor against her first husband just before the battle at Boroughbridge; and whilst she had no love for Thomas of

Lancaster, she had even less for a man who would betray his master like that. She knew that Henry hated him too, and it was just one more way in which Roger Mortimer was attempting to undermine his authority.

'And I will not permit this bullying of the king over Scotland,' he muttered. 'Edward wants to lead a campaign against Bruce, and I think that he is right. It would be stupid and unfair to men who own land there to let the Scots simply take what is not theirs.'

Alicia nodded. She knew that Henry's son-in-law, Thomas Wake, was one who had claim to Scottish lands, and that Henry Beaumont already titled himself the Earl of Buchan, by right of his wife. Thomas Wake had been brought up in her father's household and was known to both her and Eble, and she had heard hints that although he had been one of the key figures in the deposition of the late king, even he was growing wary.

'Mortimer has some hold over the boy, though I don't know what,' grumbled Lancaster. 'Edward does not like him, yet he crumbles beneath his will.'

'The boy will soon grow into a man,' observed Eble, 'and things will change.'

'But not soon enough!' snapped Henry. 'Is this what we got rid of the old king for? To be duped and sold out to the damn Scots?'

'Come, let us not talk of it now, not on this day,' said Alicia as they went inside, though she knew that there would be little talk of anything else.

18

May 1328–September 1328

The Dispossessed

Henry of Lancaster peered across the hall of Northampton Castle, where parliament had been summoned. He was relieved that some voices of dissent agreed that Scotland should not be handed back to its inhabitants.

'Because of the death of the queen's brother, Charles, it is imperative that we act to secure the throne of France for the king,' argued Roger Mortimer. 'And we cannot afford to fight wars with both Scotland and France. The only solution is to ratify the treaty with Robert Bruce.'

There were some murmurings of assent, mostly from those men whom Mortimer had promoted to influential roles. Mortimer was a cunning enemy, thought Henry. He took no power for himself, but on behalf of the king he appointed men to positions of power — the latest being John Maltravers, who was now Steward of the Royal Household, a role which gave one of Mortimer's most loyal allies control over access to the king.

'Even if I were to accept that the border with Scotland should be restored, I cannot condone the demand that men give up their rights to their Scottish land,' argued Henry. Thomas Wake, Henry Percy and Henry Beaumont all nodded. They would never agree to such a demand either. They had too much to lose.

'Men will be rewarded with lands in France as compensation for any they might lose in Scotland once we have secured the French throne,' replied Mortimer.

'What lands? Where?' asked Lord Beaumont. 'And will they come with an earldom? It is a meaningless promise, my lord. I am the Earl of Buchan, and I do not intend to give up my title or my lands. If Bruce will agree to my retaining them, then I might consider the matter of reinstating the border more favourably; but whilst he demands that all the lands are returned to him, then I cannot agree.'

'We are turning in circles,' complained Mortimer, pressing his fingers to his temples as if his head ached and he held the dissenters responsible. 'If we do not look to France, then Philip de Valois will usurp the throne that is King Edward's by right.'

'This is treason!' burst out Henry, remembering how angry the young king had been when Mortimer had allowed the Scots to retreat unharmed at Weardale. 'You have made some secret agreement with Bruce and you would force us to validate it!'

'The terms of the treaty have already been agreed and read out to parliament. And it is the king's will that the treaty should be signed,' replied Mortimer, thumping his fist on the table.

'I doubt that very much,' replied Henry. 'Do you agree to this treaty, your grace?'

The boy had sat silently as the arguments raged about him, but Henry saw the anger in his eyes. He knew that giving up Scotland was the last thing that Edward wanted. He knew that the boy was filled with admiration for his grandfather, and that he wanted to complete his ambition of uniting the kingdom rather than handing back hard-won lands.

Edward tightened his hands around the arms of the chair and glanced towards Mortimer, who was watching him with an enigmatic expression. 'I will be advised by my parliament,' said the king.

'But what do you want?' persisted Henry. 'Let us hear your wishes. Do you truly want to sign this treaty?'

The boy hesitated. 'Yes,' he said at last. 'I wish to sign the treaty.'

Henry stared at him in horror. It was

apparent that Mortimer had some hold over him. It was as if the king were afraid of him, thought Henry, although he could think of no reason why it should be so; and as head of the king's council, and as his kinsman, it angered him to see Edward crumple under Mortimer's jurisdiction.

'Then it is a shameful peace — and is none of my will,' Henry told him, and was pleased to see the boy look uncomfortable at his displeasure.

* * *

Edward placed the quill beside the parchment and stared at his carefully written name. He had been left with no choice. Without the signature, Mortimer would reveal the survival of his father, and there would be civil war. And if his father's supporters were successful, his mother would stand accused of treason. At the very least, she would be sent into imprisonment, and he could not allow that to happen.

'You have forced my hand,' he complained to Mortimer. 'But I will never recognise an independent Scotland, and I will not go to Berwick to see my sister married to the son of my enemy!'

'Then you can stay behind.' Mortimer

shrugged, looking unconcerned as he supervised the sealing of the treaty with the privy seal. 'The Earl of Lancaster also refuses to attend, so you may remain under his care.'

'Then I will,' said Edward defiantly. He had thought that Mortimer would rail at him and insist that he go, or would try to persuade him by saying that his mother would be angry and upset if he did not accompany them. But the man merely rolled and secured the signed treaty and passed it to a clerk for safekeeping.

'You may even keep the privy seal,' he remarked, tossing it down in front of the king, 'as long as you are not reckless with it.'

As Mortimer strode from the chamber, Edward stared after him in frustration. It seemed that there was no way in which he could better the man. But one day soon he would be king by right — and then things would change.

*   *   *

In her chambers at Berwick Castle, Isabella gazed at her daughter Joan, dressed in a gown of virginal blue for her marriage to the son of Robert Bruce. She bit hard on her lower lip and forced a smile to reassure the little girl. On the long journey, Joan had talked about her marriage as if it were a great adventure, and Isabella was not sure, even now, that she understood what was about to happen.

She stroked a hand down the long blonde hair that hung almost to her daughter's waist and tried to fix the image of Joan in her mind; an image to carry with her in the days to come. She had barely been reunited with the child after her return from France, and now she was being forced to part with her again.

Lady de Vescy came in with a wreath of fresh summer flowers and arranged it on the bride's small head. 'I have decided to leave court once this wedding is done,' she said without looking at Isabella.

'Why?' she asked, not able to comprehend that her friend would want to desert her.

'Do you need to ask?' said Lady Vescy. 'My brother has been robbed of his lands by this treaty.'

'But my lord Mortimer means you no harm,' protested Isabella as she watched Joan skip around the chamber. 'He thinks well of you. He has told me so. Don't go,' she pleaded, reaching out her hand to grasp Lady de Vescy's. 'I need your friendship.'

Lady de Vescy sighed. 'I am sorry,' she said. 'I know that it is not a good time, but it has been on my mind for many days, and I have not been able to find the words to tell you.'

'Then you are still undecided,' replied

Isabella with a glimmer of hope. 'Think on it some more, and you may change your mind. I would be lost without you. Would it help if I asked my lord Mortimer to speak to you? To reassure you?'

'No,' said Lady de Vescy. 'I do not wish to speak with him. My mind is made up. I am sorry.'

Isabella tried to dismiss what had been said from her thoughts. Later she would persuade her friend to stay. But there was not time now. The escort was at the door.

'Shall we go?' she said to her daughter, forcing a brave smile. Joan nodded, almost dislodging the circle of blossoms, and placed her tiny, cold hand inside her mother's.

As she led Princess Joan from the chamber, Isabella felt as if she were giving her precious child as a sacrifice. The Scots had already named her Joan Makepeace, and despite her reassurances to the girl that she would be well cared for and would find happiness, Isabella was finding it hard to disguise her tears. She had pleaded with Roger, told him that Joan was too young, but he had said that there was no other way, and the Scots would only accept the treaty if the marriage went ahead. He had told her that, as queen, she must put the needs of her country and her people before her personal feelings. She had begged him to change his mind, but he had been adamant. With Charles gone, and the threat of the revelation that her husband still lived, he had a hold on her that she could not break, and she was beginning to fear him.

⋆　⋆　⋆

Alicia watched as a tray of sweetmeats was laid on the white linen tablecloth. Now that Roger Mortimer had banned all tournaments so that men could not meet up to hatch plots against him, the business of politics was being brought to the tables of castles and manor houses, and it pleased her because it made it easier for her to take part.

'Are you attending the parliament at York?' Henry asked Eble. 'I have made up my mind not to,' he continued without waiting for an answer. 'Thomas Wake will stay away as well — and the Earls of Kent and Norfolk. Mortimer has gone too far this time.'

'Do you plan to oppose him openly?' asked Alicia.

'If I can garner enough support, yes,' he said after a moment. 'Will you join me?'

Alicia toyed with the piece of marchpane on her platter. 'Has the king said anything to you about the treaty?' she asked.

'He says that he has no wish to give up Scotland.'

'Then why did he sign the treaty if it was against his wishes?'

'Mortimer appears to wield great power over the king. His anger and his frustrations are apparent, but he will not speak of it.'

'Does he act to please his mother?' she asked.

'No.' Henry shook his head. 'It is more than that. The boy is afraid of something. I think that if we can be rid of Mortimer, Edward would be grateful. I know that you have not yet succeeded in reclaiming your lands, but if I were advising the king it would be a different matter.'

'I am grateful for that, but do not forget that I am a married woman,' she reminded him, 'and so must act in accordance with my husband's wishes.'

She watched as the earl stifled a wry smile. 'I would not presume to come between man and wife,' he replied, then turned his attention to Eble. 'So, what do you think?' he asked him. 'Will you join me?'

'I will do whatever is necessary to ensure that the lands belonging to my wife are returned to us,' he told Henry.

★　★　★

At York, Isabella was missing the reassuring presence of Lady de Vescy, even though Jeanne de Bar had come to join her, and was now laying a tray of dainties on the coffer near the window.

'I cannot believe she is really gone,' said Isabella. 'I keep thinking that at any moment the door will open and she will come in.' She pressed the back of her hand to her lips. Losing both a daughter and a friend was too much for her to bear, and she had done little but weep since leaving Berwick.

'It would have been too difficult for Lady de Vescy to stay,' reasoned Jeanne. 'And my lord Mortimer may not have allowed it.'

'He does not choose the ladies who wait on me, as you well know,' replied Isabella, sitting down on one of the cushions that Jeanne had plumped for her. 'That is my business alone.'

Jeanne raised an eyebrow as she poured the wine. 'Lord Mortimer seems to make every decision these days, and no one dares to gainsay him.' She put the flagon down and brought the cups to the bench. 'Do you entirely trust him?' she asked.

'Of course! I trust him with my life.'

'And your son's life?' asked Jeanne.

Isabella stared at her friend. 'He would never harm Edward,' she said, wondering why

Jeanne would suggest such a thing. It was unthinkable.

'Can you be certain?' persisted Jeanne. 'Forgive me for speaking so openly, my lady, but surely a man who could arrange for the death of the late king to enhance his position, might do the same to the son? My husband says that Mortimer's eyes are fixed on the throne, and that he will never be content until he wears the crown himself.'

'That is nonsense!' protested Isabella. 'My lord Mortimer seeks only to serve the king. And my husband died after an accident. Lord Mortimer had no hand in it. It is ridiculous to say that he arranged it. What makes you suggest such a thing?' she demanded.

'There are many rumours that the late king was murdered,' said Jeanne. 'You must have heard them.'

'There are always rumours. The common people thrive on lies and speculation. I'm surprised that you give such gossip any credence.'

'My husband gives it credence,' said Jeanne.

'Then he is mistaken,' Isabella told her, wondering why John de Warenne would fuel such lies. She had thought him to be their ally. 'My lord Mortimer would never harm my son, and he never harmed my husband.'

'He may not have harmed your husband personally, but Edward was in his care.'

'My lord Mortimer did not have him killed,' repeated Isabella, growing impatient at Jeanne's refusal to believe her.

'You cannot be certain of that, my lady.'

'Oh, but I am,' replied Isabella. 'Edward is alive,' she told Jeanne, pleased to be able to prove her wrong. 'He is at Corfe Castle, where he wants for nothing, and my lord Mortimer tells me that he is happy and content to be spared the burdens of kingship.'

She watched with satisfaction as Jeanne's face took on a look of incredulity. 'Are you sure?' she asked after a moment. 'Have you seen him?'

'No,' admitted Isabella. 'My lord Mortimer says that it is safer for us both if I do not visit him, but I have no reason to doubt him.' Her friend did not reply, and Isabella began to regret the confidence. 'I should not have told you of this,' she said. 'You must promise me that you will reveal it to no one. You must not tell your husband. Promise me,' she insisted.

★   ★   ★

It was not in Eble's nature to eavesdrop, but as he walked into the stables at Kenilworth Castle, he found himself transfixed by a

270

conversation coming from one of the stalls.

'And not only did Mortimer have him murdered, but they killed him with a red-hot iron . . . up the fundament!' said the voice of one of the grooms.

'Why would they do that?' asked his companion.

'Because of what he and Despenser did. You know . . . '

Eble cleared his throat and the boys fell silent. 'It isn't wise to repeat gossip,' he warned them as he walked around the partition to Trebnor's stall. 'You never know who may be listening.'

'No, my lord. Sorry, my lord,' they said, and the boy who had been telling the story unfastened Trebnor's reins and led him out, ready-saddled for the journey.

Eble reached into his purse and flipped a coin for the boy to catch. 'Mind what you say in future,' he told him, wondering where the tale had come from but not wanting to add to its credence by asking, although it would not surprise him if the story had originated with Henry of Lancaster. He could well be spreading it to discredit Roger Mortimer.

Henry had kept his word not to attend parliament at York and, after the exchange of many messages, the queen and Mortimer had eventually agreed to bring the king to

Barlings Abbey in Lincolnshire to meet Henry and hear his grievances. Eble had agreed to take charge of the men-at-arms who would protect the earl.

As they approached the abbey, Eble saw one of the men allow his horse to stray from the narrow road that the monks had built across the marsh. 'Keep to the causeway!' he yelled. 'You may sink into the mire from your own incompetence if you desire, but I will not have you lose a valuable horse!'

The man reined his mount back onto the track, and Eble saw him mutter something to his companion. He turned away and decided to let it go. He was aware that many of the men were resentful at his promotion by the Earl of Lancaster and did not like having to take orders from him. But let them think what they wanted, Eble told himself. He was familiar with this area and knew that the bog was treacherous after heavy rain.

Although the towers of the abbey church did not rise as high as those of Lincoln Cathedral in the distance, it was an imposing building. Henry strode in ahead of Eble and, although they had left their weapons at the door, their armour betrayed that they had not come entirely in peace. The king was already seated in the abbot's chair, and his gaze strayed between Mortimer and Lancaster as the two men took stock of one another.

'Your grace,' Henry acknowledged the king. 'I have come with a list of demands.'

'Then let us hear them,' suggested Mortimer, making himself more comfortable on his seat and crossing his legs as if he were to be treated to a tale. Eble bristled. Mortimer spoke to the earl as if were a child to be cajoled, a source of amusement — a notion reinforced by his sly glance towards Isabella.

Lancaster saw it too and glared at them. 'One,' he began, 'the queen holds lands which are not hers by right. Those lands must be returned to their rightful owners. And two, you, Roger Mortimer, must be banished from court and go to live upon your own lands, of which you have plenty, seeing that you have disinherited so many people to acquire them.'

Eble watched as Mortimer raised his eyebrows in mock surprise, then smiled. His fingers itched for the hilt of his sword as his growing dislike of Mortimer was confirmed. Power had changed him, as it changed all men when they were tempted to rule for their own ease rather than the ease of those they ruled over.

'Three,' continued Henry, ignoring the sniggering of his enemy, 'I demand that there is an official enquiry into the shameful retreat at Weardale. I would like it to be known who betrayed the king!'

Eble glanced at Edward. The boy was sitting very still, and there was nothing in his expression that betrayed his inner thoughts.

'And four, I want an inquiry into why it is that the king's council is ignored when its twelve men, headed by me, were ordained at the king's coronation to guide and control him!'

Mortimer uncrossed his legs. 'Is that all?' he enquired.

'No!' shouted Lancaster. 'I want to know why you took the late king from my castle at Kenilworth by force and without the permission of parliament. I want to know why you took him and held him where none of his kinsmen were allowed to see him or speak to him ever again. And I want to know why you traitorously murdered him!'

The gasp that followed the accusation bounced off the stone walls of the chapter house. The king stared at Lancaster, who was glaring at Mortimer, and Mortimer held his gaze in a battle of wills.

'Furthermore,' went on Lancaster, 'you have frittered away the king's treasure without his consent, and the advice you have given him on the matter of Scotland has disinherited not only him but his successors, his vassals and all Englishmen forever. And you have married the Princess Joan to the son of a traitor! Shame on you!'

With these words, Henry of Lancaster turned on his spurred heel and marched towards the door. 'I have an army!' he shouted back at Mortimer. 'And I am not afraid to use it!'

19

December 1328–January 1329

Defeat

The messenger wore the livery of John de Warenne. Eble hoped that he did not carry bad news, and from the frown on Alicia's face he could tell that she was having similar thoughts as the man came into the hall and proffered the letter.

'Go to the kitchens and ask for whatever you want,' Alicia told him.

'I will call for you if there is need to send an urgent reply,' added Eble, breaking open the seal and eyeing the letter suspiciously.

'What does he say?' asked Alicia, trying to peer over his arm to read it herself.

'Not a lot,' remarked Eble, handing it to her. 'It's typical John. He hints at some matter that he needs to discuss with me but tells me nothing.'

'And there was no verbal message,' said Alicia when she had finished reading. 'I wonder what this information is that cannot be written down or spoken of openly. Trouble with Henry of Lancaster?' she suggested.

Eble shook his head. 'I can't imagine what this might be about, so I had better go and discover what his great secret is, although I would wager it will be something and nothing.'

★ ★ ★

Trebnor pricked his ears, and Eble wondered if it was because he recognised his former home that his pace increased as they approached the high walls of Conisbrough Castle. By the time he had dismounted, John had come out to greet him.

'So what's this all about?' he asked as the groom led Trebnor away to the stables and he pulled off his heavy leather gauntlets to unfasten his mantle.

'Come inside,' said John, and he led the way into the hall, where refreshments had been laid out on the trestle and where Eble was surprised to see Jeanne de Bar. She handed him a cup of wine. Then John dismissed the servants and turned a serious face to him.

'You are not going to believe what I am about to tell you,' he said.

'Try me,' replied Eble, raising the cup to his lips to cover his amusement at John's clandestine manner. Whatever it was, he thought, it had better be good to merit such mystery.

'The king is alive!' he announced.

Eble stared at him, wondering if he had gone quite mad.

'Yes,' he said.

'Not the boy king,' explained John, seeing that he had misunderstood. 'Edward of Caernarfon is alive!'

Now Eble was convinced that his friend had lost his mind. Firstly he had sent away Maude, the one woman he had ever truly loved, and replaced her with the wife he professed to hate. And now these wild claims about a man whose funeral they had both attended, and who they had seen buried beneath the pavement at Gloucester with their own eyes.

'It explains so much!' continued John. 'It explains why the young king signed the treaty with Scotland. And it explains the hold that Mortimer has over him.'

Eble put his cup on the bench beside him and held up a hand to silence his friend. 'Surely you give no credence to this rumour?' he said. 'What proof is there that this could be true?' He looked at Jeanne to see what her reaction might be, and her expression was earnest.

'The queen told me herself,' she confided.

'She says that Mortimer holds my uncle secretly at Corfe Castle.'

Eble stared at her until he recollected his manners and looked back at John, who was watching him with a look of triumph.

'Has the queen seen him?' asked Eble, still unsure whether to believe what he was being told.

John looked to his wife. It was obviously a question that he had not thought to ask.

Jeanne hesitated. 'No,' she said. 'But why would Mortimer convince her that Edward was alive if it wasn't true?'

'For many reasons,' replied Eble. 'Perhaps the most important being that he does not want her to believe the rumours that he had Edward murdered. And, as you say, his survival would mean that he has a hold over her and her son. But surely it is too incredible to be true? The king's body lay in state at Gloucester. Hundreds of people saw it. And what of the funeral? And the tomb? How could all of that have been a deception?'

'Do not underestimate Roger Mortimer,' warned John. 'Remember that we are speaking of the man who arranged his own escape from the Tower of London.'

'Well it would be remarkable if it were true,' agreed Eble, picking up his cup again and drinking.

'I believe it is true,' insisted John, 'and so does my wife.'

'And what do you intend to do about it?'

John twisted his cup in his hands. 'I'm not sure,' he admitted. 'If it is true, there will be war for sure.'

'There will be war anyway,' replied Eble. 'Lancaster is not content to allow Mortimer to rule the kingdom.'

'And will you fight for him? For Lancaster?' asked John.

'I have pledged myself to him, as I once pledged myself to his brother,' said Eble. 'But you know that I am not skilled at choosing the winning side.'

'Do you think Mortimer will win?'

'What do you think? You have already spoken of how wily he is. And once Mortimer has rid himself of Lancaster, he can rule with impunity, whether Edward is alive or not.'

'Until the boy becomes a man,' said Jeanne. They both looked at her. 'You say that you must not underestimate Mortimer,' she told them, 'but do not underestimate the king either. I have seen him, and with every day that passes he grows taller and more confident.'

'Does he know about his father's supposed survival?' asked Eble.

'I believe he does.'

'And do you think he has told anyone? Has he told his uncles?'

'I do not think that the Earls of Kent and Norfolk are aware that their brother lives,' she said.

'Then the king keeps a closer secret than his mother,' observed Eble.

'But they will know soon enough,' declared John, leaving Eble in no doubt that he would be the one to inform them. 'Mortimer may think he is clever, but with our combined forces he can be stripped of his power and Edward set free.'

'And will Kent and Norfolk fight against a man who rides with the royal banner in the name of the king? Especially if they have no proof that their brother is indeed alive. Be careful, John,' he warned his friend. 'Is this rumour worth risking your head for?'

★   ★   ★

Four days after the Christmas feast, Roger Mortimer declared war on Henry of Lancaster in the king's name. He marched on Kenilworth and demanded access to the castle, and when refused, instructed his men to sack Lancaster's manors. The results were a grim sight, thought Eble as he rode south to meet up with Lancaster's army. Manor houses, cottages, barns, sheds and fences all destroyed; fishponds emptied; livestock slaughtered; woods cut down and deer taken from the parks. The villagers had been spared, but as Eble saw them standing in huddles, staring at the ashes of what had once been their homes, he wondered how they would manage to find shelter from the freezing weather or food to give to their wailing infants. He had a pouch of silver at his belt, but what use were coins to these people when there was nothing for them to buy?

Angry and powerless, he called down a curse on Mortimer for his brutality, determined that he would play his part in bringing the man to justice for this. He turned Trebnor's head to the south, eager to get away from the acrid stench that caught at his throat, and to take the news of what he had seen to the Earl of Lancaster.

It was a gruelling journey. The weather worsened, and the biting north wind blew snow-laden showers at his back as he crouched low in the saddle. He was cold, hungry and exhausted when, four days later, he caught sight of the welcoming smoke of Henry's camp near Bedford.

He asked to be taken straight to the earl's tent, and Henry looked up as he ducked in under the flap. He was wrapped in several layers of clothing and huddled near to a brazier for warmth, but still looked pinched and blue.

'Have you come with a message from Mortimer?' he asked suspiciously.

'No, my lord. I am sworn to you,' Eble reassured him. 'But I do not bring good news,' he said as he related what he had seen of Henry's lands in the north.

Eble had expected him to be angry, to shout and curse and threaten that he would see Mortimer swing at the end of a rope for what he had done, but he remained strangely subdued, and turned his head away to stare into the flames that were doing little to warm the tent.

'As soon as I am able, I will ensure that food is sent, though where we will find materials to rebuild the houses, God alone knows,' Henry said, rubbing at his eyes with his fingers.

'We will be revenged on Mortimer for this,' said Eble, surprised when Henry did not take up his cry. 'Surely you are even more determined to see the man removed from power now?'

He watched as Henry began to shake his head. 'He has me defeated,' he replied. 'Kent and Norfolk have decided to join the king's army rather than risk being presumed traitors against their nephew, and I cannot fight him alone. I do not have enough men to face him in battle, and he knows that. I am left with no choice but to make peace, no matter how much it grieves me to do so.'

Eble watched as Henry seemed to sink even lower on the stool. 'All may not be lost,' he ventured.

'I doubt there is anything you can suggest that will make a difference,' snapped Henry.

'I have spoken with John de Warenne,' began Eble.

'Will he fight alongside me?' asked Henry, looking up with slight hope.

'No. He remains at Conisbrough, but his wife is with him, and she says that your cousin, the Lord Edward, is still alive.'

'I had heard a rumour,' he said. 'But I gave it no credence.'

'Jeanne de Bar is certain,' Eble told him, but Henry continued to shake his head.

'Even if it were true, how could it help us?' he asked. 'It isn't as if Edward has an army. Those who continue to support him are mostly vassals and monks. They're no match for Mortimer.'

★ ★ ★

At daybreak the next morning, Eble was woken by horns sounding urgently through the camp. He unrolled himself from his cloak and struggled up, stiff with cold, to push back the flap of his tent and see what the alarm was. His breath clouded the air as he watched the approach of Mortimer and his army. The man must have ridden through the night to take them by surprise like this, he thought. With fumbling fingers he laced his boots and reached for his sword, but by the time he reached the earl's tent it was to see him walk out, unarmed, towards where Mortimer and the king were waiting.

Eble watched with shame and disillusionment as Lancaster knelt down before them in the mud.

'Sire,' said Henry of Lancaster. 'I beg your forgiveness.' Once more, Mortimer had made the winning move.

Part Four

1329 to 1330

20

August 1329

The King of Folly

There were pavilions of all colours stretching across the valley as far as Alicia could see. Roger Mortimer was holding a round table tournament at Wigmore that threatened to rival even the most lavish that his grandfather had arranged. The event was a celebration of the weddings of two of his daughters, but it was Mortimer himself who was taking the central role. The costume he wore as King Arthur was rich with silks and furs, and his rings and jewels had caused much comment. With Isabella beside him as his Guinevere, it was plain to see that he considered himself king.

Eble had agreed to joust on the team of John de Warenne. He could hardly refuse when his friend had provided him with such an able horse, thought Alicia as she walked across the grass towards him with the favours in her hand. He was running his fingers under Trebnor's girth to check that it was secure before he mounted, and his face was serious.

'Do not look so worried,' Alicia said as she handed him the lengths of purple and saffron. 'You will account yourself well. You always do,' she added as she watched him tie the silks to the end of his lance.

'I would be happier if I were not set against one of Mortimer's new sons-in-law in the first round,' he remarked as he allowed her to take the place of a squire and hold the lance whilst he gathered Trebnor's reins and put his foot in the stirrup. 'It is only done because they are certain I will lose.' He mounted, closed the visor on his helm and bent to take the lance, balancing it carefully in his hand.

'I will cheer for you,' Alicia shouted above the chanting and singing of the crowd. 'Ensure that you do not let me down,' she instructed, although she knew that he would allow the bridegroom his victory.

Alicia watched as he touched his spurs to Trebnor's sides. The horse moved away at a graceful, controlled canter, and she returned to her seat whilst offering up a prayer for her husband's safety. She had seen too many men injured and killed at such tournaments to be able to watch without a fluttering of anxiety.

Mortimer had already taken his place under the cloth of gold alongside Isabella and the king, with his young wife. Mortimer's son, Geoffrey, was leaning against the edge of the berfois as she approached. He moved aside for her and caught her eye as she passed. 'The king of folly,' he remarked, with a nod towards his father. Alicia laughed politely and allowed him to help her up the step, but as she settled herself onto the cushion she glanced back at him and realised that he had not spoken entirely in jest.

She looked closely at Roger Mortimer and wondered what his son knew. When Eble had returned home from his visit to John de Warenne at Conisbrough, she had been amazed by what he had told her about the Lord Edward, and even now she wondered if Mortimer was really capable of such an elaborate subterfuge. She watched the queen smiling up at him. They appeared to have grown even closer of late, and Isabella looked radiant in her fashionable gown. But as they leaned towards one another and shared some private words, Alicia noticed the bitter look on the face of the king. He was no longer a boy, she thought, and they were foolish to ignore him.

The wind tugged the purple and yellow silks as she turned to watch Eble lean forward and urge Trebnor on. He did not hesitate, and she wished that her father were here to see him. She knew as the clash of lance on shield reverberated across the lists that he would not win, but she believed that he was capable if he chose to. Neither lance was broken in the first run, and in the second Eble leaned away so that his opponent missed him entirely. On the final run, Alicia saw him ease his horse onto the wrong leg so that his opponent's lance broke against his shield. The young bride of the Earl of Pembroke leapt to her feet in delight. The victor bowed to his lady and the crowd applauded, but Alicia was applauding her husband for his chivalry. She knew that he would never give up until the wrongs that had been done to her were righted.

★ ★ ★

Trebnor had been unsaddled and tied up in the makeshift stables that served the Warenne camp at the bottom of the meadow. With the silks still attached to his lance and his helm under his arm, Eble began to walk back to his tent when he saw a group of young men making their way towards him and recognised the king at their centre. He went down on one knee as Edward approached.

'I hope that your wife is not too disappointed that the colours of the Earl of

Lincoln were not upon the winning lance,' he remarked as he gestured for Eble to rise.

Eble leant on the lance to get to his feet. The blow he had taken had been a jarring one, and he was still in some pain.

'I have not spoken to her yet. I may have some explanations to make,' he replied with a self-deprecating smile.

'I have been remiss in not seeking you out earlier, to thank you properly for what you did at Weardale,' said the king.

'It was no more than my duty,' said Eble, appraising the boy — although it was time that he stopped thinking of Edward as a boy. The king had grown tall and his shoulders had broadened. He had the fair good looks of his mother, and shrewd blue eyes, which were fixed on him.

'You let the Earl of Pembroke win,' he observed.

'I'm sure that his victory was well deserved.'

'Wisely spoken,' remarked the king. 'But are you a member of the household of the Earl of Surrey now?' he asked. 'I thought that you were with my uncle, the Earl of Lancaster, at Weardale. You have not deserted him, have you?'

'No, indeed I have not,' said Eble. 'But as he declined the invitation to this tournament,

I agreed to join Sir John. We have been friends for many years, since we were squires together in the household of my wife's father.'

'Then you remain on good terms with the Earl of Lancaster?'

'I do, your grace, although my loyalty is to you as my sovereign,' he added, wondering where this conversation was leading. He suspected that the king had purposely sought him out and that his questions were not idle conversation.

'I need men who are loyal,' replied the king. 'I hope that I may count on you, Eble le Strange.'

'Be assured that you can,' replied Eble, and he inclined his head as the king and his men moved away.

He watched them go and wondered who else the king intended to speak to as he made his way through the pavilions — and he wondered whether Mortimer and the queen were aware of what he was doing.

21

February 1330

Rescue

Eble and Alicia travelled to Conisbrough Castle to meet Lady de Vescy.

'My brother has gone to France, but I have remained in England to help,' she told them. 'The Earl of Kent knows that Edward is alive and being held at Corfe. He intends to rescue him, but he needs trustworthy men. Will you help us?' she asked.

'What would you have me do?' Eble asked warily, exchanging a glance with Alicia.

'Edward is carefully guarded at Corfe, but there is a man there, John Deveril, who can obtain a key to the chamber where Edward is being held and will unlock the door. But there needs to be some way of getting Edward out without raising an alarm. My chaplain, Brother Richard, will help us. He will go to Corfe as if on a journey, and ask to be admitted for refreshment. If John Deveril can free Edward from his chamber, Brother Richard may be able to get him out, but we need another man to complete the plan.'

'Go on,' said Eble as Lady de Vescy paused. He was beginning to suspect that the other man might be him.

'It would raise suspicion if Brother Richard were to travel alone,' said Lady de Vescy, 'and although there are other friars who might agree to accompany him, we think it might be better if the man who goes has some skills other than those of a monk.'

'What skills, exactly?' asked Eble.

'Someone who is willing to give up his monk's habit to the king — and someone who is not afraid to cut a throat to silence its owner. Are you willing to do it?'

'What will happen if he is freed?' asked Eble. 'Will you seek to place him back on the throne?'

'There is no plan to make him king again. I do not think that Edward would do battle against his son.'

'Yet surely he would do battle against Mortimer?' asked Eble, wondering how becoming embroiled in this plot sat with his vow of loyalty to the young king.

'The plan is simply to free him and get him out of the country.'

'To France?'

'Or maybe to Lombardy. Edward would be content to live out his life in peace.'

'Unlike you, I think he may be suited to the monastic life,' remarked John as he offered the flagon to Eble, who shook his head. He needed to think clearly. He looked at Alicia, who had said nothing yet, but whose face was strained with concentration.

'Have you thought about how this rescue is to be managed?' asked Eble. 'If I were to agree, I would want to be sure of what was expected of me.'

Lady de Vescy looked to John. 'Nothing can be defined except a fluid plan,' he said. 'That is why we need a man who can think on his feet. And we know that we can trust you; and with all you bookish habits and your fluent hand, you will pass easily for a monk if challenged.'

'But I will have to shave my head!' protested Eble, running a hand over his thick fair hair.

'It will grow back,' said John irritably. 'What is more important — the life of your liege lord, or a few lost strands of hair?'

'That is easy to say for a man whose bald pate grows wider by the day,' retorted Eble, knowing how prickly John was about his thinning hair.

'Would you really say nay over this?' Lady de Vescy asked him.

Eble shrugged his shoulders. He was far

from sure that he was in agreement, even without the need for a tonsure, but he was at a loss to know how to refuse. 'What do you think?' he asked Alicia.

'Will you be guided by your wife?' snapped John.

'Yes,' Eble told him. 'I will.'

'If the Lord Edward is alive, then I do not want him as the captive of Roger Mortimer,' she said. 'If this can be done, and if you are willing, then you have my blessing.'

'But I will take no part in returning Edward to the throne,' said Eble. 'As long as our present king is not hurt by this — '

'Do you think he would be happy to see his father remain imprisoned?' interrupted John. 'And do not forget that once Edward is removed from Mortimer's grasp he will be free to rule.'

⋆　⋆　⋆

Eble was cold. The icy wind was flapping the monk's habit and, although he had insisted on being allowed to wear his own braies rather than a communal pair from the abbey, his legs were bare and mottled with the cold, and the monkish shoes were not keeping out the wet snow that had transformed the Dorset countryside overnight. It was mid-morning, and he and Brother Richard would reach Corfe well before the bell was rung for the dinner hour. Despite his anxiety about their plans, Eble was eager to reach the castle, if only to sit down for a while and ease some feeling back into his extremities. He was used to travelling, and he was used to deprivation, but he had never appreciated before how hard the life of an itinerant friar was. He would insist that they ate more and rested longer the next time such men presented themselves at the door of the manor house in Swaveton, he decided.

Above them, the castle rose in a gap between the Purbeck Hills. The plan was that they would ask for food, and whilst the household was eating, Eble should pretend some malady of the stomach and beg leave to visit the latrine. Once out of the hall, he would be followed by John Deveril on the pretence of ensuring his welfare, and they would go to the chamber where the king was held. Eble would give his cloak and hood to Edward, who would return with Deveril to the latrine, and then leave with Brother Richard when the meal was over. Just beyond, in the forest, the Earl of Kent was waiting with horses to spirit Edward away. How Eble was to leave the castle had not been discussed.

'You'll think of a way,' John de Warenne

had said as he slapped his back in farewell. 'And don't keep scratching your head. Monks don't do that.'

'But it itches like the devil,' Eble had complained as he reluctantly took his fingers from the round circle on his scalp where the shaven hair was beginning to grow back.

No one paid much attention as the two monks walked into the bailey. Eble mimicked Brother Richard's behaviour as he kept his head bent and his hands clasped together, although his own hand clasped a dagger within the wide sleeve of his habit. After Brother Richard had begged for alms, they were shown into the hall, where the tables were already set for the meal. But it was John Maltravers rather than the expected guardian, John Deveril, who came forward to greet them.

'May God's blessing be upon you, my lord, for your welcome and hospitality,' said Brother Richard as he made the sign of the cross to accompany his blessing.

Eble's fingers tightened around the dagger, fearful that it might drop from his sleeve and betray him. He sensed danger and hoped that the absence of Deveril did not mean that they had walked into a trap.

Maltravers led them between the two rows of trestles to the table on the dais, where they were seated with the esteem that was routinely afforded to travelling friars.

'Will you say grace?' asked Maltravers, and Brother Richard obligingly blessed the food on the platters.

'Your face looks familiar,' said Maltravers as the dishes were shared out. Eble glanced up in alarm, wishing that he could have kept his hood up to eat; but it was Brother Richard whom the man was addressing and Eble withdrew his hand from the temptation of the food, recalling that he was supposed to feign a stomach ache.

'I have visited your castle at Berkeley,' said the monk without hesitation, 'although it is some years ago. I am surprised that you remember me.'

'Oh!' groaned Eble, thinking that this was a good moment to change the topic of conversation. He pressed a hand to his stomach and tried to look as if he was in pain.

'Are you unwell, Brother?' asked Maltravers. Eble kept his face averted and nodded his head.

'I must beg your forgiveness, my lord. May I be excused?' Eble got up and raised the rough cloth of his habit to climb over the bench. 'Forgive me,' he muttered again, and with one hand on the dagger he hurried out of the hall. 'Where is the nearest latrine?' he asked the chamberlain, and went off in the direction that the man pointed, only pausing when he was out of sight to take account of his whereabouts.

The castle was huge and there was no indication of where a prisoner might be held. Eble knew that they would not hold Edward in a dungeon, and that it was likely he was in a chamber high up from where escape, or rescue, would be more difficult. So, with a glance around to ensure that no one saw him, he began to climb the twisting stairs.

'I am seeking the latrine,' he told the guard, who grasped at his sword when he saw him.

'Down there!' growled the man, and Eble retreated. Without Deveril to guide him, it was hopeless.

At last he conceded defeat and returned to the hall as the meal was finishing. His stomach growled with hunger, and he shook his head as Brother Richard approached him.

'I am no better off than I was before,' he told him.

'Do you need the physician?' asked Maltravers.

'No, thank you, my lord. It is an old affliction, and I will be better presently,' he said.

'Do you need beds for the night?' he asked.

'No,' said Eble quickly before Brother

Richard could reply. 'We would prefer to go on our way. We have troubled you enough.'

'As you will,' replied Maltravers, and he fumbled in his purse for some coins. 'Pray for my soul,' he requested as he handed them over, 'and the souls of my ancestors.'

Brother Richard took the money and gave him a blessing, and Eble began to breathe more easily as they made their way across the bailey to the drawbridge.

'What happened?' asked Brother Richard once they were clear of the castle walls.

'There was no sign of the king,' said Eble. 'But it was impossible to search everywhere without the help of John Deveril. Where do you think he is?'

'Prisoner or turned traitor,' replied Brother Richard. 'In either case, it is not good news. We had better make our way to our rendezvous and give the unwelcome news to the Earl of Kent.'

★ ★ ★

Edmund, Earl of Kent, hurried forward when he saw them approaching, and did not disguise his look of disappointment when Eble drew back his hood.

'Where is my brother?' he demanded, as if Eble had personally cheated him.

'I am sorry, my lord. I could not find him.'

'Maltravers has taken custody of the castle,' explained Brother Richard. 'There is no sign of Deveril.'

'Damnation!' swore the earl, his eyes scanning the heavens for inspiration. 'Were you followed?' he asked, looking behind them for any sign of approaching danger.

'I don't think so, my lord,' answered Eble. 'I don't think that Maltravers suspected us.'

'Let us hope he didn't. But this is not good news. I thought that I could rely on Deveril. Take these two,' he said to Brother Richard and Eble, pointing to two palfreys that had been led forward, 'and head in the opposite direction to that which Maltravers saw you take.'

'What will you do, my lord?' asked Brother Richard.

'Keep searching until I find my brother and procure his freedom,' replied the earl as he mounted his own horse.

22

March 1330

Behold the Head of a Traitor

'He has done what?' exploded Edward.

'He has issued a warrant for the arrest of the Earl of Kent,' repeated his mother. 'And once he is captive, my lord Mortimer will denounce him as a traitor to the parliament in Winchester.'

Edward stared at his mother and wondered how this could be true. 'How can he be a traitor?' he asked. 'He is my uncle.'

'So is the Earl of Lancaster, and he did not hesitate to rebel against you,' Isabella reminded him.

'I think you will find his rebellion was aimed at you and Mortimer rather than me,' replied the king tersely. 'What charges has he against Kent?'

'That he sent a letter to Edward of Caernarfon at Corfe Castle, telling him that he would be freed and placed back on the throne.'

'No.' Edward shook his head. 'He does not know my father is alive,' he said. 'Does he?'

'I do not know.' Isabella came towards him and reached up to touch his cheek. 'I know that you are fond of your uncle, but his wish to free your father and make him king again in your place makes him your enemy now.'

'I only have one enemy,' said Edward, pushing her hand away.

'Who?'

'You know that I speak of Mortimer.'

'That is not true. You know that my lord Mortimer and I have always had your best interests at heart,' she protested.

'Really?' Edward drank his wine but did not offer a cup to his mother.

'You need him, Edward,' she said. 'You cannot rule without him.'

'You think not?'

'Edward, you must not act in haste. Think of your father. Think of me. Think of yourself.'

The young king appraised his mother as she stood before him. She looked afraid, and it angered him that she allowed Roger Mortimer to hold the power over her that he did. If they acted together, they could be rid of the man, but his mother would hear no word against him.

'If you acknowledge that your father is alive and that you have known it all this time, then you will destroy us all. Please, do not act in anger before giving the matter careful thought,' she pleaded.

Edward slammed the cup onto the table, spilling wine. He yearned to bring Mortimer down; but despite everything, he loved his mother, and did not want her to be harmed.

'And if I keep up the pretence that my father died at Berkeley and my uncle is mistaken? What then?' he asked.

'I am sure it can be made right,' she said, laying a hand on his arm. 'Perhaps my lord Mortimer will only exact a fine and a plea for forgiveness as he did with the Earl of Lancaster.'

'You speak as if Mortimer rules!' snapped Edward. 'Why is it for him to say what will or will not happen? Am I not the king?'

He watched his mother step back as if he had physically struck her. He should not have shouted at her, he knew that. But the frustration that was building inside him was making him want to tear down the walls that confined him. He wanted to be king in truth rather in name only — and the only thing preventing him was Mortimer.

★   ★   ★

Eble was crossing the courtyard to the hall where the parliament was to be held at

Winchester, when he was suddenly tugged aside. His hand flew to the dagger at his belt to defend himself, and he was about to draw it when he saw that it was John de Warenne. 'What's wrong?' he asked.

'Mortimer has arrested the Earl of Kent.'

'Why?' whispered Eble, glancing around.

'He must have discovered the rescue attempt. Deveril must have betrayed us.'

'Do you think Mortimer knows who else was involved?' asked Eble. He fingered the dagger again, wondering how safe it was to stay, and if they would both be arrested before sundown if Kent had talked. 'Should we go in?' he asked.

'I don't know what to do,' admitted John. 'If we run, we will show ourselves to be guilty.'

'And if we stay, we may put ourselves in danger.' Eble looked into John's clear grey eyes and saw that he was afraid, and it angered him that Roger Mortimer had brought them to this. 'We cannot allow him to intimidate us,' he said, remembering the way that they had often planned to stand up to the bullying of Thomas of Lancaster when they were both squires at Pontefract. 'And surely people will not allow him to harm the Earl of Kent. He is the king's uncle, for goodness' sake.'

'And you think that will matter to Mortimer?' demanded John. 'He'll stop at nothing until he wears the crown on his own head.'

'Perhaps we had better go in,' said Eble. There were only a few latecomers hurrying towards the entrance now. 'It will look suspicious if we linger any longer, but we must keep our wits about us.'

They walked across to the entrance, where the chamberlain nodded briefly and, having checked that they were the last, closed the heavy oak door behind them.

Inside, a gradual hush quietened the chamber, and men knelt as the king came in, flanked as always by his mother and Mortimer; and as the more privileged lords took their seats on the benches at the front, Eble lost sight of John. He could see no sign of the Earl of Kent either, although his brother, the Earl of Norfolk, was seated near the king, and even from this distance Eble could see that he looked troubled. Mortimer stood and gave a slight bow towards the king before beckoning to someone, and Kent was brought forward. His hands were bound, and Eble listened in growing horror and alarm as Mortimer read out the charges against him.

'Sir Edmund, Earl of Kent, it behoves us to say on behalf of our liege lord, Sir Edward,

King of England — whom Almighty God save and keep — that you are his deadly enemy and a traitor!' The Earl of Kent was gazing at the floor in front of him as if he wished some tunnel would appear down which he might escape. 'You are also a common enemy to the realm,' Mortimer told him. 'You plotted to free Sir Edward, the sometime king of England, your brother — and to help him to govern his people as he was wont to do beforehand, thus impairing the king's estate and also his realm.'

Did Mortimer really think he could accuse Kent of trying to free a dead man and have parliament take him seriously? wondered Eble.

'In truth, sir,' replied the Earl of Kent, 'it was never my intention to harm the state of our lord the king, nor his crown.'

Eble thought that the earl looked diminished and unlike the confident man he had last seen in the forest near Corfe. Mortimer, on the other hand, appeared to have an even stronger hold on the affairs of the kingdom than before. He gestured to another man-at-arms and was handed a parchment, which he held up as evidence for all to see.

'Sir Edmund, is this the letter that you gave to Sir John Deveril at Corfe Castle?'

'I sent several letters to Deveril. This is one

of them,' he agreed, 'but it is of no consequence.'

Mortimer paused for effect, then began to read aloud the words that Kent had written to his brother.

'Sir knight, worshipful and dear brother, if you please, I pray heartily that you are of good comfort, for I shall ordain for you that you shall soon come out of prison and be delivered of that disease in which you find yourself. Your lordship should know that I have the assent of almost all the great lords of England, with all their apparel, that is to say with armour, and with treasure without limit, in order to maintain and help you in your quarrel so you shall be king again as you were before.'

Many of the assembled members of the parliament averted their eyes as Mortimer's challenging glance swept around the chamber, and Eble guessed that he was not the only person to be feeling a mixture of guilt and fear. Then Mortimer gave a slight shrug as if there was nothing more to say. He retook his seat, and it was left to Robert Howel, the coroner of the king's household, to draw the conclusion and give the verdict.

'Sir Edmund, since you have admitted openly that this is your letter, enseated with your seal, and that you were on the point of delivering from captivity Sir Edward, the sometime king of England, and helping him to become king again, you are found to be a traitor, and the will of this court is that you shall lose both life and limb.'

There was a murmur of shock from those gathered. Eble shifted uneasily. The scene brought back memories of the deaths of Piers Gaveston and Thomas of Lancaster. But they had, in some way, deserved their fates. All Kent had wanted to do was free his brother. Eble watched as the king met his uncle's eyes. The boy seemed about to speak, but Mortimer ordered the prisoner removed and ended the session of parliament with rushed finality. The king was ushered out, and men spilled from the hall into the courtyard, breaking into groups and talking in anxious voices, asking if the Lord Edward truly lived and if the Earl of Kent really would be executed.

Eble pushed through the throng to find John de Warenne. His friend gave him a warning look as he approached.

'Not here,' he muttered. 'Come to me later at my lodgings.'

★　★　★

'He will name names,' said John de Warenne as they sat around the hearth of the inn where he had taken chambers. Eble had brought Alicia, not wanting her to be left alone when there was so much unrest throughout the city.

'Who will he implicate?' she asked. 'Does he know the names of all those who were involved?'

'I do not know,' replied John. 'But they will force him to confess his adherents, and Mortimer will punish those he does name.'

'But surely he will not go through with the execution of Kent,' said Alicia.

'Do not underestimate him,' warned John. 'He will not allow Kent to go free.'

'And what about Edward?' asked Alicia.

'Do you think Mortimer will have allowed him to live on after this?'

'Then you think he has truly murdered him?' she asked.

'But that would destroy the hold he has over the king,' said Eble.

'No.' John shook his head. 'Whilst Edward is unsure whether or not his father lives, the threat is still there.'

'Do you think we should go into hiding?' asked Alicia. Eble could hear the anxiety in her voice and he knew that, more than anything, she feared being taken captive again.

'I have sworn my loyalty to the king and I will not desert him,' he told them firmly.

'But if you are named, you will be in mortal danger!' protested Alicia, reaching to grasp his arm.

'Mortimer is not interested in the likes of me,' he reassured her. 'It is your friend, Lady de Vescy, who should be your concern.'

'But surely Queen Isabella will protect her?'

'Maybe and maybe not,' said John. 'I have sent word to her, and by this time tomorrow both she and my wife will have taken ship for France. Will you go with them?' he asked Alicia.

'No,' she said. 'I will stay with my husband.'

★ ★ ★

Roger Mortimer watched the king pace the chamber.

'Why can he not be allowed to do the penance instead?' demanded the boy.

'He is a traitor,' Roger explained. 'And we must not show weakness to traitors.'

'We pardoned the Earl of Lancaster. What is different here?'

'The Earl of Lancaster did not plot to remove you from your throne,' said Roger. 'If Kent is allowed to live, he will not refrain from attempting such a coup again.'

'You cannot know that.'

'Would you rather take the risk?' Roger asked as the boy paused and looked at him. He drew himself taller. Edward was of a similar height now, but the boy was yet young and inexperienced. 'He has named many men in his confession. He has even claimed that he acted with the knowledge and encouragement of the pope, who agreed to fund his plot. Look at the list!' He thrust the parchment nearer to the king. 'There is no alternative but to go through with the execution, unless you want to risk your own life — and the life of your mother,' he added, knowing that no argument would move the king as much as the thought of harm befalling his mother. 'Remember that both you and your mother will be punished if the late king is freed by your uncle.'

'And you. You would also lose your head,' Edward reminded him.

Roger shrugged. 'It is my role to give you the best advice I can, and my advice now is to execute the Earl of Kent so that he is no longer a threat or a rallying point for a rebellion.'

'There is already much talk amongst the common people that my father lives.'

'Rumours will abound, and gossips like to clutch at talk of conspiracies,' said Roger.

'What if others try to free my father?'

'From Corfe? They will not find him there.' He watched as Edward frowned.

'You have moved him?'

'He is in a safe place.'

'Have you killed him?' demanded the boy, and Roger noticed his hand stray to the dagger at his belt. He was confident that he could defend himself if the boy struck, but he was not willing to prove himself.

'Edward,' he began in the conciliatory tone that he more often used on Isabella, 'please, be seated.' He waited with his hand extended towards the bench until the boy sat down. 'I know that this is hard,' he said. 'As king it is often necessary to make unpleasant decisions. Remember that you do this not only for your personal welfare and that of your wife and your mother, but for the good of your realm and all your people. Nothing is served by this unrest. Whilst men like Kent foment rebellion against your rule, you are left weak and vulnerable.'

'But if people see him walk barefoot to London, then they will know that he is sorry . . . '

'It does not work like that,' Roger told him. 'It may engender sympathy and add to his cause. You cannot be seen to be weak. People take advantage of those who are weak.'

'As you have taken advantage of my mother?' demanded the boy.

Roger was momentarily shocked and silenced by the hatred he saw in Edward's eyes. He had had disagreements with his own sons, Geoffrey in particular, but none had ever gazed on him with such open contempt. 'I have no advantage of your mother,' he protested. 'My role has always been to advise her.'

'And to . . . ' Edward looked away and ran his fingers through his hair. Roger guessed what he had been about to say but the boy had not been able to voice such thoughts about his own mother.

'I will always do my best to protect you and your family,' Roger told him. 'And my advice is that if you do not execute the Earl of Kent, then you put both yourself and your mother in great danger. Even if you do not have a care for yourself, then consider her.'

The boy remained with his back to him for a long time, and Roger wondered what he would do if he could not gain the king's consent. It was too dangerous to allow Kent to live, even with Edward removed to Ireland. It was not a risk that he could take.

'Very well,' sighed the boy at last. His voice was coloured with defeat. 'I will sign the warrant.'

'Your grace,' replied Mortimer, going to the door to call in the clerk before the king could change his mind.

Edward scrawled his name across the parchment with tears in his eyes. He liked his Uncle Edmund and did not want him to die, but he was faced with no choice. Much as he hated Mortimer, he knew that what the man said was true. If Kent lived and freed his father, then his mother would suffer.

★   ★   ★

Alicia shook her head at the news. Kent's heavily pregnant wife had been arrested and taken to Salisbury Castle with her children and only two maids to wait on them. She ought to have been in confinement awaiting the birth, not being forced to journey across the country without proper care.

'It is worse than Despenser,' she said when Eble was finished. 'I cannot believe that we strove to be rid of him only to find ourselves with a devil twice his incarnation. Will they truly execute the earl?'

'The date is set for the day after tomorrow,' Eble told her. 'I wish that something could be done.'

'What does John say?'

'He is as sad as the rest of us, but he does

not have the men to challenge Mortimer in an open battle.'

'It is a travesty of justice. I am glad my father is not alive to see such things. It would have broken his heart,' said Alicia.

'There are few men left with the integrity of your father,' said Eble. 'Except perhaps the king.'

'Yet he signs the warrant of execution for his uncle,' said Alicia angrily.

'The boy's hands are tied by Mortimer.'

'Then it is time someone untied them!' she told him.

⋆   ⋆   ⋆

Roger Mortimer pressed his face into his hands. It was not often that he prayed. It seemed that he only bothered God in moments of extremity, and he now found himself begging for guidance in a moment of self-doubt. Wasn't it enough that he had built the chapel at Ludlow? he wanted to demand. Why was he to be tormented like this, as those who had once supported him turned against him with their acts of treason? Edmund of Kent and his wife had been with him in France when he had escaped from the Tower. Kent had supported him, along with Henry Beaumont and Thomas Wake, as he had striven to free England from the tyranny of Hugh le Despenser. Why had they turned against him now?

God remained silent, and after some time had passed Roger rose from his knees, neglected to cross himself, and made his way to the courtyard where the execution was to take place. Kent had already been brought down from his cell and was standing by the block with a heavy guard surrounding him.

'Where is the executioner?' asked Mortimer, eager to have the thing done and finished with.

'He is gone, my lord,' one of the men-at-arms replied.

'Gone? Gone where?'

'My lord, I do not know. No one has seen him since yesterday.'

'Then find someone else.'

'No one is willing, my lord.'

'Then you do it!' shouted Mortimer, grasping the axe and thrusting it into the hands of the unwilling man.

'My lord, I cannot.'

'Cannot? Or will not? Who here is willing?' He glared at the assembled guards, but none volunteered. Instead they averted their gazes and looked uncomfortable, and Roger knew that he could not order them all thrown into the dungeon. 'Someone must be found!' he raged. 'We have waited long enough already. Find someone — anyone. Give some man his freedom in return for the deed if need be!'

'Yes, my lord,' said the man.

Mortimer walked away from the scene, not able to look at Kent as he stood waiting with a resigned air of patience. He went inside where he sat at the table, drumming his fingers on the board as he waited, watching through a narrow window as the gathered crowd grew restless with the prolonged delay.

At length a message was sent that a man had been found — a latrine cleaner who had murdered a man and was under sentence of death himself. He had agreed to strike off the earl's head in return for his own freedom.

'Good. Tell him to get on with it,' muttered Mortimer. 'It will be too dark to see, if the thing is not done directly.'

He stepped outside to where a bent and filthy man, covered in sores from his time in the prison, stood blinking in the daylight. One of the men-at-arms pushed the heavy axe into his hands, and Kent was pulled to the block and forced to kneel. He laid down his head, and the latrine cleaner approached him slowly.

'Get on with it!' shouted Roger, fearful that this man too was about to throw down the axe and forfeit his own life rather than kill a prince of the royal blood.

Roger felt as if time had paused, but then the man gripped the haft of the axe, and in hands that were visibly trembling he brought it down blade first on the neck of the earl. Blood rose in a fountain. Kent made a choking noise as a river of red liquid spewed from his mouth, and with another blow the head was severed. One of the men-at-arms grasped it by its fair hair and held it aloft for the crowd to see, proclaiming the usual cry of: 'Behold, the head of a traitor!' But rather than the rapturous cheering that commonly followed such an event, the crowd remained silent. People shuffled their feet and glanced at one another in discomfiture, as if they had just witnessed judicial murder.

★　★　★

After the messenger had gone, the king sat on the bed in the palace at Woodstock — the bed where his uncle had been born — and wept. He felt as soiled as if he had executed him with his own hand. Gradually, Edward became aware that someone was beside him. He felt a gentle hand on his shoulder and was about to shirk it off, thinking that it was his mother come to offer false comfort, when he realised that it was Philippa.

'Should you not be in your chamber?' he asked her as he felt her huge belly against his arm. He turned to her, wiping his eyes on the heels of his hands. 'Do you think me weak to cry?' he asked.

'It is not weakness to mourn the loss of those we loved — especially when the death comes in such an unfair fashion,' she told him. Her dark eyes were watching him steadily. She was no great beauty, but her face pleased him, and he was glad that she had come.

'What am I to do?' he asked her in despair. 'I am powerless before him.'

'It will not always be so,' she reassured him. 'Our time will come.'

'I am glad that I agreed to marry you,' he said. 'I know that it was done to fund Mortimer's invasion, but I do not regret taking you as my wife.' He reached to grasp her hand in his and kissed it, and then held it against his wet cheek.

'And I do not regret taking you as my husband,' she said. 'One day you will be a great and powerful king.' She pulled her hand from his face, took hold of his and pressed it to her belly. Beneath his palm he felt a sturdy movement. 'Do you feel the child, my lord?' she asked him. 'This is your heir, and you must claim back your kingdom for him.'

'But how?' he asked with a desperate shrug.

'You have men you can trust. Men like your friend William de Montagu. I have seen you confide in him,' she said. 'Wait until this child is born, and then the time will be ripe for you to act. You must rid yourself of Roger Mortimer,' she told him. 'And then we can be free.'

23

June 1330–October 1330

Pater Sancte

Edward gazed at the tiny child. He had rarely seen a baby so young, and certainly never held one, and he was surprised at the weight of it in his arms and in awe of the symmetry of its tiny features. Although his son's eyes were tightly closed in sleep, he could see that the arch of the dark eyebrows and the thick hair that covered the baby's head were reminiscent of Philippa's, although there was a familiarity about the child that reminded him of the image he saw when he looked in his own mirror.

He was surprised by the sudden rush of desire to protect the child and keep him safe from all harm, and as he traced the curve of the tiny cheek with his forefinger he admitted to himself that his fears for his son were justified — as were his fears for himself. He was still angry that his pleas for his uncle's life had been ignored, and now Mortimer was creating allies within the country by sharing out his uncle's lands amongst those he believed would support him. Mortimer was becoming a threat, and whispers had reached Edward's ears that the man planned to have him murdered and snatch the crown for himself.

The baby snuffled and moved in his arms, and Edward was overwhelmed by feelings of love and pride. He wondered if his own father had held him like this and whether he had experienced the same emotions. But his joy at the birth of his child was tempered by an intense sorrow for the loss of his father, for he was certain that Mortimer would not have allowed him to live after the debacle of the failed rescue attempt from Corfe. And he did not even know where his body was buried. His few trips to the tomb at Gloucester were meaningless when he knew that it was the body of an impostor who was interred there. Yet he was also aware that if his father were truly dead, it meant that he could not be resurrected to be made king again, and that the way was now clear for him to act. He was still concerned for his mother, but his love for his son was more powerful. He had tried to protect her to the best of his ability, but she had made her choice; and now, for the wellbeing of all his subjects as well as this child in his arms, he resolved that he would strive to take control of England.

'What is he to be named?' asked Amie de Gaveston, one of the ladies of the queen's chamber.

'Edward,' he replied as he carefully placed the baby in her arms to be taken back to his mother. 'Tell my wife that she has done well,' he added, 'and that I will come to visit her when she is ready.'

He was eager to go in to see Philippa, if only to reassure himself that she was indeed well, as her ladies had told him that she was. She and his son, and the future children they would create together, were his concern now. His mother and Mortimer had had their time, and it would soon be over.

It was approaching dinnertime when the chamberlain came hurrying in. 'Your grace, Sir William de Montagu is here,' he told him.

'Bring him up to my chamber,' said Edward with his foot already on the step. He had been unaware that his friend was back from France, and he would be pleased to see him.

Edward had barely had time to begin to wash his hands when William was shown in. 'I hear that congratulations are in order.' He grinned. 'A son and heir!'

'It is a day for good news,' said Edward, throwing the towel over his shoulder. 'I hope that you bring me more.'

William's face grew serious. 'The news I heard of Kent's execution was not good,' he said quietly.

'I tried,' said Edward, sitting down on the edge of his bed and spreading his hands in a gesture of defeat. 'He pleaded to do penance, and I was agreeable, but Mortimer would not allow it. I was powerless.'

'Soon you will not be,' William told him. 'I was granted a private audience with the pope, and I advised him of the troubles within your realm. He was concerned by what he heard and asked that in future, when you write to him, you give him some sign, so that he may know which letters contain your true wishes and which are requests made by Mortimer in your name.'

Edward nodded. 'Tell Robert de Bury to write to the Holy Father and inform him that all letters from me will contain the words 'pater sancte' written in my own hand.'

★ ★ ★

Eble was glad to be back in Lincolnshire, away from the intrigues of life at court. He found it difficult to sit in the parliament whilst lacking the knighthood that would place him on the same ranking as the other men. He always felt embarrassed when those who were not aware of his lack of status addressed him as Sir Eble. He found it awkward to correct them, yet he was reluctant to claim a title that was not his by right.

He was speaking with the steward in the hall, discussing whether the weather would hold, when he heard someone ride into the courtyard outside. He hurried to the door, hoping that it did not mean trouble, to find Sir William de Montagu, a member of the king's household, dismounting from a large roan.

'My lady,' said Montagu as he saw Alicia come out, 'please excuse my arriving unannounced like this, but I have come on urgent business from the king.'

Eble exchanged a worried glance with Alicia, but she remained calm, calling for refreshments and urging Montagu to take a seat on the best chair.

'You will find that we live plainly here,' she told him by way of apology for their impoverished state. 'It is a far cry from the castles that were my father's.'

'Indeed, I am sorry for your circumstances, Countess,' said the man, waiting for Alicia to seat herself before he sat down himself. 'I know that the king will do more for you when it is in his power to do so.'

Eble watched Alicia give the man a sharp look as he helped himself to the bread and cheese that were offered on a platter. 'You said that you have come from the king?' she said.

'Yes, from the king,' reiterated Montagu, 'not from Roger Mortimer. A son has been born to Edward.'

'Is the baby strong? And the queen well?' she asked.

'Both are strong and healthy, my lady,' Montagu reassured her before turning to Eble. 'The king has almost reached his maturity, and he has asked me to find trustworthy men who will help him claim his throne, but my inquiries need be discreet and not reach the ears of Mortimer's spies. Edward is afraid,' he added.

'Afraid?' said Eble, taking a seat on the bench beside Alicia.

'Edward believes that Mortimer may seek to kill him and take the throne for himself. It is more than idle gossip,' Montagu told them. 'I think the threat is real. I think that Mortimer does want the crown for himself.'

'He favours those he thinks will help him to achieve it,' remarked Alicia.

'I have already pledged my loyalty to the king, both in public and in private,' Eble told

Montagu. 'Edward already knows that I am his liegeman.'

'The court will soon be at Nottingham,' said Montagu. 'Will you come to join us?'

Eble glanced at Alicia, and she nodded. 'We will come,' he agreed.

'The king also has many friends abroad,' said Alicia. 'I have letters from the Lady de Vescy. She and her brother have gathered much support. I would not be surprised if there is an invasion that would ensure that the king takes his rightful place on the throne.'

'Edward is aware that they support him, and he is grateful, but what he needs now are men whom he can trust at court; men who can help to keep him from danger. The king already owes you his life,' said Montagu to Eble. 'And he tells me that he would feel safer if you and others were guarding him closely.'

★　★　★

Roger Mortimer listened with incredulity and growing trepidation as John Wyard confirmed what his other spies had already told him. The king and his friends were holding secret meetings and plotting against him.

'Are you certain?' he asked again.

'I am, my lord. And I thought that you ought to know.'

Roger nodded. 'You have done the right thing,' he told the man. 'And it will not go unrewarded.' He watched as a sly smile twitched at Wyard's face and wondered if there was a man alive who could not be bought with the lure of money and lands.

He was still wondering how little reward he could get away with giving Wyard when the door was flung open, and Isabella came in with the agitated castellan in her wake.

'Henry of Lancaster is here, and he has been allowed in!' she protested.

'Surely not? We cannot have that man within the castle. Who has given him entry?' he demanded.

'My lord, he is the Earl of Lancaster,' protested the castellan, 'and the king said he could have apartments. I did not see any reason to refuse him. Besides, the man is almost blind. What harm — '

'What harm?' thundered Mortimer, wondering how the man could have risen to such a position when he showed such misjudgement. 'The harm is that the man is an enemy of Queen Isabella, and you have given permission for him to be housed within the same walls!'

He was so close to the man now that he

could see him quivering under the onslaught of his anger.

'What should I do?' he bleated.

'Get rid of him!' shouted Roger. 'Can you not see how afraid you have made the queen?'

'But my lord, where will he go?'

'In the name of everything that is holy, do I appear to care? Just get him out of the castle and tell him that he must seek lodgings in the town. And give me the keys to the castle!'

'But my lord — '

'The keys!' roared Roger. 'From now on they will be kept by the queen!'

The castellan fumbled at his belt and unhooked the heavy iron keys that secured the front and postern gates and reluctantly placed them on Roger's outstretched hand.

'Get out of my sight! And make sure that the guards understand that they are to ignore any commands of the king and obey only mine!'

'Yes, my lord.'

The man fled, and Roger took the keys to where Isabella was looking down into the courtyard where the men and horses of Lancaster's household were milling in disarray. He put his hand on her trembling arm and pressed the keys into her grasp.

'He will soon be gone,' he reassured her. 'I will not allow any harm to come to you.' Her eyes were wet with tears when she turned to him, although whether it was from fear or anger he could not tell. 'Lancaster assumes too much. Perhaps we let him off too lightly last time,' he mused, wondering whether the time had come to be rid of the man altogether. Surely it would not be hard to bring charges of treason against him as well. One earl had already been executed, and the world had not ceased turning, so why not be rid of another?

★　★　★

The king dismounted outside the house where Lancaster had been lodged. It was adequate, he thought, glancing at the thatched roof and shuttered windows, but his uncle should be safely housed within the walls of the castle, not dwelling on the lower streets of Nottingham.

He stooped under the low doorway and approached the central hearth. His uncle did not acknowledge him. His sight had failed and he needed someone with him to guide him, but his mind was as clear as ever.

'Uncle,' Edward said, and the earl looked up. 'No, do not rise. I have come to say that I am sorry for the way that you have been treated by Mortimer and my mother. It is a gross insult to turn you away from the castle, and it was done against my wishes.'

'What do they fear?' asked Lancaster. 'I am hardly equipped to be an assassin, am I?'

Edward put a hand on the older man's shoulder in a gesture of remorse and affection. He was sure of his uncle's support of him as king, but it was true what Lancaster said. His failed vision meant that he could take no personal part in any toppling of Mortimer.

'You will have your chamber in the castle before long,' Edward promised him.

'So it is true that you and your friends plot against Mortimer?' asked Henry.

'Yes, it is true.'

'Then I hope you have surrounded yourself with brave and courageous men who will watch your back as they follow you.'

'I know who I can trust,' replied Edward.

'Who guards you now?' asked Lancaster.

'Have no worries, uncle. It is Eble le Strange who is standing in your doorway.'

'Then I can speak with confidence,' he said. 'I have had a visit from William Eland. He has been the castellan here for a long time and knows of places that are not commonly known. He tells me that there is a passage that runs from the castle and ends in the woods beyond the town. It begins in the cellars beneath the tower where your mother has her apartments, and Mortimer is always with her. You will need a trustworthy man inside the castle to draw back the bolts, but once inside it should be possible to overpower the guards and arrest Mortimer before the alarm can be raised.'

'I know someone,' said Eble. 'I will ensure that it is done.'

24

October 1330

To Depose a Traitor

The sun had sunk in a blaze of blood-red glory when Eble joined Sir William Montagu and about twenty other men in sparse woodland on the outskirts of Nottingham. But as the moonless night rendered them reliant on their ears rather than their eyes, the silence told them that many others had been too afraid to come. Eble could hardly blame them. Men had always been in awe of Mortimer, and now they feared him; feared that they would be the next to feel his wrath.

Eble slid down from Trebnor's saddle as he recalled how he had come face to face with Mortimer in the castle and how he had been asked what his business was. 'I am seeking the Earl of Surrey,' he had told him, and Mortimer had stared at him long enough to make him feel uncomfortable.

'Down there,' he had said at last, and Eble had thanked him politely and hurried on his errand.

John had looked unsurprised when Eble arrived at his chamber and only betrayed his curiosity with a raised eyebrow. Eble's glance at the servants had told his friend all he needed to know, and John had suggested that they go outside into the fresh air as his head was aching.

'How well do you know this castle?' Eble had asked him as they went down a spiralling stone stairwell, and when he was certain that they were alone and could not be overheard, he had told John about the secret passage. His friend had agreed to be the one who would draw back the bolts.

Afterwards, he had gone to Alicia and told her to pack a few clothes and leave Nottingham.

'No,' she had replied when he had explained why.

'You cannot refuse. I am your husband!' he had shouted in exasperation, wondering how other men managed to rule their wives.

'I can refuse,' she had replied with her dark eyes blazing, 'if only to save your head! Think about it, Eble. If I am seen fleeing the city, then suspicion will fall on you.'

He had seen the sense in what she said and had hugged her to him for her bravery and good sense. 'I only seek to protect you,' he had whispered. 'If it goes wrong and I am captured, then Mortimer will be revenged on you.'

'Then you had better ensure that you are successful,' she had told him.

Now Eble stood in the soaked grass with Trebnor's reins in his gloved hand. It was too dark to see the horse, but he could feel the animal's hot breath on his cheek and could smell the familiar scent of its coat. He sensed the tension in the men around him.

'Word should have reached Mortimer by now that we have fled,' said Montagu, who was standing beside him. 'He will be surprised to meet with us again so soon. Where is Eland?' he asked.

'I am here, my lord,' came a disembodied voice from nearby.

'I hope to God you can find this tunnel entrance,' said Montagu, 'or we will all be swinging on ropes before the new moon.'

'I know the way,' said Eland's voice, 'but we must leave the horses here and go on foot. It will be marshy, so you must tread carefully.'

Eble tethered Trebnor to the branch of a tree. 'We will not be long,' he told him. 'There is an errand I must do.'

Eland lit the small lantern that he was carrying. 'Stay close and keep your eye on the light. If you lose it, stand still, even if you have to stand there until sunrise. The ground is a bog, and if you step into it you will not be able to step out,' he warned.

Eble was aware that he was nodding, though no one could see him. He felt a slight breeze as men pulled their cloaks more closely around them, over their armour. As the bobbing light of the lantern moved off through the thicket, Eble heard a snicker from Trebnor, who was not happy at being left behind.

Someone cursed as a low-hanging branch whipped at his face, and Eble ducked to avoid it. Underfoot the ground was soft and cushioned their footfalls. All Eble could hear was the steady breathing of his companions, and his mind turned to stories of dragons that breathed fire from the heart of dense forests. If any peasant or poacher was abroad that night, they would surely run home with tales of some mysterious and frightening creature at large, he thought.

They followed the lantern, and the ground grew increasingly soft and springy underfoot as they approached the riverbank. Someone cursed, and there was a squelch as a boot was pulled from the mud. With each step, Eble prayed that he would not stray into the mire. He did not want to be left stranded until daylight or risk sinking to his death.

He could hear the distant sound of the

river as it rushed past the rocks on which the castle was built. The ground beneath his feet was harder now, and they had left the shelter of the trees behind. Once or twice he saw the light hesitate and stop. Each time he felt his heart beat faster, but then the light moved on again and he followed it. Though he knew they were walking into danger, he was eager for the moment to come when they would emerge from the tunnel and claim England for its king.

At length the light hovered for longer. 'This is it,' whispered Eland, and the light disappeared for a moment and then reappeared. 'Yes, this is the entrance,' he said.

'I think we should take off our cloaks and hide them here,' suggested Eble. 'It will be best if we are not encumbered.'

'And draw your swords,' said Montagu. 'We must be prepared.' Then, each warning the man behind him to lower his head, they ducked inside the tunnel.

The ground became steeper beneath Eble's feet. He couldn't see it, but he could feel the strain on his thighs as they climbed. He reached out a hand to feel for the rock through which the tunnel had been cut, and with the other he gripped the handle of his sword. There were men ahead of him and men behind him, and he could not have escaped even if he had changed his mind. But he felt no qualms. He had made his vow to the young king and, although he prayed that God would save him, for Alicia's sake he knew that this was his duty.

They stopped, breathing heavily with the climb; and as Eland raised the lantern, Eble caught sight of a wooden door.

'Are we ready?' asked Montagu. There was a murmur of assent, and Eble readied himself as the trap door was slowly pushed up.

★ ★ ★

Edward pressed a hand to his abdomen and uttered a groan that he hoped was convincing, but not too dramatic. Mortimer looked at him sharply.

'Are you unwell?' asked his mother, suddenly solicitous.

'Over-indulgence,' muttered Mortimer to the Bishop of Lincoln, who was sitting with them at the high table.

'I think I will go to my bed,' the king told them. 'I have a stomach ache.'

'I will have someone call your physician,' said his mother. 'He will give you something that will settle the discomfort.'

'Thank you,' said Edward, remembering to get up slowly and keep his hand clenched to his guts as if there were a danger of his spewing the contents of his stomach or voiding his bowels — or both.

Mortimer gave him a look of distaste and suggested that as the king was retiring, he and the bishop should continue their conversation with the queen in her private chambers. He gave Edward a brief nod and bade him a curt goodnight as his physician hurried in with his bag of cures clutched in his hand.

'Double the guard on all the outer doors,' ordered Mortimer as Edward slipped away.

Once in his own apartments, the pretence of any illness was abandoned, and he paced the floor as he and his allies waited by the door for the Earl of Surrey to come up. At last there was a soft knock and the physician admitted him.

'Is it done?' asked Edward.

Surrey nodded. 'The bolts are drawn back and Montagu is ready.'

'Tell them that Mortimer is with my mother in her chamber,' replied the king.

★   ★   ★

Eble stepped through the doorway and waited until the mail-clad legs of the man above him disappeared around the turn of the stair before he followed him up from the cellar. They climbed in silence, but suddenly there was a shout from above, and Eble cursed that they had been seen before reaching Mortimer.

'Traitors!' cried a voice, and Eble heard the clash of fighting above him. As he stepped through the doorway, he caught a glimpse of Hugh Turpington, the royal steward, who had raised the alarm. The man ran at Montagu with his dagger raised, but he neatly sidestepped and brought his mace crashing down on the man's unprotected head. Eble watched as a gurgle of blood foamed from his lips and he slumped against the wall.

But his cries had raised the alarm, and guards came running. The door to the queen's chamber flew open, and Eble saw Roger Mortimer grasping his sword as he glanced this way and that to assess the situation. Metal grated on metal, and there was a scream as one man fell and blood began to puddle around his boots. Eble recognised Mortimer's squire, Richard de Monmouth, as he leapt to defend his lord, but Montagu sliced at his undefended throat and he sank to the floor. Montagu leapt over his prone body, pushing another guard aside. He was closely followed by other men, and Mortimer stood no chance against their sudden and unexpected onslaught. His sword clattered to the ground, and within moments they had seized him and forced him back into the chamber.

Eble heard Queen Isabella before he saw her. She was screaming hysterically at the sight of the armed men overpowering her lover. Eble pushed past them and grasped her arm, shaking it to try to get her attention, but her eyes were fixed on Mortimer.

'Have pity! Have pity!' she screamed. 'Do not harm him!'

Eble sheathed his sword and bundled the queen into the antechamber, where he saw the Bishop of Lincoln disappearing through the door that led to the latrine, no doubt in some futile attempt to escape down the chute that led to the moat below. He knew that the king did not want his mother harmed, and he judged that she was safer out of the melee, but she continued to scream and pull from his grasp, calling for her son to have pity on Mortimer and not to kill him. Eble pulled her against him, pinioning her flailing arms to her sides.

'Do not let them hurt him,' she sobbed.

'Please, calm yourself, my lady,' he told her, wondering if it was a treasonable offence to physically hold the king's mother against her will.

Edward stared at Roger Mortimer. His hands were fastened tightly in front of him with rope, and a cloth had been pushed into his mouth and tied there to silence him.

'You are finished!' Edward told him. 'England is mine, and you are a traitor, and a dead man!'

Mortimer threw him a look of contempt, and Edward drew his knife as if he would finish him there and then by his own hand, but Montagu laid a hand on his arm. 'Not here,' he said.

The king glanced towards the antechamber where his mother's screams and sobs were competing with the moans of those who had been injured. 'Take him to the Tower,' he said.

Epilogue

Eble walked into the chapel with John de Warenne. He had bathed and was dressed in a clean robe. The king was waiting for them with his sword in his hand, and after John had fastened the golden spurs to his heels and buckled the belt of knighthood around his waist, Eble knelt and felt the gentle pressure of the blade on his shoulder.

He stood and bowed to Edward, his liege lord and King of England. The boy was gone, and in his place stood a man they could trust to rule with a fair and generous hand.

'I have a favour to ask of you, Sir Eble,' said the king.

'You know that I am yours to command, sire.'

'Will you bring my mother from Berkhamsted to us here at Windsor for the Christmas festivities?'

'Willingly, sire.' Eble watched as a frown creased the king's forehead.

'The physicians say that she is improved and is strong enough to travel,' he said. 'But I do not want her to be alarmed, and I know that she thinks well of you and trusts you. She spoke of you in her letter, and said that you gave her much comfort that night . . . ' The king fell silent. There was no need to remind Eble of which night he spoke. After Mortimer had been taken away, Eble had stayed with Isabella. She had sobbed in his arms all through the dark hours until, as dawn crept over the shadowy sills of the windows, her head had drooped against his shoulder and she had slept with exhaustion.

As he rode to Berkhamsted, Eble hoped that his small Christmas gift would bring the dowager queen some comfort. In his pack he carried a small book of his own stories that had been bound for him by Osbert, the scribe in Lincoln. The stories were about love and chivalry, and he hoped that they would show her that Roger Mortimer had failed her on both counts: he had set himself above his peers and revelled in his power. Eble had written a story of a wiser ruler, a new King Arthur, who knew that his knights were as important as himself. This wise ruler had paid a carpenter to make a table that was not set up on a dais in a great hall for him alone, but was round so that no man could set himself above another.

In the hall at Berkhamsted, he knelt to Isabella and presented her with the carefully wrapped package.

'What is this, Sir Eble?' she asked after she had bidden him to rise. Her face looked very white and she seemed frail, as if she might break apart if she were touched.

'They are some words of mine,' he said. 'I hope that you might draw some pleasure from them. I know that you like stories.'

'Do they have happy endings?' she asked, raising her blue eyes from the gift to look at him.

'They do, my lady.'

'That is the pleasure of romances,' she said. 'They rarely end badly — unlike life.' The tears brimmed in her eyes and Eble, who was usually good with words, could think of nothing to say. He gestured for one of her ladies to come to assist her. The woman was unknown to him. Isabella had lost her closest friends as well as her lover. Jeanne de Bar had returned to France, leaving John de Warenne alone, and Lady de Vescy was still abroad with her brother; whether things could ever be the same between the two women, Eble could not say.

'There are still good things in your life, my lady,' Eble told her. 'You have your children, and your son is waiting to welcome you at Windsor.'

'Is he angry with me for what I did?'

'As far as I know, the king bears you no

grudge, and he speaks of you as lovingly as ever,' Eble reassured her. 'He is waiting to receive you, and I will ensure that no harm comes to you on the way. You have my word. I will protect you.'

'You are a good man, Eble le Strange,' said Isabella. 'The Countess of Lincoln is a fortunate woman.'

'It is I who am fortunate that she even considered me,' replied Eble.

★ ★ ★

Lady de Vescy stood beside her brother, Henry Beaumont, at the rail of the ship as they approached the busy port of Sandwich. She could hear her teeth chattering above the swell of the waves as they slapped against the hull. The winter crossing had been rough, and she would be glad to set her cold feet on English soil once more and claim the inheritances that were rightfully hers.

'Go back into the shelter where you are out of the wind,' said Henry.

'No, I want to watch as we come into the harbour,' she said, straining her eyes for sight of where they could tie up. There seemed so many other craft bobbing on the rough grey sea, their coloured sails sodden and greyed by the mist, that she worried there would be no place for them. But it was not long before the wooden boat was manoeuvred into position, bumping against the sea wall.

The sailors secured it with ropes and slammed down the ramp for them to climb ashore. Lady de Vescy clung to her brother's hand as he helped her onto the quayside. She was growing old, she thought, as she forced her stiffened joints into movement.

As she stood and watched Henry overseeing the unloading of their baggage, she caught the eye of a hermit, as if he had been watching her. There was something familiar about the tall figure who turned his head away and adjusted his hood. He must be waiting to take ship, to go on some pilgrimage, thought Lady de Vescy. Her numbed fingers struggled with the strings of her purse and she extracted a coin to give the man as an offering, but when she looked again he was walking away from her. She wondered whether to call after him, but suddenly Henry was at her side, and urging her on towards the lodgings he had procured for them.

As she headed away from the spray of the sea, she looked back, and the hermit had also paused and was watching her. She saw his face.

'Edward?' she whispered under her breath as he turned and continued on his way.

Alicia lowered her gaze from the towering walls of Bolingbroke Castle and looked at the handsome man who rode beside her. He caught her eye and smiled. The new king had rewarded them well. Bolingbroke had always been a favourite residence of hers, unencumbered as it was by the bad memories of other castles such as Pickering and Kenilworth.

'The wheel of fortune has turned, and we have risen on its axle,' remarked Eble as they watched the heavy gates being opened for them.

'Fortuna looked on me with kindness the day you came to Pontefract,' said Alicia.

'You don't remember when I first came,' he challenged her.

'I do,' she told him. 'It was very late, and the torches had already been lit in the bailey. We had eaten supper and the squires were clearing the tables. I was with my mother and her ladies in her chamber, and they were telling stories when my father came to the door to show you to my mother. You were standing beside him with some baggage still clasped between your hands. You had pulled off your hood, and your freshly shorn hair was standing in peaks. You gazed into our chamber like a hart that has just caught sight of the huntsman with an aimed bow.'

'I recall none of this,' claimed Eble. 'What happened then?'

'You looked at me,' said Alicia, 'and you dropped whatever it was you were carrying.'

'Did I? And what did you do?'

'I looked back at you,' Alicia told him, 'and I knew that I had found the thing I had been searching for all my life. When I saw you, even though you looked so young and afraid, I knew that you could make me complete.'

The hooves of the horses clattered as they stepped from the track onto the stones that led in under the gateway. Torches had been lit to welcome them, and grooms hurried forward to help them dismount and to take charge of the horses.

Eble held out his hand and she put hers into it. The little boy was a tall, strong man now, but the eyes that met hers in the twilight were just the same — and they shone with pleasure.

'Welcome home,' he said.

★   ★   ★

Roger Mortimer knelt in his squalid cell in the Tower of London and commended his soul to God. He could hear a bell ringing, but there would be no feast-day chimes for him this day — only for those who would celebrate his death. Once again he rehearsed the speech that he would make on the gallows. He hoped that his voice would remain steady and that he would not shiver, despite the cold. He did not want the crowd which would gather to see him hanged to think that he was afraid to die, although being tied behind two horses and dragged to the Elms to face a traitor's death was no small ordeal — and there was no one in the Tower who would help him now, not even a friendly gaoler who might slip some soporific into his food to dull the pain.

He heard the voices outside his cell, the stamping of boots, the clatter of swords, and he knew that it was time. He said one last prayer, and it was for his wife, Joan. He felt guilty that he had let her down again, and he hoped that the king would treat her and his children with compassion.

He made the sign of the cross and stood up. He straightened the black tunic that he had worn for the sham funeral of Edward of Caernarfon and turned to face the door as the key scraped in the lock and bolts were drawn back. Armed men waited for him.

'I am ready,' he told them, and walked out of the cell.